sammy KEYES
and the DEAD GIVEAWAY

WENDELIN VAN DRAANEN

A YEARLING BOOK

Published by Yearling
an imprint of Random House Children's Books
a division of Random House, Inc.
New York

Visit us on the Web! www.randomhouse.com/kids

Educators and librarians, for a variety of teaching tools,
visit us at www.randomhouse.com/teachers

ISBN: 978-0-440-41911-2

Reprinted by arrangement with Alfred A. Knopf Books for Young Readers

Printed in the United States of America

May 2007

10 9 8 7 6

This book is dedicated to Martha, my swashbucklin' (and wonderfully supportive) sister-in-law.

Thanks and a mighty "Arg!" to me hearties Mark "Skipper" Parsons and Nancy "Sharp-eye" Siscoe.

I'd also like to acknowledge Mary Abatti, who walked the plank of the *Santa Maria*.

Also Philip Sinco, Deputy City Attorney, who helped me sail the high seas of legalese.

sammy
KEYES
and the DEAD GIVEAWAY

PROLOGUE

Grams says that most people have some sort of skeleton in their closet—something they really don't want other people to find out about. I always thought that was just grandma talk. Or, at least, her way of excusing the fact that *she's* got secrets from *me*.

"Skeletons are not just secrets, Samantha," she told me when I accused her of this. "They're life-*changing* secrets." Then she hurried to add, "And mind you, I'm not saying that *I* have skeletons in *my* closet, but if I did, that's exactly where I'd want them to stay."

I just laughed and said, "I bet you would!" 'cause I've learned that my grams can be pretty cagey—especially when it comes to things I'm dying to know about.

But shortly after our conversation I discovered what having a skeleton in your closet really means.

And how a closet isn't always a closet . . .

1

ONE

It's funny how you can think you know someone pretty well, and then something happens or they *do* something that makes you understand that you didn't really know them at all.

My homeroom teacher, Mrs. Ambler, is that way. I always figured she was just another long-suffering adult who was sick to death of dealing with junior high school kids. I also always thought that she was at least fifty. Probably well on her way to sixty. You know, *old*.

Then one day she came into homeroom with two lovebirds. I'm talking the feathered variety, not the gross pimply kind you see swapping spit behind the locker rooms.

Anyhow, these birds would've looked perfect on the shoulder of a midget pirate. They had orange faces, green bodies, a little splay of bright blue tail feathers, and I thought for sure they were baby parrots.

But when Mrs. Ambler parked the white domed cage on her desk and Tawnee Francisco asked, "Are they cockatiels?" Mrs. Ambler smiled at her and said, "No, they're lovebirds."

Now, this may seem like a perfectly normal exchange to you, but (a) I didn't even know there was actually such a

3

thing as a lovebird, and (b) Mrs. Ambler's voice when she said "lovebirds" was all soft and sweet and ... *feathery*.

Then I noticed her face. *It* was all soft. And sweet. And ... well, not feathery, more *glowy*.

It was not the Mrs. Ambler I was used to seeing, that's for sure. I glanced at my best friend, Marissa McKenze, who sits way up front in the corner, and she was sort of blinking at Mrs. Ambler, too.

Then Heather Acosta pipes up with, "*Love*birds, Mrs. Ambler? How *adorable*."

I rolled my eyes and Marissa did the same, because ever since end-of-the-year elections for Class Personalities started drawing near, Heather's been on the world's most revolting kiss-up campaign.

The whole idea of Class Personalities is stupid to begin with. It may be a "tradition" at William Rose Junior High School, but what it really is, is an overblown popularity contest. But since popularity is the pulse that drives Heather's blood, I guess that explains why she's dying to win something. Anything. You should see the way she's been circulating through campus lately, oozing a diabolically contagious form of congeniality. She's nice. She's sweet. She's helpful. She's concerned. And she's all that with such true-blue sincerity it's frightening.

Unfortunately for her, after nearly a full school year of her schemes and lies, I think that most people are smart enough to be suspicious, except for one thing—Heather's also been acting contrite. You know—she's just so, *so* sorry for her part in any trouble this year. I've heard her tell teachers, "I know I made mistakes, but I've learned so much!" and "You

4

know, I'm just so grateful for the experiences—I feel I've really grown as a human being!"

That's the kiss-up game she's been playing with other people, anyway. To *me* she's been whispering, "Count 'em and weep, loser."

Please. Like I care if she wins some stupid popularity contest?

She's not just after Friendliest Seventh Grader, either. Oh no. She's hedging her bets by going for Most Unique Style, too. One day she comes to school looking like a punk princess in black and chains and ratted red hair; the next she's all decked out like an old-time movie star, wearing satin shoes and a matching *hand*bag, her hair all smoothed back.

It's so transparent it's pathetic.

But anyway, the minute Heather finds out that Mrs. Ambler's birds are *love*birds, she kicks into total kiss-up mode. "Oh, how *adorable*," she gushes. Then she asks Mrs. Ambler, "Were they a gift from your husband?" like that would just have been the sweetest, dearest thing a man could do for his wife.

Well, Marissa and I may be able to see right through Heather, but not Mrs. Ambler. She goes from, like, forty watts of glow to about seventy-five and gives Heather the brightest smile. "How did you know?" Then she nuzzles her nose at the cage and says, "He gave them to me for our anniversary."

"How *romantic*," Heather sighs. "How long have you been married?"

Mrs. Ambler smiles at her again. "Fifteen years today."

5

"Fifteen years? Wow! And he buys you lovebirds? He must be terrific." Then she asks, "So how'd you meet?"

Mrs. Ambler keeps on letting herself be suckered. "In graduate school," she tells Heather. "We got married shortly after I got my master's degree."

Whoa now! A master's? A master's in *what*? Honestly, all I've ever seen Mrs. Ambler do is take roll and read the announcements and reprimand kids when they get out of line. I know she's in charge of the yearbook and has some class with special-ed kids. Oh, and she teaches eighth graders how to study or get focused on their goals or...I don't know what. But nothing that would seem to take a *master's* degree.

So while I'm busy trying to digest that, I'm also chewing on the math involved in this new Ambler Information. I mean, let's say you're twenty-two when you graduate from college. A master's is what? Two more years of college? So even if you tack an extra year on for good measure, Mrs. Ambler would have been at *most* twenty-five when she got married. And if she'd been married for fifteen years, that meant that this fifty-, well-on-her-way-to-sixty-year-old woman that I'd seen nearly every day for the whole school year was only...thirty-nine or forty?

I was stunned. I mean, forty is plenty old, but not nearly as old as I'd *thought* she was. And she was probably also a lot *smarter* than I'd given her credit for. Plus, at that moment she wasn't just my boring, worn-out homeroom teacher, she was a woman who was embarrassingly in love with her husband.

"I hope I find a man like him someday," Heather was

saying. "Somebody that'll give me lovebirds after fifteen years of marriage!"

She was laying it on thick, but Mrs. Ambler was oblivious. "I hope you do, too, Heather."

Heather nodded at the birds. "So what did you name them?"

"Tango and Hula."

Tango and Hula? Boy, this was getting weirder by the minute! Did this mean she was into *dancing*? Did she and her husband tango around the house?

Did she have a funny grass skirt in her closet?

Whatever. For the rest of the week Mrs. Ambler brought the birds to school every day. She would park them on her desk, where they'd flutter around the cage during the day making chirping and chattering noises and little *kissing* sounds, then she'd take them home at night.

They were actually pretty entertaining. Especially Tango, who'd kind of spin around on the perch or just hang upside down and make kissing noises up at Hula.

Mrs. Ambler became entertaining, too. Once when I came into homeroom, I saw her nuzzling up to the wires of the cage, cooing, "Who's so cute? Who's so sweet? Who's got little angel feet?"

Angel feet?

She was also training them to perch on her shoulder, and you'd catch her cooing at them, saying stupid stuff like, "Hula-hoop, now don't you poop!" and "Does little Tango want some mango?" She told us she didn't believe in clipping a bird's wings, so sometimes they'd flap

7

around the room, but pretty much they stayed in their cage or on her shoulder.

Anyway, it was during lunch on our second Wednesday with birds that we found out that Heather's ridiculous Vote-for-Sweet-Little-Me campaign had worked.

I also discovered that I *did* care. I choked on my sandwich when they announced the seventh- and eighth-grade candidates in all Class Personality categories over the P.A.—Heather was on the seventh-grade ballot for Most Unique Style *and* Friendliest. I actually stood up and shouted, "You have got to be kidding!"

Holly and Dot pulled me back down and told me, "Just forget it. We know she's a phony, and so does everyone else."

"If everyone else knows she's a phony, then why is she on the ballot? *Twice?*"

"Why do you think she's been kissing up to Mrs. Ambler?" Marissa grumbled.

"Wait—Mrs. *Ambler* came up with the nominees?"

"I'm sure the other teachers helped," Marissa said, "but she *is* the one running the Class Personality elections."

"But . . . what does *she* know about us? Why didn't the seventh graders get to nominate?"

Marissa nodded. "It is totally lame, huh? I wonder if we should talk to the administration about it."

"Oh right." I snorted. "Like they're going to listen to *us?*"

So yeah, the whole thing made me spitting mad, especially since Heather came strutting into science whispering, "Count 'em and weep, loser" as she passed by.

Couldn't the teachers see what Heather was doing? Did they sit around the faculty room going, That Heather Acosta has certainly turned over a new leaf. I am so impressed with the manner in which she's been conducting herself lately...?

Did they *all* have master's?

In gullibility?

I brooded about it for the rest of school, wondering if the seventh graders were going to be as blind as Mrs. Ambler when it came time to vote.

After school I went over to Mrs. Willawago's house to walk her dog. It's a new, temporary job that doesn't pay squat, but thanks to Grams I'm on the hook to do it until Mrs. Willawago's recovered enough from her foot surgery to do it herself. Grams says I'm securing my place in heaven and that this is the kind of thing you're supposed to do for recently widowed senior citizens who've had foot surgery and go to the same church as you.

I say it's one more reason to avoid church.

Anyway, Marissa went with me the first couple of times but didn't like the way Mrs. Willawago is so over the top about God and the Bible. "I can't believe she's Catholic, Sammy. She seems like a total thumper to me."

Well she was right about that, but I sure wasn't going to risk asking about it. That'd be like walking straight into Sermon City. Besides, I don't really mind hearing "Praise the Lord" and "Amen" and all her other evangelistic expressions—I just kind of ignore them. You can get away with a lot of religious mumbo jumbo around me if you just don't preach.

And the truth is, going over to Mrs. Willawago's has kind of grown on me. For one thing, she's got the coolest house I've ever seen. I call it the Train House because even though it looks pretty normal from the street—well, except for the cowcatcher that ramps up to her porch— it's got an actual caboose attached to one side of the back of the house and an old parlor car attached to the other. The caboose she uses as a guest bedroom, and the parlor car is where she and her husband used to hold Bible meetings. It's the most luxurious room I've ever seen—rich wood panels, chandeliers, brass trim, green velvet seats. . . . It's hard to believe that it used to chug along a track, but Mrs. Willawago swears that it did.

And besides the total coolness of the train cars, the main part of the house is like a museum of railroad gadgets and furniture and signs and photographs and stuff. The more I go there, the more I learn about railroads and trains, and even though I didn't really care about any of that before, now I find it, you know, *interesting*.

But the *main* reason I don't mind going over to Mrs. Willawago's came bounding across the house toward me as I stepped through the front door. "Captain Patch!" I cried as he yippy-yap-barked and dashed in a circle around me. "How are you, buddy?"

"Happy to see you, as usual," Mrs. Willawago said as she handed over the leash. "As am I, of course." Then she added, "Praise the Lord you're here. That dog needs a walk!"

Patch *is* kinda hyper and sniffs everything—not exactly the sort of dog you expect an old lady to have. He was a gift from Mrs. Willawago's kids, who live in different parts of the country and thought a dog would be good companionship for their mom after Mr. Willawago "went to be with the Lord." Supposedly he's a cross between an American foxhound and a golden retriever, but there's nothing furry or golden about him. He's got smooth brown fur and white paws and was named by one of the grandkids because of the big black patch of fur around his left eye.

Anyway, Patch always seems to get my mind off my problems at school and put me in a good mood, but not this time. This time when I walked him, I didn't forget about school, I obsessed about it. How could people have nominated Heather for Friendliest?

That's like nominating a vampire for Best Kisser!

Heather Acosta, Most Phony Seventh Grader—that was more like it! How come they didn't *see* that?

When I got back to the Train House, I guess Mrs. Willawago could tell I was upset, because after I let Patch go in the backyard, she said, "I thank the Lord every day for your help, Samantha, but if you've had enough . . ."

"Huh? Oh no. That's okay. I don't mind."

Trouble is, it came out sounding really flat. Like I *did* mind. And the next thing I know, Mrs. Willawago's opening her purse, saying, "I told your grandmother that I was willing to pay you, but she insisted that I not."

"Wait! No. It doesn't have anything to do with that. It's just . . . it's just this girl at school that's got me all, you know, tweaked." And because I was embarrassed that she thought I was grumpy because she wasn't paying me, I wound up blurting out a whole lot more than I normally would have.

When I finally shut up about Heather Acosta, Mrs. Willawago let out a little cackle and said, "Heather sounds a lot like Coralee Lyon."

"Who?"

"Coralee Lyon. You don't read the paper?"

I scowled. "I live in this town—I sure don't want to read about it."

She nodded, then said, "Well, Coralee Lyon—or Coralee Abbot, as she'll always be to me—now rules the roost of our city council, but back in junior high school she was not pleased with her place in the pecking order. She did all manner of sinful things to remedy that." She gave me a knowing look. "Lucifer still dwells deep in Coralee's heart, but people don't see him because she's learned to disguise her tactics."

"Oh great," I grumbled. "So you're telling me Heather'll never change?"

She laughed. "Who but God can write history in advance? But until she walks through the door of repentance, it'd be easiest on you to simply avoid her. I haven't spoken to Coralee in years." She looked toward the ceiling. "Thanks be to God."

So you see how much help talking to Mrs. Willawago was. And talking to Grams wasn't much better. "Good heavens, Samantha," she said. "If her end goal is to win some popularity contest, let her. Besides, the popular people in *my* junior high and high school all fizzled."

"But what if she turns out like Coralee Lyon?"

"Who?"

"Some brat Mrs. Willawago went to school with who's now ruling the roost on the city council." I hesitated. "What *is* the city council, anyway?"

Grams laughed. "A group of people who make decisions about Santa Martina's growth and development." She eyed me. "In other words, she's not ruling much of a roost."

Still. I didn't sleep very well that night thinking about how people like Heather and Coralee Lyon shouldn't be allowed to rule roosts of *any* kind, even flea-infested ones like Santa Martina or William Rose Junior High.

The next morning I woke up ridiculously early and started brooding about the Class Personality nominations some more. And since there was no way I was going to get back to sleep, I finally just got up, took a shower, ate breakfast, packed a lunch, and went to school. And instead of tearing onto campus at the last second like I usually do, I arrived a whole fifteen minutes early.

There were other kids around and everything, but I didn't see my friends, so I decided to go drop off my backpack and skateboard in homeroom. That's one nice thing about Mrs. Ambler—unlike a lot of the other teachers, she unlocks the classroom early so you *can* drop off your backpack or just meet up with your friends and get in out of the cold. Usually she's at her desk grading papers or reading a book, but lots of times she's going between the classroom and the office, taking care of teacher business.

Now, since I was so early, it crossed my mind that I might have the chance to ask Mrs. Ambler how Heather got on the ballot. Or maybe I'd just ask her how kids on the ballot were nominated.

Of course on *second* thought, that might make it look like I was sore because *I* hadn't been nominated for anything, which I didn't care about, but I didn't want it to *seem* like I cared. I mean, *looking* like you care is way worse than actually caring.

It's truly... pathetic.

But thinking all that through turned out to be a big waste of mental energy, because when I arrived at the classroom, no one was there. Well, no *people*, anyway. The birds were there, but it wasn't until I was inside that I noticed that one of them was out of the cage. And flapping for the open door.

Fast.

The doors at my school are heavy-duty metal. Every one of them has a small wire-mesh window, a kick-down doorstop, and a hydraulic closer so that it automatically shuts. Most of the classrooms have a whole wall of windows right next to the door, so I don't know *why* they're such heavy-duty doors, but they are.

And in all my junior high experience I can honestly say that I'd never been in a hurry to *close* a classroom door before. Open and dash in, yes. Close? Never.

So when I whipped around and pushed on the door to make sure the bird didn't escape, I learned something new about hydraulic closers—they can't be rushed. I mean, there I am, pushing like crazy on that door, but the stupid thing's fighting back, taking its old sweet time, closing at its own sweet pace.

So I drop my skateboard, plant both hands on the door, and really *lean* into it. And all of a sudden *shh-whack,* the closer gives way and the door slams shut.

Phew.

I look up for the flyaway bird but freeze with both hands still on the door. There, a foot above my head, is one beautiful, fluffy, blue-and-green bird butt sticking straight out of the doorjamb. And above it, pointing up to heaven, is one perfectly still, outstretched wing.

"Oh *no,*" I cry, whipping the door back open. But with a little *thwump,* the bird drops to the floor.

I pick him up and whimper, "Oh no! Oh no, no, no!" but it's plain to see—little Tango has danced his last dance. I hold him in the palm of my hand and stare. There isn't even any blood. He's just kind of . . . broken. And inside *I* feel broken, too. How can this be?

And as I'm standing there, holding this poor broken bird in my hand, I glance up, and through the door's window I see someone coming up the walkway toward the classroom.

My heart stops midbeat.

It's not Mrs. Ambler.

No, it's someone much, *much* worse.

TWO

There was only one thing I could think to do.

Hide!

I looked around frantically, then slid open Mrs. Ambler's closet and dove in, skateboard, backpack, dead bird and all. I found myself tramping lost sweatshirts, old backpacks, papers, and books. And it smelled like stinky feet, but I didn't care—I fit, and that's all that mattered. I slid the door almost all the way closed and held my breath.

Then there she was, pushing through the door— Heather Acosta.

I actually happen to be really good at hiding in closets because for almost two years now I've been living with my grandmother in a seniors-only building—something that may not *seem* like a big deal but is, seeing how me getting caught would mean her getting evicted.

In other words, we'd both be living on the streets.

So I've become real good at hiding in closets and peeking through cracks in doors because that's exactly what I do when someone unexpected comes to the apartment.

But still, experience or not, I was shaking. I mean, eviction is one thing, but Heather catching me with termi-nated Tango in hand?

That would be death by gossip squad.

So it took me a minute to realize that Heather was acting strange. She was moving sort of twitchy, glancing over her shoulder, sort of *tip*toeing. And the look on her face was almost euphoric. Like she couldn't believe her good luck.

No doubt about it—that girl was up to something.

But what?

I leaned a little closer to the opening in the closet door and watched as she hurried over to Mrs. Ambler's desk. She didn't seem to notice that the birdcage was open or that little Hula was inside it, all alone. She was focused on casing the desk.

She checked over the top of it quickly, then leaned side-ways so she had a better view of the walkway through the windows. Then she rolled open a drawer. "C'mon... c'mon, *c'mon*!" she muttered, pushing it closed and open-ing the next one. Then I heard her say, "Yes!" and sud-denly she had a stack of blue papers in her hand. She checked the windows again, then slammed the drawer closed and stashed the papers in her backpack.

What had she stolen?

Tests?

But what tests? Heather didn't have any classes with Mrs. Ambler, just homeroom. And why steal more than one test? She'd taken a whole *pile* of them.

Then it hit me—ballots! She must be stealing seventh-grade Personality ballots!

But . . . why steal them now? We hadn't even voted yet.

With a sickening *thunk*, the reason clicked in my brain. And just as I'm having the frightening thought that Heather is *way* smarter than I am, the classroom door opens and Tawnee Francisco and Brandy Cavaletto walk in.

"Hi, guys!" Heather says, cool as a breeze as she moves toward the door.

"Hey, Heather," they say back, and as they're heading for their desks to drop their backpacks, Heather sails out of the room, taking *her* backpack with her.

So there I am, an eyewitness to one of Heather's sneaky crimes, unable to do anything about it. I mean, I couldn't just pop out and say, Stop, thief!

I had a dead bird in my hand.

And yeah, Heather's crime was premeditated while mine was accidental, but still, something about what I'd done felt much worse than what Heather was doing. So she was going to win Friendliest Seventh Grader by cheating.

Me, I'd murdered a *love*bird.

Then I hear Tawnee say, "Hey, Brandy, look. The birdcage is open," and right after, Mrs. Ambler walks in. "Mrs. Ambler?" Tawnee asks. "Did you leave the birdcage open on purpose?"

There's a moment of hesitation, then Mrs. Ambler says, "No!" and hurries over to her desk. "Good girl, Hula," she coos as she shuts the cage. Then she starts looking around. "Tango?" she sings out. "Here, pretty bird, come here, sweetheart!" She makes little ticking noises with her tongue as she moves around the room. "Tweet-tweet-tweet! Here, pretty bird! Tweet-tweet-tweet!"

My heart's absolutely *ka-blam*ing inside my chest because she's moving closer and closer to the closet. And part of me wants to jump out and cry, I'm so sorry! It was an accident! and beg for her forgiveness. But I'm hiding in her closet like a criminal.

I looked guilty as sin!

"Come on, buttercup!" Mrs. Ambler twitters, only two feet away from the closet door. But just as I'm about to collapse from the shakes, she turns to Tawnee and Brandy and says, "I don't understand—where could he be?"

"I don't know, Mrs. Ambler," Tawnee says. "The cage was wide open when we came in."

"But . . . who opened it?"

Tawnee and Brandy both shrug.

"Was anyone here when you got here?"

Tawnee and Brandy look at each other. "Uh . . . Heather was."

"Acosta?" Mrs. Ambler asks, and there's a twinge of fear in her voice.

The girls nod.

The warning bell rings, so Mrs. Ambler moves around the room faster, looking all over. "Tango . . . here, pretty bird . . . come on, fella . . ."

Tawnee checks the bookcases and the floor beneath the windows. "He didn't crash into a window . . . I don't think he's here."

"Then where *is* he?" Mrs. Ambler's face is all pinched up like she's about to cry. "And who opened the cage?"

Then Brandy says, "We used to have a lovebird, and he could unlatch the cage by himself."

"He could?"

Brandy nods. "Once he figured it out, he did it all the time. We clipped his wings so he couldn't fly away, but we still kept the cage locked."

"But if Tango opened the cage, where is he now?"

I should have just stepped out of the closet right then. And if Mrs. Ambler had been alone, I would have. But Tawnee and Brandy were there, and they weren't the kind of girls to keep something like me popping out of the closet with a fluffy little bird corpse to themselves. They'd spread the news like fertilizer, and in no time the story would grow and blossom. There'd be no way of trimming it back. I'd be the Lovebird Murderer until the day I died.

So I just stood there, my knees wobbling like crazy, my hand all sweaty around the broken bird.

Then Tawnee says, "Uh...maybe you should ask Heather?"

Kids were already filing in. And pretty soon everyone was flapping their lips about Tango. Then right before the tardy bell rang, Heather slid in.

"May I see you a moment?" Mrs. Ambler asks, pulling her aside and maneuvering her over to guess where?

The closet.

"Yes, Mrs. Ambler?" Heather asks like a total innocent. I can see the profile of both their faces. Can count Heather's earrings...one, two, three, four, five...

What if they can hear me breathing?

Mrs. Ambler keeps her voice low as she says, "You were in the classroom earlier this morning?"

"*This* classroom?" Heather asks, and it's easy to see she's buying time.

Mrs. Ambler snaps, "Yes, Heather. *This* classroom. What were you doing in here?"

"What I was *doing* in here?" Heather asks.

Now, this is typical Heather tactics. Act innocent and avoid the question. If anyone *questions* your innocence, act insulted. If *that* doesn't work, threaten to sue.

So when Mrs. Ambler says, "Yes, Heather. What were you doing in *this* classroom *this* morning?" true to form, Heather gives an innocent shrug and says, "I was just dropping stuff off. Why *else* would I be in here?"

But Mrs. Ambler's got her eyes locked on Heather. "Do you have something valuable in your backpack?"

"Uh . . . valuable?"

"Yes, Heather, valuable."

"Nooo . . ."

"So why did you take your backpack with you?"

Heather hesitates, then tries to recover by saying, "Look, I just swapped books, that's all. I always take my backpack with me!"

But Heather's eyes are shifty, and Mrs. Ambler can tell she's guilty, only she doesn't know it has nothing to do with her bird!

Mrs. Ambler crosses her arms and says, "A minute ago you said you came in here to drop stuff off. What is it? Swap books, or drop stuff off?"

"Both! And why's it matter!"

"Now would be a good time to tell me the truth," Mrs. Ambler says. Her voice is hard, and it's making me shrink way back in the closet.

"I *am* telling you the truth!" Heather whines.

Mrs. Ambler shakes her head. "You never come to homeroom early, Heather. I may have been a fool to think you'd turned over a new leaf, but I'm not stupid."

"I . . . I don't know what you're talking about!"

"I can see in your eyes that you do! Just tell me, okay? Where is he?"

In a heartbeat, Heather's face smooths back. "Where is *he*? Where is *who*?"

"Tango!" Mrs. Ambler cries. "Where'd you put my bird!"

"How should I know where Tango is!" Heather puffs up and starts squawking like an angry jay. "I can't believe you're accusing me of this. I didn't *touch* Tango!"

"You're lying, Heather. I saw it in your eyes."

Heather gasps. "You can't just call me a liar! It's against the law!"

"So is stealing my bird."

"Why would I want to steal your stupid bird? And where is he, huh? Where is he if I stole him? Here—you want to check my backpack?" She swings it off and rips it open.

But Mrs. Ambler doesn't even look. "Where did you go after you were in here, Heather? Where did you take my bird?"

I'd never seen Mrs. Ambler like this before. And she sure wasn't following proper protocol or whatever teachers are supposed to do when they're mad at a student. She was just letting Heather have it.

So Heather zips up her backpack, swings it on, and gives Mrs. Ambler a steely look as she says, "I've got a roomful of witnesses here. You've called me a liar, and you've called me a thief. Apologize, or I'll sue for slander!"

Mrs. Ambler just stands there, looking her in the eye.

"Fine!" Heather huffs, then spins around and storms out of the room.

The class is dead quiet as Mrs. Ambler goes to her desk and plops down in her chair. And everyone seems to be holding their breath as she just sits there, staring at her birdcage.

Time ticks by. Mrs. Ambler doesn't lead the Pledge. She doesn't read the announcements. She just sits there.

Then finally, she stands and says, "A show of hands, please. How many of you come to homeroom early, re-arrange your books, and leave again *with* your backpack?"

Not one hand goes up.

"Sometimes I drop something off," Cassie Kuo offers. "Like my lunch? Or a project?"

Mrs. Ambler heads for Heather's desk. "What does she have first period?"

"Math," Monique Halbig says.

"Second?"

"Social studies," Derrick Stern says.

Mrs. Ambler digs through Heather's desk, then announces, "Both books. No lunch. No project." She shakes her head. "She's lying. I could see it in her eyes."

At this point I'd gone from facing the gossip squad to

23

seventh-grade suicide. If I got caught now, kids would think I'd tried to frame Heather. I could just hear them: Sammy was in the closet the whole time, can you believe that? And we thought *Heather* was sneaky... man!

And I know it would have *looked* that way, but I really wasn't trying to be sneaky. I was just scared. And if it had been Marissa out there getting blamed, I would have bit the bullet and stepped out. But this was Heather the Horrible—the person who'd terrified me into diving for the closet in the first place.

Then a little voice started whispering in my ear. *This is perfect!* it told me. *Heather's framed you for all sorts of things this year... so what if she gets blamed? It would serve her right!*

So I stayed hidden. And when the passing bell rang and kids filed out, I listened to the little voice some more. *Put the bird down,* it whispered. *Put him under that old jacket. That way if you get caught leaving the closet, you may still be able to lie your way out of it.*

Now, I know from experience that the trouble with one lie is that it usually takes more lies to cover it up. And if you don't watch out, you wind up telling lies to cover up the lies that are covering up the *original* lie.

But the fact is, I saw no way of telling the *truth*. So I ditched Tango under a jacket, wiped my hand on my jeans, and let my mind turn to the business of cover-up lies: I'd "missed" homeroom, so I needed a note from Grams excusing me for being late. But getting a note from Grams would mean having to explain things to her, and let's just say that it's been a long time since Grams attended junior high. There was no way she'd understand why confessing what I'd done would be seventh-grade suicide.

Besides, just thinking about telling her I'd killed a bird and hid in the closet made me queasy. It sounded so . . . cowardly.

So I decided to do what lots of kids do when they miss school—forge a note.

But I couldn't exactly forge a note in the closet. And I couldn't exactly go to the media center to compose one, either.

No, I had to get *off* campus, then come back with the note and act like I'd overslept or something.

The trouble was Mrs. Ambler. How long would I be trapped in this closet, waiting for her to leave the classroom?

Lucky for me, she must've been anxious to talk to Vice Principal Caan about Heather and the bird because she grabbed her birdcage and filed out with the rest of the kids when homeroom was over.

I didn't waste a second. I slipped out of the closet, out of the classroom, and beelined over to the service alley that delivery trucks use to bring in cafeteria food. The coast was clear, so I ran down the alley, squeezed my backpack, my skateboard, and myself through the chain-link gate, then hit the sidewalk.

My heart was like a jackhammer inside my chest as I escaped school, praying that no one had seen me. And when I reached the end of the block, I dared a look over my shoulder.

Nobody was watching.

Nobody was chasing.

I took some deep breaths and tried to calm down. Just a few simple lies, I told myself. I could handle this. Just a few simple lies, and it'd be all over.

No one would ever know.

THREE

It was weird being off campus during school. I felt like I was ditching, even though I was really trying to get *in* to school.

The first chance I got, I pulled over and started writing the note.

> To Whom It May Concern:
> Please excuse Samantha for being late. She overslept.
> Thank you,

Then I forged my mother's signature.

Well, I forged the signature my grams uses when *she* forges my mother's signature. Goes with the territory when you live illegally with your grandmother because your mom's in Hollywood trying to make it as a movie star.

Anyway, my version of my grandmother's forgery was awful. It looked like a little kid trying to forge their forged parent's signature.

So I practiced the signature a bunch of times, then started over on a new piece of paper. But I got nervous when it came time to sign my mother's name, and once again it was awful.

So *this* time I tried the signature *first,* and when I finally had one that looked pretty pro, I wrote the note above it.

I checked it over. Good enough. Then I packed everything up, rode back to school, and tried not to shake as I handed the note to Mrs. Tweeter, the office lady.

She read it and smiled, saying, "Well, you certainly look wide awake now."

Was I ever. But I just nodded and asked, "Are we still in first period?"

She checked the clock. "Yes, dear."

So off to class I went, my heart fluttering with excitement.

I'd done it!

It was over!

No one would ever know.

But later when Marissa saw me, she said, "Sammy! Where have you been?" and since there were other people around, I said, "Uh . . . I overslept."

"Well, you'll never guess what happened in homeroom!"

So I had to act like I didn't know a thing while she went on and on about Heather getting in trouble for snatching Mrs. Ambler's bird. "You should have seen Mrs. Ambler go after her! She was like a detective!"

I played dumb. "Mrs. Ambler?" I said with a laugh. "A detective?"

But Marissa was right—that's exactly how she'd seemed. And it made my stomach queasy again. What if somebody *had* seen me leave campus? What if they were discussing it in the office? What if they were checking my signature against the one on file? What if they were calling

Grams—or, they thought, my mother—to verify? Or what if Mrs. Ambler figured it out a different way? She would think I was the most despicable person to ever walk the halls of William Rose Junior High.

And believe me—that's saying something.

So I was in the middle of a total panic attack when Marissa nailed the Vault of Truth closed by saying, "Knowing Heather, she *killed* poor Tango and hid him somewhere so Mrs. Ambler'll never know what happened to him." She sighed and shook her head, adding, "This is an all-time low, even for her."

It felt like there was a dark spot on my heart. Like a bruise. And it was getting deeper and wider with every lie I told. Marissa was the one person I might have spilled the truth to, but after what she'd just said, there was no way I could tell her what I'd done.

So I just listened and nodded and acted surprised. And at lunch when Holly asked me, "Are you feeling all right?" I said, "Huh? Oh yeah. Just a little tired, that's all."

Heather was gossiping like crazy during science, playing the wounded innocent. She was so, so hurt that Mrs. Ambler had accused her. "I can't believe it," she moaned. "I just can't believe it. I really liked Mrs. Ambler... and I thought she liked me, too..."

Class Personality ballots were passed out the last ten minutes of school. The seventh-grade ones were blue, all right, and Heather's name was still on them. So I voted against her, hoping that the rest of the school was doing the same.

But when Miss Kuzkowski collected them and said,

"Can I have a volunteer to take these to the office? They go in Mrs. Ambler's box," I knew that Heather was going to win both categories. Wherever she was, she'd find some way to get to the office, then she'd slip her filled-in stolen ballots alongside the legitimate ballots that had been delivered to Mrs. Ambler's box.

Heather Acosta, Friendliest.

Heather Acosta, Most Unique Style.

She was a shoo-in.

When the dismissal bell rang, I just wanted to escape. School, my enemies, my friends...I wanted to get far away from anyone who knew me.

Or, at least, anyone I'd lied to.

So when I saw Marissa and Holly at the bike racks where we always meet, I came up with an excuse.

Scratch that—I came up with another lie.

"I've got to get over to Mrs. Willawago's early today," I told them.

Marissa frowned. "Why?"

"Uh...I've got to do some yard work for her."

"*Yard* work?" Marissa asked. "Now you're doing her *yard* work?"

I forced a laugh. "Not exactly. I, um, I just clean up after Captain Patch."

She blinked at me. "So let me get this straight—you're in a hurry to clean up dog poop? For a lady who's not even *paying* you?"

"Well, I...I've also got a lot of homework."

Marissa's eyebrows shot up. "You're kidding. Who's giving you homework?"

"Yeah," Holly said. "I've got *none*."

God. Was I lame, or what? I could feel the weight of the lies stacking up. And all of a sudden they seemed to be smothering me. "Look," I snapped, "you guys may not have any homework, but I do."

And with that I jumped on my skateboard and tore out of there.

Mrs. Willawago may live in the coolest house I've ever seen, but it's flanked by other houses that are pretty dilapidated, and it's on Hopper, the funkiest street in Santa Martina. Hopper's got no sidewalks or curbs or gutters, just a four-foot strip of asphalt that's all worn through, cracked, full of holes, and runs right alongside the railroad tracks.

Now, I don't know what the railroad tracks are actually used for anymore. Lights still flash and bells still clang when the safety arm lowers across certain streets in town, but all that ever seem to go by are locomotives. No boxcars, no cabooses, just one locomotive pulling another locomotive backward. They don't even switch tracks. They just *toot-toot* as they hold up traffic and take turns pulling each other across intersections.

Anyway, if all the roads in that part of town were like Hopper Street, you'd think the area was just poor, or "economically challenged," as my English teacher, Miss Pilson, likes to say. But since Hopper Ts off McEllen—which is a wide, pristine street that has the great big municipal pool complex, lawn bowling, and the fire station on one side, and the library, the historical society,

31

and city hall on the other—well, discovering Hopper Street can be a bit of a shock.

But anyway, *I* wasn't shocked because I'd been visiting Mrs. Willawago every day for three weeks. What I *was*, was out of breath. I'd ridden my skateboard really hard the whole way from school, and actually, being out of breath felt good. Like I'd cleansed my lungs of lies-and-deceit pollution.

Now, since you can't exactly ride a skateboard on what's left of Hopper Street, I popped up my board and headed down the road on foot, passing by the abandoned Santa Martina Railroad Office, where *Mr.* Willawago used to report to work.

"It was the cutest office you ever saw," Mrs. Willawago told me. "Oh, there were desks and the like, as any old office has, but the boys built a miniature railroad that went around the walls, complete with trestles they'd fashioned above the doors. If someone came into the building, *chuga-chuga-chuga-whoo-whoo*, it would trigger the train. Praise the Lord, what a sight! It would take a trip clear round, then come to a rest until the next person went through the door.

"They had the place decorated with pictures of the men working the line, crossbucks and a gantry, a semaphore, steel gangs and spikers . . . all manner of railroading paraphernalia. Frank adored the place, which is how we got our start collecting and decorating in here. It was a real ferrophiliac's delight."

Now, I didn't know what half the things she'd mentioned were, but ferrophiliac? I couldn't let that one slide. So I asked, "Uh . . . ferro-*what*?"

She laughed. "Ferrophiliac. Someone who loves railroads."

Before Mrs. Willawago told me about the railroad office, I thought it was just another old building ready for the dozer. There's chain-link clear around it, and all the windows and doors are boarded up. And slashed all over the plywood and the building's brick are layers and layers of graffiti. It was hard to imagine it ever being anything cute or, you know, *vibrant*.

But now that I knew its history, it made me kind of sad every time I walked by. It felt like the tomb of the railroad guys. A place where they'd spent their lives. A place that was now just fading memories.

Anyway, I walked by the railroad office, then the weedy vacant lot next door, past two houses with more car parts out front than a wrecking yard, past another weedy lot, and then the Stones' house.

The only reason I knew their name was because they lived next door to Mrs. Willawago, and she had joked that they were just a "Stone's throw away." Their house was definitely weathered, but at least their front yard wasn't a car-parts graveyard. It didn't have flowers and a white picket fence or anything, but it did have the finest lawn I'd ever seen. Not fine as in great—fine as in fine hair. The blades were thin and delicate and cropped really close to the earth. Actually, the first time I saw the lawn, I thought it was fake, but even in Santa Martina most people don't mow fake grass, and that's exactly what Mr. Stone was doing as I walked by.

He was pushing a little antique lawn mower. You know, no seat, no motor . . . just a handle and a wide spiral blade.

And he was wearing the same thing he always seemed to wear—blue coveralls, work boots, cop-style glasses that turn dark in the sun, and one of those ball caps with the built-in safari cloths in back.

I waved because it seemed pretty stupid not to, seeing how I was walking right by, but I might as well not have because he pretended not to see me.

No big surprise. Mr. Stone's a bit of an odd duck, if you ask me. His weight's all in the middle, plus he's got an overgrown brown-and-gray moustache that curves around his mouth. So between that and the shades and the hat, he looks like a dressed-up walrus.

He's also not very friendly, but Mrs. Willawago says he's actually nicer than he used to be. Apparently he injured his back at work, but she says she thinks he's been humbled by other medical problems—like skin cancer.

Whatever. Humbled or not, he's still not very friendly.

Anyway, it was trash day, so I moved Mrs. Willawago's empty bin into her garage, then picked up her mail and opened her front door. She likes me to just call hello and come in because it saves her from having to hobble over to answer the door. But this time I kind of choked on my hello because she was standing right there, flushed and flustered, clenching some papers in her hand. And she was breathing funny. Sort of shallow and *panty*.

If she had been alone, I would have worried that she was having a heart attack. But there was another woman standing right beside her. A very *patriotic*-looking woman, which somehow made her seem, I don't know, *safe*. The lady was wearing a royal blue skirt, a white blouse, and a red blazer that had a blue-and-white scarf peeking out of the little scarf pocket. Even her *feet* looked patriotic in blue-and-white pumps with little red buckles across the tops.

Something about this woman seemed familiar. Not like I'd met her before, but like I'd *seen* her before . . . maybe on TV? But before I could figure it out, Mrs. Willawago grabs me by the arm and says, "Oh, Sammy, come in!" like she's never been so relieved to see anyone in her whole entire life.

"Are you all right?" I ask, looking from her to the patriotic lady, trying to imagine what this woman could have done to Mrs. Willawago. I mean, she was probably about as old as Mrs. Willawago and way too beauty-parlored to look threatening. Her hair was all pouffy and dyed, her nails were a perfect candy-apple red, and her face was covered in pressed powder. But where Mrs. Willawago was casual and friendly, this patriotic lady had definite airs. Like a politician who pretended to be one of "the people" but really thought "the people" were a breed beneath them.

"I'll be all right," Mrs. Willawago was saying, but her voice was definitely shaking, "as soon as this woman gets out of my house."

"This woman?" Blue Butt says, her penciled-on eyebrows arching high. "Annie, honestly, I'm here as a friend to warn you, is all. It's going to happen whether you want it to or not." She laughs softly, but it's a slick laugh. A practiced laugh. Then she tags on, "You know what they say—you can't fight city hall."

And that's when it hits me—this woman *is* a politician.

Someone Mrs. Willawago hasn't seen in years.

Someone she would live happily ever after without ever seeing again.

Someone who, it turns out, had just delivered some very bad news.

FOUR

"What are you doing here?" I asked ol' Blue Butt, and let me tell you, I didn't ask it nicely.

She ignored me. "I'll be going now," she said to Mrs. Willawago. "But honestly, Annie, look at the bright side." She spread her arms a little, hands up. "Surely you'll wind up someplace better than this!"

"OUT!" Mrs. Willawago shouted.

I whipped open the door, and as she crossed the porch and started down the cowcatcher ramp, I said, "And feel free to stay away."

"Oh, I'll be back." She laughed. "To cut the ribbon."

I closed the door quick and said, "That was Coralee Lyon, wasn't it?"

"The Devil herself!" Mrs. Willawago said, hobbling into the kitchen.

I chased after her. "What ribbon was she talking about? Why was she here?"

Mrs. Willawago didn't answer me. She just thumbed open a worn leather address book, her hands shaking. Then she picked up the telephone that was mounted on a wall near the kitchen sink and muttered, "She will not get away with this!" as she dialed.

37

She stretched the phone cord so she could see out the kitchen window toward the street, so I looked, too.

No Blue Butt.

No Mr. Stone to tell her to take a hike.

Rats.

Then someone on the other end picked up, and Mrs. Willawago said, "Teri? It's Annie. Next door? I just learned that despite our protests, the city *is* moving forward with their plans!" She relaxed the tension on the phone cord and turned away from the window, saying, "You did? Why didn't you call me?...Oh, oh, that's right. I was at the physical therapist." There was a long string of "Uh-huh's" and "Yes, I know's," and finally Mrs. Willawago said, "Why don't you and Marty come over and we'll discuss what to do...Fine. Fine. That'll be fine."

When she hung up, I asked, "What is going on?"

She frowned. "Our illustrious city council had decided to seize all the properties on Hopper Street."

"To seize them? As in *take* them?"

"That's right. If they pass a 'resolution of necessity,' my property becomes theirs in as little as three days!"

"But...how can they do that? Don't you own this house?"

"Heavens yes, I own this house! And the Stones own theirs, as do the Quinns next door that way! And the lawyer on the corner owns his, too! He's put a heap of money into renovating that place! But the city council has decided to exercise eminent domain to acquire all of them!"

"Eminent domain?" It sounded vaguely familiar, but more like the end of the world than something you exercise. "What's that?"

"A law. A very *old* law. And it was designed to be used in national emergencies or times of war or some such. It certainly shouldn't be used to expand a *sports* complex!"

"Wait—*what* are they planning to do?"

"They want to tear down all the buildings on Hopper Street, pull out all the lovely pines that divide us from the ball fields, and put in batting cages, a sports café, and a community rec center. Instead of my house they want batting cages!"

A rec center? A sports café? Batting cages?

It sounded great!

"They offered piddles because that's what they say the house is worth, but that's really irrelevant—I am not going to sell. Not for a million dollars!"

I'm afraid *Really?* was written all over my face, because she frowned and said, "It may not seem like much to you, but this home took a lifetime to create. It's my honeymoon cottage, the place my three children were raised . . . I have countless memories here, and . . . and . . . Frank's ashes are scattered in the backyard!"

"I didn't—"

"When I think of the painstaking care he put into the additions . . . You can't just buy a Pullman parlor car anymore, you know." She pointed across the house. "And that one was a positive wreck when we got it. Frank restored it completely! It took him *years* to track down all the parts, not to mention refinishing and installing them."

The doorbell rang and she said, "That'll be the Stones. Do you still have time to walk Captain Patch?"

"Sure. And I'm sorry, Mrs. Willawago. I didn't mean to be—"

"Never mind," she said, waving it off. "A million dollars sounds like a lot, I know. Especially when you're young. But you can't let money erode your principles or you'll wind up with nothing."

It sounded like something my friend Hudson Graham would have said. Hudson's seventy-two, and I've learned that if I'll just take a second and actually *hear* the things he tells me, his advice can be really good. And since this felt like one of those Hudson statements, I found myself just standing there for a minute, letting what she'd said sort of sink into my brain.

Then Mrs. Stone stepped inside the house, saying, "Marty has to rest. His back's flared up from mowing the yard," and since I had a dog to walk, I grabbed Patch's leash and headed for the French door that leads from the living room to the backyard.

Before I was even outside, Patch saw me through the glass and started wagging and wiggling like crazy, spinning in a circle. I laughed and said, "Hi, boy!" then latched him to the leash and let him drag me through the side gate, out to the street, and up Hopper the way I'd come.

He kept his nose to the ground, sniffing his way along, and when we got to McEllen, I pulled him back, trying to get him to quit yanking on the leash. But he wiggled and wagged some more, yippy-yapping at me like, C'mon! You can't be tired yet!

So up McEllen we ran. Only as we were passing by the municipal pool, I heard someone call out, "Sammy!"

I skidded to a halt and looked around.

"Over here!" the voice called.

Then the body that went with it stepped out from under the pool entrance awning.

"Brandon?"

He looked taller.

Older.

Cuter.

How could that be?

My heart started bouncing around a little as he came toward me, saying, "It's been ages!" He broke into a blinding smile. "I ask Marissa about you whenever our families get together...she always has some wild story to tell."

I shrugged and looked down, toeing a line in the sidewalk with my high-top.

"So who's this?" he asked, ruffling the fur behind Captain Patch's ears. And since he was looking at the dog, I stole a look at him. Flip-flops. Swim trunks. A thin towel hanging around his neck. Swimmer muscles.

More swimmer muscles.

And tan, tan everywhere.

"Uh, his name's Captain Patch," I said, but it came out all cracked and funny sounding, and I could feel my cheeks getting hot. "I walk him for Mrs. Willawago."

The second it was out of my mouth, I knew it was the lamest thing in the world to say. I mean, who in the world is Mrs. Willawago to a shiny-haired, almost-junior-in-high-school swim star, anyway? So real fast I point back toward the railroad tracks and sputter, "She lives on Hopper. Had foot surgery. Needs to take it easy…"

He stops petting Captain Patch and asks, "On Hopper? In one of those old houses they're going to tear down for the rec center?"

I blink at him. "How do you know about that?"

"Coach Yabi's on the development committee. It sounds like it's going to be great." Then he grins at me and says, "So, how's Heather?"

Now, something about him jumping topics like that really bothered me. I mean, okay. There's a definite demolition quality to Heather, so maybe it wasn't actually *that* much of a mental leap, but the idea of tearing down someone's *home* didn't even seem to come into play. He was also acting like it was a done deed. Like even though they were still standing, in people's minds the houses on Hopper Street were already gone.

But before my tongue could untie enough to say anything to him about Mrs. Willawago not wanting to sell her house, not for a million bucks, *he* said, "Or should I ask, how's her brother?"

Mrs. Willawago vaporized from my mind. And if I was red before, I was purple now. I knew who he meant, too, but what came out of my mouth was, "Her brother?"

"Yeah," he said with a shrug. "I heard you were going out with him."

"Going *out* with him?" All of a sudden my tongue cut loose. "We're not going out! We're just friends! You know, people who know each other. And talk to each other. That's it! That's all. No hand holding, no kissing, no hanging out behind the gym." I scowled and actually looked straight at him. "Who told you that, anyway?"

Like I didn't already know—his blabbermouth cousin and my best friend, Marissa.

He shrugged and shook his head a little. "It's not like it's a *crime*."

I reined in Captain Patch because he was sniffing Brandon's leg. "What *is* a crime is spreading rumors that aren't true. What *is* a crime is being someone's best friend and talking about them at family pool parties, or whatever. What *is* a crime is betraying someone's trust, and believe me, I trust Marissa not to spread rumors about who I'm going out with! Especially when I'm not!"

"Hey, hey, hey," he said. "Sorry I brought it up. Casey's a cool guy and I was, you know, happy for you."

"Well, don't be!" I said, then leaned toward him and added, "He's Heather's brother," like, You chow-der-head!

Now, with the way I'd railed on him, I wouldn't have blamed him for just saying, Later! and walking his tan swimmer muscles back up the walkway and out of my life for good. But he didn't. Instead, he laughed and said, "You better come to the pool party on the Fourth! It won't be any fun without you!" *Then* he walked his tan swimmer muscles back up the walkway, calling, "See ya!"

No fun without me? Yeah, I'd gone to their Fourth of July party the year before, and yeah, I'd put up a big fight against Brandon's team playing water hoops, but . . . no fun without me?

I just stood there like an idiot. Of course. That's how I

43

always act around Brandon McKenze. Well, unless I'm laying into him about who I'm not going out with. Then I go on and on about *that* like an idiot.

Anyway, after he disappeared inside the pool complex, I let Captain Patch drag me along some more. Up McEllen we went to Cook, where he hung a right and powered past the fire station and police station. And since he was on the trail of something awfully sniffing good, he would have just charged into the traffic on Miller Street if I hadn't yanked him back. "Maniac mutt," I grumbled, and pulled him south along Miller, past the courthouse and baseball fields, all the way to the lawyer's office on the corner of Miller and Hopper. Patch was still zigzagging all over the place, sniffing every stick and stone in sight, but then he caught whiff of the lawyer's sign. To humans it may read:

LELAND HAWKING, ESQUIRE
ATTORNEY-AT-LAW

But to dogs? I think it must be like their society gossip page or something. No dog can seem to walk by without sniffing the daylights out of it and then adding his two cents, of course.

I find the sign pretty entertaining myself. It's the esquire part that cracks me up. I mean, an *esquire*? In Santa Martina?

Please.

But Mrs. Willawago was right—he had put a lot of work into remodeling it into an office. It used to be one of the little houses *on* Hopper Street, but when they'd fixed it up and added rooms, they'd changed the entrance so it faced Miller Street instead.

Anyway, I tugged Captain Patch away from the sign before he tried to throw his two cents in, then turned right onto Hopper and walked along the hedge that divides the office from what's left of the street.

The hedge is only about waist height, so it's easy to see over. And it's not like I was *spying* over it or anything, but I did happen to look, so I did happen to see the blue car that was parked behind the office.

I did a double take because in all the times I'd walked Captain Patch, I'd never seen a car parked back there. There were often cars parked out front, but not *behind* the house. And it's not like a car parked at a business is any big deal—Leland Hawking, Esquire had to have clients, right? But it was the *way* this car was sucked up against the house, hiding in the shadows of a big tree, that made me look again.

And then I noticed the license plate: CNCLOWN.

So okay. I'm a sucker for personalized plates. I always try to figure out what they mean, partly because it's a puzzle, and partly because lots of times they sum up a person for you, which saves you a lot of time trying to figure them out for yourself. I mean, if a person has a plate that is, say, BABMGNT, well, there you go. Might as well say BIGJERK. But if it reads HI-TOPZ, I'd probably shake my foot and give them a thumbs-up as they cruised by.

Anyway, the car caught my eye, and my brain got busy trying to figure out the plate. And I'm going, Seen Clown? Seein' Clown? wondering why someone with a car that was trying a little too hard to say luxury would want to advertise anything about clowns. You know the kind of car I'm talking about—spoked hubcaps, hood ornament, velour seats.... People who drive cars like that just don't seem to fit with circus creatures like *clowns*.

But then I realize that the *O* is a *Q*. It's really CNCLQWN. And *that's* when it hits me what the license plate says.

I pull back on Captain Patch and stop.

There's no way I can just go by—I've got snooping to do!

FIVE

CNCLQWN wasn't Seein' Clown at all. It was CNCL QWN.

Council Queen.

This was Coralee Lyon's car.

Not that I knew anybody else on the city council, but from the two minutes I'd been exposed to her, I knew—ol' Blue Butt was the sort of person to crown herself queen, even if no one else wanted her to be.

Just like Heather Acosta.

I pulled Captain Patch in tight and snuck around the hedge, my mind zooming with questions: Was she really trying to hide her car? Or was she just after a little shade. Was she visiting a lawyer's office for legal reasons? Or was this another one of her courtesy visits. After all, it was the last house on Hopper Street, even if the entrance had been changed so it faced Miller.

But why would you tuck your car way behind the house like that if you were just there to tell someone to start collecting packing boxes? And if she was there for legal services, why *this* lawyer? I mean, there was a whole barracks of lawyers over by the mall—why use one that had his office on land you were planning to take over?

No, something about her car being parked that way smelled sneaky.

Sneaky like stinky feet.

So I kept Captain Patch close and made my way over to the car as inconspicuously as I could. There was a blue pillbox hat decorated with red and white feathers on the seat, and next to the hat was a pair of white gloves. A pillbox hat and gloves? Good grief. But I could just picture ol' Lyonhead wearing them. The whole package said patriotic like her car said luxury.

Anyway, there wasn't much else inside—just a stack of clipboards and a map and a Diet Coke can in the cup holder. So I told Patch, "Shhh," and led him over to a small open window at the side of the house.

Now, looking inside someone's house—or office, even—is a little more dangerous than looking inside someone's car. Even if the house is small and you can see straight through the windows like you can with a car, it's not the same as looking in a car.

Not even close.

So my heart started doing a bit of *ka-boom*ing as I peeked inside the window. And it was supposed to be like a warm-up. You know, check out the kitchen, see no one, move up to the next window, see nothing, move up to the front-room window, see *some*thing. Kinda like they warm up big bells and gongs. *First* they give a little rumble, *then* they go for the big whack—it helps prevent cracking or exploding parts.

Trouble is, looking in the small window was like going straight for the big whack. Coralee Lyon was standing right there. I'm talking *right* there. If there hadn't been a screen in the window, I could have reached right in and pinched her patriotic butt.

I jerked back and held my breath, trying to contain my exploding heart. Then I heard the faint clink of a spoon and Coralee laughing. "Oh, Leland, you worry too much. She can't stop it. You know that!"

"But what about the Stones? I thought you said they'd jump at the chance."

"Well, yes, they are the one surprise in all of this. But don't you see? This is good for us!"

"But if they fight too hard, aren't you worried how it'll reflect on you?"

"On me? Oh, darlin', you're not worried about me. But have faith, would you? Everything will be fine. But be more forceful. You've been much too reserved!"

What I was hearing didn't seem to make any sense at all. It seemed like the opposite of what she *should* be saying.

I inched an eye back over the windowsill. Leland Hawking was jetting around the small kitchen, moving things in and out of the refrigerator, pouring coffee, wiping up a spill.... He sure didn't *look* like a lawyer, at least none of the ones I'd seen going in and out of the courthouse. I mean, lawyers always look pressed. Like they've got some secret lawyer facility where they can go right before court to get sharp lines steamed into their slacks and shirtsleeves. This guy's clothes were rumpled. Not *quite* like he'd been sleeping in them, but close. And they were *tan*.

Real lawyers never wear tan.

Coralee checked her watch and put down her coffee cup. "I'd better go, darlin'. Lots to do before tonight."

I hurried off the property and hid behind the vine-covered fence that divides Leland Hawking, Esquire's office from the little square stucco house next door. The vines were really dense, so I crept along between the fence and a graveyard of old washer and dryer parts that were stored alongside the stucco house's driveway. And when I finally found a place to peek through the fence, there was Coralee, sneaking out the back door.

I watched her scurry to her car and check over her shoulder as she unlocked the door. But just as she's pulling up on the door handle, Captain Patch lets out a ferocious growl, straining to my right against the leash. Coralee's head snaps toward the fence, mine snaps toward Captain Patch, and Patch is snapping at a man with biker written all over him—long scraggly hair, long scraggly beard, tattoos, and a gut the size of Milwaukee. "Hey!" he shouts at me. "Whatcha doin' back there?" But before I can come up with an answer, he says, "Oh, Patch! Hey, dude, mellow out," and produces a dog biscuit from the pocket of his faded black sweatpants.

In an instant, Captain Patch turns from guard dog to glutton. And while he inhales the biscuit, Coralee's car zooms away and the biker dude says, "He had to take a dump, huh?" He gives me a bushy grin. "Don't sweat it. Dogs are like that. When they gotta go, they gotta go. Just kick some dirt on it, would ya?"

So I turn around and kick some dirt on a pretend doo-

doo while he gives Captain Patch another biscuit and says, "Sorry if I scared ya, boy. I thought you was some poachers messin' with my stuff."

I almost choked out, Poachers? I mean, that'd be like calling gulls at the landfill thieves. But whatever. I just smiled at him and said, "Thanks for not being mad."

"Like I said, don't sweat it." Then he adds, "So, uh . . . you're friends with Annie, huh?"

Now, I could tell there was a reason he was asking me this and that he had more questions lining up in his head, depending on what my answer turned out to be. But before I could figure out what to say, a beer-bellied *woman* with long scraggly hair and tattoos comes out the front door, calling, "Andy? Your loser son's on the phone. You want me to tell him to go to hell?" Then she notices me and says, "Who the hell are you?"

Andy gives me a sheepish look. "Sorry 'bout that. My old lady gets kinda possessive." Then he calls over, "She's walking Patch. He had to take a dump."

"Ah," she says, like, Well, okay then. "So are you hanging up on PeeWee, or am I?" she says to Andy.

He lets out a heavy sigh. "I'll do it."

So I left Andy the Appliance Guy and his Old Lady and hurried back to Mrs. Willawago's. And after I let Captain Patch loose in the backyard, I went inside through the French door, saying, "Guess what!"

Mrs. Stone was still there, and she and Mrs. Willawago both turned to look at me but didn't say, What?

Did that stop me?

No way!

51

I blurted out, "That lawyer on the corner is in cahoots with Coralee Lyon!"

Mrs. Willawago blinked at me. "In cahoots? What are you talking about?"

"They had a secret meeting! I spotted Coralee's car parked behind the house, and when I peeked in the window, there they were, having a little chitchat about how nobody will be able to stop these properties from being taken over and how you guys fighting them is a good thing."

They both squinted at me. *What?*

"I know. It doesn't really make any sense to me, either, but for some reason Coralee wants him to be more—what did she say? Oh yeah, *forceful*. She told him to be more *forceful* tonight." I cocked my head a little. "What's tonight, anyway? Is there a hearing or a meeting or something?"

"Wait a minute," Mrs. Stone said. "You're talking about Leland Hawking? The lawyer on the corner?"

I nodded. "That's right."

She looked at Mrs. Willawago. "I thought you said he was *against* the project."

"That's what he told me!"

"When?" I asked.

"A month ago! Right before my surgery, when they sent around that appraiser! He told me not to worry— that he was a lawyer and knew just what to do." Mrs. Willawago shook her head. "Surely you're mistaken. Surely you misunderstood."

"I don't think so." So I told them the whole thing, right from the personalized license plate straight through seeing Coralee sneak out the back door. And when I was all done, Mrs. Willawago's eyes were wide, but Mrs. Stone's were hard and narrow. "You went right up and looked in the window?" she asked.

I shrugged and kind of pulled a face, and Mrs. Willawago came to my defense, saying, "She saw how upset Coralee had made me...." She turned to me and smiled. "I think it was very brave of you, and you're a saint for trying to help." Her face sort of fluttered as she added, "But maybe the bits and pieces you overheard weren't meant to be put together the way you've put them together? Maybe Coralee was really there for the same reason she was here?"

"I know what I heard, and it wasn't bits and pieces."

"Well, it certainly is odd . . ."

Now, inside I'm getting sorta steamed because I can tell she *still* doesn't believe I heard what I heard. And *why* doesn't she believe me?

Because I'm a kid.

Then all of a sudden she says, "Oh! Your grandmother called while you were walking the Captain—she wants you to go see her as soon as possible."

Grams had called? In the three weeks I'd been walking Captain Patch, this was a first. But before I could ask, Was anything wrong? a wave of acid flooded my stomach.

Of course something was wrong!

I'd killed a bird.

Cut school.

Forged a note.

There was no doubt about it—Grams knew.

❖ ❖ ❖

53

Grams and I have a deal. I don't lie to her, she trusts me. But on my way home from Mrs. Willawago's the little voice in my ear was back, telling me that this deal I had with her was just not fair. *Why should you tell her the truth about everything when she keeps secrets from you? Important secrets. Like who your dad is . . .*

Yeah, I told myself, good point! And by the time I was sneaking up the fire escape of the Senior Highrise, I'd convinced myself to do what Grams and Mom always do—plead the Fifth. Change the subject. Fake an illness.

Lie.

Why should I tell her that I'd killed a lovebird. Hid in a closet. Ditched class. Forged her signature.

Well, she obviously already knew about the forged signature part, but the rest of it concerned her a lot less than who my father was concerned me, right?

So I braced myself as I tiptoed into the apartment. I'd find some way around the truth. I didn't exactly know *how*, I'd just have to wing it.

"Grams?" I whispered. "I'm home."

"In here, sweetheart!" she called from her bedroom.

Sweetheart? Was this a new tactic? Or did she really not know?

I went into her bedroom and found her clipping her toenails. "Hey," I said, trying to act casual as I sat on the edge of her bed.

"How was school?"

Hmmm. Was this a test?

I tried to analyze the tone of her voice. Seemed calm. Normal.

So I tried to sound normal, too, as I said, "Fine."

"Nothing to report?"

Uh-oh. Was she fishing? Was this a new, sly granny strategy?

My brain scrambled around for the right response and finally settled on, "Uh, not really."

She switched feet and started clipping the big toe of her left foot. "These get so tough when you get older," she grumbled. "They're like toe tusks."

I laughed. "Toe tusks?"

"That's right." She lopped off a chunk. "Look at that. It's hideous."

So there we were, talking about toenails. Not dead birds, not ditching class, not forging notes.

Toenails.

And I wanted to ask her, Why did you call Mrs. Willawago's? What was on your mind? Did the school call and ask you about the note I forged? Did you pretend to be Mom? But she just sat there, clipping away. And I didn't want to give myself away by asking anything, so I just sat there watching. Wondering.

Sweating.

"So," she finally said when she was done. "Marissa called earlier. She was concerned about you." She looked me square in the eye. "She said you weren't feeling well and that you were acting strangely."

I looked down.

Shrugged.

Toed the carpet with my high-top.

"Are you okay?" Grams asked. "Did something happen with Casey?"

I snapped to attention. "No!"

"Heather?"

I shrugged. "Nah."

"But Marissa said—"

"I was just kinda in a frump, okay? Do I always have to be cheerful?"

She hesitated, then tried to be nonchalant as she asked, "Maybe it's puberty?"

"Gra-ams!"

"Samantha, we all go through it."

Well, fine. If she wanted to think I was moody and frumpy and irritable because of puberty, that beat her knowing the truth. So I shrugged and said, "Can we not talk about it?"

"Would you be more comfortable talking to your mother about it?"

I rolled my eyes.

She laughed.

"Okay then," she said. "I'm glad that's all it is. Marissa made it sound so...well, anyway, you should give her a call, let her know you're all right."

I told her I would, but I didn't. Instead, I just moped around. And let me tell you, there was a raging battle going on inside my head. I'd killed Mrs. Ambler's lovebird.

Scratch that—her *adored* bird.

And I'd accidentally framed my archenemy for it.

It was beautiful!

Brilliant!

Beyond any payback I could ever have plotted on my own.

So what was wrong with me? After the year I'd had with her, Heather deserved a *hundred* brilliant paybacks.

But the dark spot on my heart seemed to be spreading. Weighing me down. Casting a shadow over everything I felt or thought or did. I'd plotted ways to lie to Grams when all she was, was concerned. I didn't want to talk to Marissa because I couldn't think of anything to say. Suddenly I felt like a stranger. To her. To Dot and Holly.

To me.

I went to bed early, thinking that maybe I'd feel better in the morning. Maybe time would make all of this fade away. People would quit asking questions. Quit wondering. After all, no one knew what I'd done.

No one but me.

SIX

Marissa did try calling again, but I just pretended to be asleep when Grams answered the phone. I wish I *had* been asleep because my brain kept fluttering with thoughts about Tango. I could see his broken little body in my mind. Could almost feel his soft little feathers in my hand. Poor thing! I'd just left him under an abandoned jacket in the closet. He deserved better than that! Maybe I should retrieve him. Bury him. I mean, what would happen to him if he just stayed there?

Would he shrivel up?

Decompose?

So I had one of those nights where you can't turn your brain off and every time you look at the clock it's half an hour later, until the hour before you're *supposed* to wake up and then you finally, *finally* fall asleep. Waking up after a night like that is like diving after a twenty-pound brick at the bottom of the deep end. It's hard enough to touch, let alone bring to the surface.

But anyway, at least one thing was back to normal—I was running late for school. And you'd think that being all out of breath from riding my skateboard so hard would have made walking past Mrs. Ambler's closet easier, but it didn't. I mean, panting and pumping blood around for oxygen sort of supersedes panting and pumping blood because of nerves, but when I walked into homeroom, I got like a double dose of panting and pumping.

I tried not to look at the closet. Tried not to look at Marissa. Or Holly. Or Heather. Tried not to look at ... the substitute? Oh no! Was Mrs. Ambler so wiped out because of her missing bird that she couldn't bear to come to school?

I stumbled over to my desk, light-headed and wobbly. I stole a look at the closet. Had anyone been inside? I looked again. Had I left the door open that far?

The final bell rang, but instead of clanging in my ear, it sounded miles away. Kids' voices sounded like they were under water. Everything seemed a little ... fuzzy.

The substitute ran through the morning routine. Roll. Pledge. Announcements. Through it all I stole looks at the closet. Was the bird still there? Had Mrs. Ambler found him? Was that why she was absent?

"Sammy!"

I jumped. "Huh?"

Marissa was kneeling beside my desk. She laughed, "It's just me."

"Oh, hi."

"Hey, why didn't you call me back last night? You're not mad at me, are you?"

"Mad at you? No!"

She laughed again. "Well, good, 'cause guess what?"

"What?" I asked, trying to forget about the closet.

She dropped her voice even further. "You and I ..." Her

eyes darted from side to side, and a little smile danced across her face. And that's when it hit me—she was about to drag me into dangerous territory. I'm not talking gang territory.

Or drug territory.

Or even trespassing territory.

Those I can handle.

I'm talking something much more dangerous.

Much more frightening.

Boy territory.

All of a sudden fuzzy edges became sharper. Sounds became louder. I fully focused on her and said, "What are you up to?"

"Shhh!" She leaned closer. "There's a limo ride in our future."

A limo ride? My mind flashed with the image of chiffon dresses and blue carnations. "Marissa!" I hissed. "What have you *done*?"

"I've said yes."

"To?"

"Danny Urbanski."

"About?"

"The Farewell Dance."

"You're going to that? In a *limo*?"

"*We're* going to that in a limo."

"What?!"

"Shhhhhh!" she said again, her eyes darting around like crazy. "I'm not supposed to tell you this at all, but I am 'cause I know how spastic you get, and how in denial you are, so I thought a little warning would stop you from doing something totally stupid."

"Like?"

"Like saying no!"

"About what?"

She rolled her eyes. "Do I have to spell it out?"

"Yes!"

"But then I can't say I didn't tell you! And I'm under strict orders not to tell you!"

"By who?"

She rolled her eyes again, and this time she stood up. "Look. You have to go with us because I *want* you to, but also because I can't go if you don't. My mom said."

"So you're saying I'm a chaperone?"

She let out a heavy sigh. "You are the densest person I have ever met, you know that?" She knelt again. "We are going out. On a date."

"Hey!" I said, shoving her shoulder. "I *am* mad at you! I ran into Brandon yesterday, and I found out you told him that Casey and I are going out!"

She blinked at me, then stood up again and said, "Don't tell me you still have a thing for Brandon!"

Everything else she had whispered.

This she announced.

I yanked her back down and said, "No! And for the record, I never had a 'thing' for Brandon!"

"See? See what I mean? When it comes to guys you are, like, some bean-brained ostrich." Then she smirked at me and said, "And I told Brandon the truth. You are."

The bell rang. And before I could say anything or get my books together, Marissa jetted out of class, dragging Holly along with her.

61

"Hey!" I called, but they completely ditched me.

Heather, however, was still hanging around looking mighty suspicious. My stomach started churning again. Had she overheard about Brandon? Did she know about the limo and ... well, whatever Marissa was talking about?

Or maybe it was the bird.

Had she put it together about me and the bird?

I just acted like she wasn't there and tried not to look at the closet as I beat it out the door. Trouble is, I ran right into Casey. "Oh hey," he said. "There you are. I was starting to think you were absent again."

Again? Did that mean he'd been waiting for me the day before? While I was hiding in the closet? Framing his sister?

"You okay?" he asked, then he saw Heather coming out behind me. Glowering. He grabbed me by the arm and pulled me aside, calling over his shoulder, "You know what would be really scary, Heather? Act like you're in a good mood sometime."

"Shut up, moron," she growled.

"Back at'cha," he said with a laugh. Then he pulled me over to the end of the building near the service alley, where I'd snuck through the gate the day before.

When he saw that Heather had taken off in the opposite direction, he smiled at me and said, "A bunch of us are getting together for a limo ride next Friday. We're going to get some dinner, cruise around town, then go to the dance. It's a group thing, so I'm hoping maybe your mom'll let you come along?"

He was standing so close. His eyes were so clear. So brown.

I managed a real intelligent "Uh..."

"It'll be fun. It's me, Danny, Billy, and Nick...we're all inviting a friend."

I blinked at him. That's all, just blinked.

"We're going casual, so there's no, you know, pressure. What do you say?"

My eyes switched from blinking to darting around.

He laughed 'cause I'm sure I looked pretty freaky, but finally he said, "Can I take that as a yes?"

"No! I mean, I can't! I mean...I'm not...I don't...I can't..."

He looked away. "Yeah, I know. Dances are lame. But Danny's mom set it up and..."

His voice trailed off, and I started feeling really bad. I mean, yeah, dances are lame—at least they seemed like it in my head. I'd never actually *been*. But there was Casey, shifting from side to side with beads of sweat popping out of his forehead, and it hit me that he'd been really nervous about asking me to go.

So I said, "No, really, it does sound like fun..."

He looked up. He looked hopeful.

It was my turn to look away. "But aren't you supposed to be hanging with *eighth* graders?" I shrugged. "It's the Farewell Dance and everything...?"

He laughed. Then he laughed again.

"What?"

"In case you haven't noticed? Eighth-grade girls are really stuck up."

63

I laughed, too. "Well, yeah. They can be."

"Look. I want you to go, and if you can't, well, I'm not into asking anyone else. I'll probably just bail on the whole thing."

In my mind I could hear Marissa screaming, Sammy! You idiot! GO! I could also hear her saying, Plus, remember—if you don't, I can't!

She would hate me forever.

So finally, I shrugged and said, "Can't have you bailing on your own Farewell Dance."

He hesitated, then broke into a grin. "Are you saying you'll go?"

I gave a little grin back. "Are you saying I can wear my high-tops? I mean, you said it was casual, right?"

"You bet!"

"Then sure. Sounds like fun." He was positively beaming, so I added, "But I should warn you—I can't dance."

He laughed. "Neither can I!" Then he skipped a few steps backward, laughed again, and raced off to class.

The fastest way for me to get to my next class was to go up the service alley. But when I rounded the corner, who was beating it around the far end of the building?

Heather.

Well, great. Just great. She'd probably heard my whole conversation with Casey. Which meant only one thing.

Trouble.

And later, when Marissa pounced on me between classes and said, "Well?" like she thought I was holding a winning lottery ticket, I started really regretting that I'd

64

said yes. I mean, my head was telling me that this trip-in-a-limo was not a big deal, but my stomach kept fluttering and my heart wouldn't settle into a normal rhythm. It galloped. It skipped. It just kind of slammed around like it couldn't decide whether it wanted to hide or explode.

And now with Marissa's eager little face in mine, I wanted to say, Forget it! I'm not going! No can do!

She grabbed my arm and bounced up and down. "You said yes! I can tell! You said you'd go!"

I rolled my eyes. "But I'm changing my mind as we speak."

She stopped bouncing and her eyes got all wide. "You can't change your mind. It's against the rules of dating! If you said yes, then you *have* to go!"

I looked her square in the eye. "This is *not* dating. It's . . . it's get-together-ing."

"Get-to*gether*-ing?" she asked, her face all contorted. She leaned in. "Get over it already. It's a date! And it's going to be fun. Nick's nice, and Billy's a hoot. We'll get our yearbooks, dance, laugh . . ."

"Heather knows."

"What?"

"She was eavesdropping. I'm pretty sure she knows."

Marissa hesitated, then said, "So what? Look. She'll be so wrapped up in them announcing Class Personality winners at the dance that she won't have the time or energy to mess with you. Just forget her, would you?" She gave my arm a squeeze. "And thank you for saying yes. I know you're a little freaked out, but it'll be fun. I *promise* you, it'll be fun."

I raced to my next class, telling myself, She's right. Of course she's right. We'll just go and have fun.

Everything'll be fine.

The good thing about the stupid date was, it kept my mind off the stupid bird. I didn't actually think about how I'd terminated Tango until the end of school, when I went back to homeroom to get my skateboard. Then *wham,* it all came slamming back.

Mrs. Ambler was sitting at her desk, looking off in the distance like she was far, far away in her mind.

"Oh, hi," I stammered when she looked my way. "You were . . . you were absent this morning."

She gave me a weak smile. "Yes, I'm sorry. I . . . I overslept."

Her too?

She leaned forward on her desk and said, "Have you heard anything about Tango? Are the kids talking at all?"

No one else was there. This was my chance. My chance to confess.

But . . . but I hadn't had time to think this through! I hadn't expected her to be there. Or to ask me!

So I looked down and shrugged. "I, um . . . I haven't heard anything . . ."

She let out a heavy sigh and said, "I'm sure it's Heather. I'm *positive* it's Heather." She eyed me with a scowl. "And I now empirically know what a rough year you've had with that girl. I am so sorry for what you've had to endure—she is *vicious.*"

That was it. The one word that best described Heather.

Vicious.

But I couldn't say, Yes, ma'am. I couldn't say *anything*. I felt cold. And drained. Like the blood in my body had oozed through the soles of my shoes, straight through the floor, and into the darkness of earth.

"If it weren't for kids like you," Mrs. Ambler was saying, "I'd be totally disillusioned about teaching." She shook her head. "Kids today don't seem to know right from wrong. They're disrespectful and unappreciative and cruel." She eyed me. "You know what I'm talking about because you've been on the receiving end of a lot of that this year. And I really admire you because through it all you always held your head high."

Other kids were in homeroom now, exchanging books or picking up stuff to take home. So she dropped her voice and said, "If you ask me, Mr. Caan should have expelled Heather with that first incident—the one when she pretended you broke her nose? Okay, granted, we all thought you were a hothead, punching her like you did, but how about when she made those embarrassing phone calls to Jared Salcido saying she was you? Or the time she framed you for that graffiti and lost us the Sluggers' Cup? That should have been the last straw! But no, they let her stay in school, and now she's absconded with my bird. What's it going to take? Is she going to have to commit a *murder* before they finally get rid of her?"

The voice in my ear was going, *See? Heather deserves this!* But my heart seemed hollow and my hands were clammy and I felt cold and shaky all over. One second I wanted to blurt out the truth—the next I just wanted to die. She was so convinced it was Heather...and she admired *me*? She thought I knew right from wrong? That I always held my head up high? Well, maybe I *used* to, but I sure didn't feel like it now.

What had I done?

What was I *doing*?

And what in the world would she think of me if she ever, *ever* found out.

Mrs. Ambler gave me another weak smile and said, "Do let me know if you hear anything, okay?"

I nodded.

Then I grabbed my skateboard and bolted out of there.

SEVEN

It was a relief to get to Mrs. Willawago's. And she was relieved to see me, too. "Sammy!" she called, covering the receiver of her phone. "Mrs. Stone says the Captain's digging under the fence again. Could you run out and stop him?"

I looked through the French door and laughed. It was like a scene out of a cartoon. Clear in the back part of the yard, Patch was halfway under the old wooden fence that divided the Stones' yard from Mrs. Willawago's, his tail wagging, dirt flying out between his back legs.

"Patch!" I called, going outside. "Captain Patch, no!"

He stopped digging for a second, his eye-patch eye turning to face me. *"Arf, arf!"* he barked, happy as a pig in slop. Then he wagged his tail and yippy-yowled like, Come on, join the fun! and went back to spraying dirt in the air behind him.

I raced over and pulled him up by the collar. "Patch, no!" I wagged a stern finger at him. "No, no, no!"

"Arf, arf, arf, yip, yip, yip, aroooooo!"

He yanked free and dove back in.

Mrs. Willawago was outside now with the leash. "Here! Use this," she said, handing it over.

A minute later Mrs. Stone's head popped over the top of the fence. "Look at the size of that hole! He's nearly clear under!"

"I don't know why he's been doing this," Mrs. Willawago said. "Are you putting anything different in your compost heap?"

"No!" Mrs. Stone snapped. "Just grass cuttings and vegetable peels, same as we've always done."

I clipped the leash to Captain Patch and strained to see over the fence. The compost heap didn't look like much of anything—basically, it was like a big sandbox of leaves and grass clippings—but the truth is, it did sort of smell.

"Have you been rotating it?" Mrs. Willawago asked. "Or perhaps you've got too much water on it." Her eyes got wide. "Merciful God! I hope it's not attracting vermin. Compost heaps can do that, you know. Maybe Captain Patch sensed a rat!"

Now, it's funny—if someone had told me my yard stank and was attracting rats, I'd probably get a little defensive. But Mrs. Stone just went, "Hmmm," then said, "I'll make sure to rotate it more." She shook her head and tisked. "Rats is about the last thing I want around here. Gophers are bad enough. I'll have Marty set a few traps and see what we catch."

Then I noticed that her vegetable garden was about twice the size it had been the last time I'd looked over the fence. "Wow!" I said. "Your garden's looking great."

"Thank you! Which is why I don't want that dog diggin' his way over."

Mrs. Willawago nodded and said, "Well, since Captain

Patch seems to be digging in the same spot every time, maybe Marty could put some cement in the hole?"

"You know he can't do that with his bad back!" Mrs. Stone snapped. "And it's not our problem, it's yours!"

"Good heavens, Teri," Mrs. Willawago said to her.

Mrs. Stone took a deep breath as she held a hand to her forehead. Then she let the breath out and said, "I'm sorry. That meetin' last night completely fried my nerves. I *can't* lose this house."

"Praise the Lord you feel that way," Mrs. Willawago said. Then she added, "The truth is, I'm more than a little surprised. You've cursed having to live here for years."

Mrs. Stone looked down. "I know it probably seems strange to you, but . . . but things do change."

"I understand," Mrs. Willawago said in a real wise, supportive way. "How is Marty, anyway?"

Mrs. Stone's eyes darted up, then away. "He's . . . he's in pain a lot."

Very gently Mrs. Willawago said, "I wasn't referring to his back, Teri. I was referring to his cancer."

Now, at this point I've retreated from the fence and am ruffling Captain Patch behind the ears, pretending not to listen. But I can hear just fine as Mrs. Stone says, "Who . . . who told you he had cancer?"

"Why, no one had to tell me. I've seen firsthand what cancer can do. Frank's cancer was different, of course, but it does change a person." She shrugged. "Marty used to be quite . . . vocal? But lately he's been very subdued. And with the way he's been shielding himself from the sun, why, I can read the signs."

Mrs. Stone looked over her shoulder to her house, then whispered frantically to Mrs. Willawago, "Please don't say nothin' to him about it. He's a real private person and insists on keepin' it to himself."

"But, Teri, talking can be very therapeutic. That's why I go to confession. And surely Marty didn't go through that other substantial change without help."

Now the way she said "that other substantial change" was like she was talking in code. But Mrs. Stone wasn't deciphering it, either, and finally just asked, "What other change?"

"Oh, you sweet angel." She dropped her voice. "Why, the drinking, of course."

Mrs. Stone's face went blank, her eyes just staring at Mrs. Willawago.

"It's okay," Mrs. Willawago said. "Praise God, he tackled it! It must have helped a lot with . . . other things."

Mrs. Stone's face was still blank, her eyes still stared, but out of her mouth came, "How'd you know he'd stopped?"

"Well! It's been much quieter *and* I can see your recycle bags through my kitchen window. Used to be piles of beer cans, and now?" She smiled at her. "None!"

Mrs. Stone looked over her shoulder again, then whispered, "Please, Annie. If Marty knew I was talkin' to you about any of this, he'd be so mad." Then she said, "I . . . I've got to go now," and made a beeline to her house.

"Wow," I said when she was gone. "She seems really afraid of him."

Mrs. Willawago frowned for a moment, then said,

"With good reason." Then she added, "We all have the potential to fall into sin, but Marty Stone has a devilish cruel streak. Exacerbated, I'm afraid, by alcohol."

"He just seems like a middle-aged loner to me."

"He's that, too. In all the years they've lived there, he's said hello to me but a dozen times. Frank and I used to invite them over for Bible meetings, but it was always no, no, no." She took a deep breath. "For years I prayed that he would learn to walk with God but saw no signs of redemption." She chuckled. "The Lord works in mysterious ways, doesn't he? Strike a man with cancer and watch him mend his ways."

"But why's she still so afraid of him?"

"Rome wasn't built in a day, you know! This is enormous progress. Why, a few months ago he wouldn't allow her to talk to me at all." Then under her breath she muttered, "Probably afraid I'd see the bruises on her."

I cringed. "Did you ever call the police?"

"In the beginning. I'd hear screaming . . . Lord a'mighty. But Teri always denied he'd hurt her. What can you do but turn the matter over to God?" She straightened her posture and said, "But I shall keep my tongue from evil, as the words of a talebearer are as wounds!"

So she led Captain Patch to the gate, saying, "On to a different kettle of fish. Have you heard what happened at the council meeting last night?"

I followed along. "No . . ."

"Well, they went through the motions of hearing both sides, but it was all just a farce. They've already made up their minds—they see this land as theirs."

73

"Was Leland Hawking there?"

She stopped and faced me. "Yes! And he gave a very spirited argument against the project. He was very articulate and, praise God, made what I thought was a very strong case."

"That's exactly what Coralee *told* him to do!"

She unlatched the side gate and said, "But why? And honestly, Coralee gave no indication whatsoever that she knew him. I watched her very carefully."

"But...you do believe me, don't you? About seeing her in that lawyer's kitchen?"

She hesitated long enough for me to know she didn't.

"Mrs. Willawago! I know what I saw. I know what I heard!"

She stopped again. "But it doesn't make any sense, lamb. There must be some mistake."

"A mistake? No, you don't understand! I'm *positive*."

"I'm sorry, angel, I know you mean well, but as I said, there must be some mistake."

What she was saying, of course, was that *I* had made a mistake. And maybe I was being overly sensitive, because this sort of thing seems to happen to me a lot, but her not believing me totally ticked me off. I mean, why do adults automatically assume that they know more than you do? Are their ears better? No! Is their eyesight better? No! Do they move around quick and eavesdrop under windows?

No and no!

Mrs. Willawago, though, was oblivious, saying, "I'll have you know I *have* come up with a plan, and Teri's on board with it."

Goody, goody.

She chattered on. "The city council voted to continue the meeting to next Monday, so I don't have much time, but Lord willing I'm going to get community support behind *us,* starting with the *Santa Martina Times.*" She checked her watch. "The reporter's supposed to be here any minute, so would you be an angel and take the Captain on a really long walk? I want him good and worn out when the reporter's here."

I did say, "Sure," but inside I'm going, Yeah, great. I'm good enough to walk your dog for free but not good enough to believe.

I took off with Patch, thinking someone had made a mistake all right and it sure wasn't me.

I went the opposite direction than I'd gone the day before—past Andy and his appliance graveyard over to ol' Esquire's office.

No Council Queen car.

Big whoop.

I kept on trucking, and since Mrs. Willawago wanted me to take Captain Patch out for a long walk—and, I could tell, a good long time—I had the perfect excuse to go blow some steam at someone I knew would understand.

Hudson Graham.

"Say…!" he said when he saw me coming up his walkway. He swung his boots off his porch railing. "And who's this happy creature?"

"Not me," I grumbled. But it sounded so pathetic that it actually made me laugh. "His name's Captain Patch," I said, holding him back. "Or just Captain. Or just Patch. Or *the* Captain. He belongs to Mrs. Willawago. You probably know her 'cause she goes to St. Mary's."

"Sure I do," he said.

I moved closer to the porch, looking around for Rommel, Hudson's ancient wiener dog.

"He's sleeping inside," Hudson said. "And too old to care." He patted his leg for Captain Patch to come closer, saying, "So why are you walking Annie's dog?"

"She had foot surgery. I've been doing it every day for three weeks. Grams calls it heaven insurance, but as of today I think I'm canceling my policy."

Hudson didn't miss the serious grumble in my voice. He nodded and said, "Feeling taken advantage of?"

I plopped in a chair. "Yeah, and ticked off."

"Because . . . ?"

"Because I heard and saw something that may not make sense, but I heard and saw it, okay? And instead of trying to figure out a way to *make* it make sense, they figure I'm just a kid who doesn't know what she heard and saw!"

"*They* being . . . ?"

"Mrs. Willawago and her natched-out neighbor, Mrs. Stone."

He stifled a grin. "She's got a natched-out neighbor, huh?"

I rolled my eyes. "Okay, earthy. She grows her own vegetables, has a compost heap, wears Birkenstock sandals with *socks,* if you can believe that."

"Ah," he said, then asked, "So what is it you heard and saw?"

76

I flopped back and let out a real dramatic sigh. But right away I sat up a little and laughed because the sigh was so, you know, teen-tantrum. Then I shook my head and said, "It's so convoluted. Involves lawyers and the Council Queen and eminent domain."

"The Council Queen? Eminent domain?" He got up and headed inside the house, saying, "Stay put. This is going to take some refreshments."

"You know what eminent domain is?" I called after him.

"Sure!" His head poked back out through the door. "I also know that you saw what you saw and you heard what you heard . . . and *I* want to hear all about it." Then he disappeared inside.

Good ol' Hudson. I already felt a ton better. Captain Patch seemed to like visiting Hudson, too, because he let out a big, contented snort and got comfy under my chair. When Hudson returned with a tray of iced tea and double-decker brownies, he said, "Eminent domain is how the Town Center Mall got built, you know."

I sat up straight. "You're kidding!"

He poured me some tea and handed it over. "This shocks you?"

"Yes!" I took a sip. "Are you telling me there used to be houses where the *mall* is?"

He nodded. "The mall, the parking lots, the lawyers' offices . . . that whole area used to be houses."

"And what? They kicked all those people out of their homes? For a *mall*?"

"They were bought out, but yes, quite a few were forced out against their will."

"But...why didn't all those people get together and say forget it!"

"They tried."

"So?"

"So in the end it comes down to the law, and the law states that so long as the government pays just compensation, it can acquire properties for public use. There's usually not much you can do about it except sue for greater compensation."

"I can't *believe* that!"

Hudson nodded. "Originally it was designed for use in national emergencies or for building railroads...that sort of thing. So instead of jogging a railroad track around privately owned parcels, they could run straight through them. Unfortunately, governments now exercise eminent domain for things like malls and parking lots."

"That absolutely stinks."

He nodded and took a sip of tea. "Goldie Danali would agree with you."

"Goldie Danali? Who's that?"

"A woman who used to live on the corner of Cook and Miller. She had a cute little place, white picket fence, flowers...the kind of house you get a real warm feeling from just walking by."

"So she didn't want to move and they made her anyway?"

"More than that. She had a job at the courthouse, which as you know is right across the street. And since she had problems with her legs, she went everywhere in a little motorized golf cart."

"Oh, you've got to be kidding."

"About the golf cart?"

"No! About them making a lady who's basically in a wheelchair move! How could they do that?"

Hudson gave me a wry smile. "They 'relocated' her in the name of the community. The community, they said, needed a mall. The irony is, they can't seem to rent the offices on the spot where Goldie Danali's house was." He grinned. "Rumor is they're haunted."

"No! By Goldie?"

"That's right. She died shortly after they forced her out."

"Aw, come on. You're making this up . . ."

He put up a hand like he was taking an oath. "On my honor."

I thought about it a minute, then said, "Well, it would serve them right if it's haunted. But still. If they kicked a lady in a wheelchair out of her house, there's no way they're going to let Mrs. Willawago keep hers."

He nodded. "I figured this had to do with the proposed rec center." He took the newspaper out from under his chair and flipped it open to the community section. Beneath the heading NEW REC CENTER GAINS SUPPORT was a picture of Coralee in her patriotic suit watching attentively as a man held a pointer to a drawing. There was also a picture of Leland Hawking giving a "spirited rebuttal," and to the side of the article was a diagram of the "proposed improvements": batting cages, café, and rec center.

I studied it and couldn't help thinking, Wow . . . these

79

proposed improvements look great! And then there it was again, that voice in my ear. *Yeah,* it whispered. *You and Marissa would use this a lot. And what do you care if ol' Willy-whaddya-know has to move? You try to help her and she doesn't believe you! She practically called you a liar...*

From the base of my neck, halfway down my back, and then around my chest, I felt a core-chilling shiver. Like my brain had touched something very cold and was sending it down to cage my heart.

It was a frightening feeling. My heart began beating faster—like it was banging against the cage, trying to break free. So I shook off the voice and tried to get my mind back on track. "So explain this," I said to Hudson. "Why would Coralee Lyon hold a clandestine meeting in the kitchen of Leland Hawking, Esquire's office, telling him to speak out *against* the rec center at the city council meeting?"

Hudson's bushy white eyebrows shot up. "Is that what you heard and saw?" He pointed to the newspaper. "This councilwoman told this lawyer to argue against the takeover?"

"That's right."

He took a brownie and sat back. "All right. I need details."

I felt the fear of the chill start to lift from my heart as I threw myself into telling the story of how I'd been walking Captain Patch and noticed Coralee's car and figured out the license plate and started sniffing around. And let me tell you, I gathered a good head of steam telling him how ol' Fanny Flag told Esquire Eyes that it was a *good* thing that the Stones didn't want to sell and how he started worrying and she started insisting. By the time I was describing how she'd snuck out the back door to get to her car, my mouth was like a runaway train, and when I finally put the brakes on and quit talking, I didn't feel the chill at all anymore.

I felt good.

Hudson, though, just sat there chewing endlessly on a bite of brownie.

So finally, I said, "See? It doesn't make any sense. But I heard what I heard and I saw what I saw, and it wasn't out of context or anything else, in case that's what you're wondering."

"No, no. I'm not wondering that." He shook his head, and for the first time since I'd met him, he looked stumped. "I'm wondering why she would say that when the more expensive the project becomes to the taxpayer, the worse the project—and Ms. Lyon—looks to the community."

"What do you mean, the more expensive it becomes?"

"Well, when the city was acquiring land for the mall, some of the homeowners didn't like the amount of money they were being offered. So the homeowners sued, and a lot of them wound up with substantially more money."

"So . . . so the only reason you'd want to fight city hall is if you *owned* property on Hopper Street."

He shrugged. "*Or* if you didn't want the development going in next to your property, *or* if . . . ," but then he got what I was saying. He faced me, his eyes opened wide.

"That's got to be it!" I whispered. "Coralee Lyon owns property on Hopper Street!"

He shook his head. "But that would be a conflict of interest. Probably even illegal."

I jumped up. "I bet she owns that lawyer's office! I bet Leland Hawking is renting from her."

Hudson pointed to the newspaper. "But it says that *he* owns that property. That *he's* made a lot of improvements to it."

"Well, what if they went in on it together? *Or* what if she owns one of those other houses on Hopper? There are two vacant lots and two run-down houses with wrecked cars all over the yards—we don't know anything about who owns those!"

Hudson nodded. "If she has *any* financial stake in them, she should have recused herself from the proceedings instead of pushing them along." He stood up, too, and said, "The truth does have an interesting habit of finding its way to the surface, but in this case I think it could use a little help. And since property ownership is a matter of public record, why don't you go do your dog-walking job and let me see what I can find out."

"Really?" I tugged on the leash, waking the Captain, who was snoring under my chair. "You know how to look it up?"

"I'm going to start by making some phone calls."

"Well, when you find something out, call me!" I said, heading down the walkway.

"Will do!"

On my way back to Hopper Street it hit me that I wasn't ticked off anymore. I just wanted to get back and tell Mrs. Willawago what we'd figured out. So I ran the whole way, and when I got to the Train House and spotted a white pickup truck in the driveway, I remembered that Mrs. Willawago was talking to a reporter.

So much the better! I'd tell them both what we suspected.

I went right in, taking Captain Patch with me. And when I found Mrs. Willawago and the reporter in the living room, I blurted out, "Guess what!"

But just as their heads are turning to face me, there's a mind-jolting *crash,* and shards of glass shoot through the room.

Mrs. Willawago screams and drops to the floor while the reporter dives for cover behind a chair. I yank Patch back and hide behind the hallway wall. My eyes are cranked wide, my heart is whacking against my chest, and when I peek out around the corner, I see that the French door now looks like the mouth of a glass shark.

And then I see a big rock sitting on the carpet right in front of it.

I jet down the hall, shove Captain Patch in a bedroom, then hurry over to Mrs. Willawago, who's holding her heart and breathing like she's just run a mile. "Are you all right?" I ask her.

"Did somebody *shoot?*" she asks back, her voice all shaky.

The reporter is half standing behind the chair, and his

83

eyes are like little planets doing a half orbit of his head, back and forth, back and forth.

"No," I tell her. "It was just a rock."

But even from across the room I can see that this is not just some wayward rock.

It's a message.

EIGHT

The rock that's crashed through the French door is smooth and shaped like a large, flat egg. And on it, written in black marker, is SELL OR SUFER.

For a minute it's like I'm trying to make out a license plate again, because the words are kind of crammed together. And either it's a puzzle I'm not getting or a word's misspelled.

And what kind of moron busts your window with a misspelled threat?

But just as I'm deciding that, yeah, this was definitely a misspelled threat, the doorbell rings. And before anyone can react to *that,* Mrs. Stone comes busting through the front door in her Birkenstocks and socks, shouting, "Annie! Annie!" She spots her and cries, "Look what somebody threw!"

She's flushed. Out of breath. Shaking.

And she's holding a smooth, egg-shaped rock.

"It says sell or suffer!" she cries. Then she sees all the broken glass. "Did you get one, too?"

So I nod and show Mrs. Willawago the rock that had crashed through her French door. "You got the same message."

"Why...it's misspelled!" Mrs. Willawago says, blinking at me. Then she looks at Mrs. Stone's. "So is yours!"

"Let me see," the reporter says.

So there they all are, in a huddle around these rocks, and I don't know—something about it seems funny: (a) someone's just busted their windows with a menacing threat and they're worried about the spelling? And (b) how embarrassing would that be? To toss a rock through someone's window and misspell the message? I mean, what if they'd written CELL OR SUFFER! Or MOVE OR DYE!

Anyway, the good thing about it is that Mrs. Willawago and the reporter don't seem scared anymore—they're actually laughing about how the person who'd thrown the rock must be an uneducated oaf.

Mrs. Stone finally stops them, saying, "Look at all this glass!"

The reporter nods. "That must've been a very old window—definitely not safety glass."

"It could have killed you!" Mrs. Stone says, her eyes all wide. She wags her rock and says, "And this one could've killed Marty! He was just going out the slider—it missed him by inches!"

The reporter nods. "You ladies should call the police."

So Mrs. Willawago goes to the phone, saying, "I can't imagine that whoever did this thinks it'll make us move. Good Lord, do they really believe they can get away with this?"

Now, while Mrs. Willawago's on the phone, the reporter produces a small notebook and says, "You must be Teri Stone, Annie's neighbor?"

"That's right."

"She told me a little about you. I'm Cal Torres, ma'am. From the *Times*. Did you say your husband's name is Marty?"

Mrs. Stone nods.

"The two of you have lived next door how long?"

"Twelve years."

The reporter glances over at Mrs. Willawago talking on the phone in the kitchen, then turns to face Mrs. Stone. "I'm going to do everything I can to help you. What's going on here is just wrong."

"Oh, thank you!" Mrs. Stone says, her face smoothing back. "You don't know what that means to us."

Mrs. Willawago's back a minute later, saying, "The police are on their way." She turns to the reporter. "Will you stay?"

"Yes, ma'am! And I'm going to ask my editor to give this story some front-page coverage."

Now, something about knowing that the police are coming always makes me want to get going. Maybe it's just in Santa Martina, I don't know, but around here if you see someone rob a bank or something, the cops won't let you say, He went thataway! First they've got to know who you are and where you live and what you had for breakfast.

Well, okay. The breakfast part has only come up once, but the other questions come up every time, and in my case they're questions that make me very nervous.

And since I didn't feel like trying to figure out how to avoid their questions, and since the police station is about

87

ten seconds by squad car from Hopper Street and I didn't have enough time before they arrived to explain my theory about Coralee Lyon possibly owning property on Hopper Street, I just told Mrs. Willawago, "I, uh, I've got to get going." Then I added, "Oh—I put Captain Patch in your bedroom."

"In my bedroom?" she asks all kind of hyper, then takes off down the hall. So I grab my skateboard and backpack and hurry east on Hopper Street—the way I think the police *won't* be coming.

There's no blue car lurking behind Leland Hawking, Esquire's, so I just keep on trucking, heading north on Miller Street with one eye on the lookout for cop cars while my brain tries to make sense of things.

The trouble, though, is that the more I think about it, the more things *don't* make sense. The rock-through-the-window business was messing everything up. I mean, if Coralee Lyon wanted people to resist selling their property because she owned something on Hopper and resisting would mean she'd get more money for it, well, that didn't go along with 'sell or suffer.' The rocks had been a real threat. Done by someone who was worried that Mrs. Willawago and Mrs. Stone *wouldn't* sell. But from what I'd overheard in Leland Hawking's kitchen, Coralee *wasn't* worried about that.

Leland Hawking, on the other hand, *had* been.

Hmmm.

But he had to know how to spell *suffer*. He was a lawyer! Weren't they always trying to get money for "pain and suffering"?

'Course maybe he'd misspelled it on purpose to make people think it was an *un*educated person.

But who delivers a threat through a window these days? It seemed like something out of an old mob movie.

Besides, if this eminent *insane* law was strong enough to get Goldie the Golf Cart Lady kicked out of her house, what were they so worried about? Why threaten?

Unless...unless there was some loophole. Some way that Mrs. Willawago and the Stones *wouldn't* have to give up their houses.

I sure didn't know anything about that. But still. I couldn't help wondering: Who would that hurt the most?

By now I was almost at the mall, which in my life is pretty unavoidable. I pass it on my way to school, on my way home, on my way to Hudson's, on my way to Marissa's.... It's a big, blocky behemoth of parking, stores, and office buildings. And although I've never been big on the mall itself, I do like the winding walkway that goes clear around it. It's fun to ride a skateboard on, and it's actually kinda scenic, too. There are trees and shrubs and flowers and grass...it's like a pathway through a really skinny park. It can almost make you forget that you're riding alongside the Mammoth Shrine of Merchandise.

But anyway, as I crossed over Cook Street, I remembered what Hudson had said about Goldie Danali living on the corner straight ahead of me.

A little house with a white picket fence? *Here?* I almost couldn't picture it. The stack of office buildings seemed to *belong* there because that's what I was used to seeing.

But then I noticed the signs in the corner office windows. In big bold lettering, on all three levels, they all said the same thing.

AVAILABLE.

I smiled. Maybe Goldie Danali had found a way to fight city hall after all.

When I got to the other side of the street, I put down my skateboard and started riding again. And actually, I was feeling pretty good, thinking about lawyers being spooked away from renting those offices.

Seemed very poetic.

But just as I'm starting to clickity-clack along the winding walkway at a decent speed, a jaybird dive-bombs me. I'm talking *whoosh*, he blasts right across my face, cawing at me like a big blue crow. And he startles me so bad that I jerk back, stumble off my board, and practically bite the dirt.

"Stupid flying gizzard!" I shout after him. But as I stand up and collect my skateboard, I suddenly remember.

Tango.

I couldn't believe it—between eminent domain and flying rocks and people not believing me, I'd actually forgotten about Tango.

But now I was remembering, all right, and my stomach was suddenly queasy.

I looked around for the jay. He'd been like an agent from the God of Dead Birds, crying, Killer! Killer!

I got back on my board and shook off the thought. I mean, how ridiculous is that? The God of Dead Birds. Please.

Trouble is, once I was rolling down the walkway again, I started noticing tweeting. It was just birds-in-the-trees type of tweeting, which I'm sure is there all the time, but once I noticed it, it seemed to get louder and louder.

Tweet-tweet-tweet. Warble-warble-warble. Tweet-tweet-tweet.

Then I started *seeing* birds. They were everywhere. Flapping around, pecking at bugs, warbling in the trees, in the phone wires…everywhere! I'm not talking big ugly ones like in that Alfred Hitchcock movie. These were scarier than those.

These were pretty little *tweety* birds.

They sounded so cheerful. So carefree.

So…*alive*.

And I know this is going to sound crazy, but I swear on my high-tops—these birds were tweeting at *me*.

Sammy, Sammy! they seemed to be singing. *Pretty day! Pretty day to be alive!*

I zoomed along faster, trying to get away from the birds. But the trouble with birds is, they can *fly*. And the faster I rode, the faster they seemed to fly.

Do you think we don't know? Do you think you can hide? Do you think what you're doing is right?

"Leave me alone!" I shouted at a stupid little red-breasted finch.

Tweet-tweet-tweet.

"It was an accident! An ac-ci-dent!"

Warble-warble-tweet.

"No! I liked him! I would never have hurt him on purpose!"

Tweet-tweet-tweet.

"Stop it! Stop following me!"

Warble-warble-tweet.

I was never so glad to get home. But as I slipped through the door, I heard Grams say, "Oh, here she is now!" Then she held the phone out to me and whispered, "It's Marissa."

Grams kissed me on the cheek as I took the phone, then rubbed my arm in a real comforting way and left the kitchen.

"Hey," I said into the receiver.

"Where'd you go after school?" she asked. Not mean or anything. Just more, you know, conversational.

"Sorry. Mrs. Ambler hung me up."

"Mrs. Ambler did? I thought she was absent."

Was she saying she thought I was lying? Did she think I'd *ditched* her?

Well, I had, kinda. I mean, I always meet Marissa at the bike racks. But after Mrs. Ambler had gone on and on about kids disappointing her and her admiring me, well, I hadn't wanted to see anyone.

"Sammy?"

"Huh?"

"Sam-my!"

"Sorry! Uh, Mrs. Ambler. Right. I think she only missed homeroom. She said she overslept."

Marissa tisked. "Poor thing. She was probably up all night about her bird." Then quicker than you can flick off a tear, she said, "So? What are we going to wear?"

"What are we going to *wear*?"

"To the dance!"

Now, I know I should've just said, Jeans and high-tops, what did you think? Or maybe, Casey said it was casual, so don't even start about dressing up. But I sort of freaked out. I mean, I'd *just* been chased clear around the mall by agents of the Dead Bird God, Marissa'd *just* said that bit about Mrs. Ambler being up all night because of Tango, and I was stuck in a tiny apartment with Grams hovering somewhere around the corner. I felt trapped. Suffocated. I didn't want to talk about what to wear to a stupid dance. I wanted to be left alone. I wanted to sort things out.

I needed some time to *think*.

So instead of saying, High-tops, of course! I said, "I . . . I can't talk about this right now."

"Why not?"

"I . . . I have to go . . . pour cement."

"You have to go pour *cement*?"

Grams appeared from around the corner. "You have to go pour *cement*?"

"*Where?*" Marissa asked.

"*Where?*" Grams echoed.

It felt like the tweety birds chirping at me again. "Never mind! Never *mind*!" I snapped at both of them, then slammed down the phone.

"*Sa*man*tha!*" Grams said, her eyes all wide as she tracked me to the bathroom.

I spun on her. "You're following me into the bathroom now?"

The phone rang.

Grams put her hands on her hips and wagged her head.

93

"That's probably Marissa calling back to find out why you were so *rude* to her."

"Well, you go answer it! Tell her it's because you were both talking to me at once! Why can't I have a private conversation? Do you have to know every little thing that I do?"

Grams' face fell, and without a word she left the bathroom doorway to answer the phone.

Great. Just great. In one big spastic moment I'd hung up on my best friend and alienated my grandmother. And yeah, it had bought me some privacy, but now that I was alone, I felt worse than ever.

Thirty seconds later Grams tapped on the bathroom door and said, "Hudson wants to talk to you."

I hesitated, then opened the door. "It's Hudson?"

"Yes." She turned to go, saying, "I'll be in my bedroom." She eyed me over her shoulder. "With the door shut."

"Gra-ams," I said, but she kept on walking. "Look, I'm sorry, I—"

Slam.

I heaved a sigh and went to the phone. "Hudson?"

"Sammy! Say, I thought you'd like to hear what I unearthed."

Poof! Like magic, my problems with Grams and Marissa and Dead Bird Gods flew out of my head. "Does Coralee Lyon own that lawyer's office?"

"No, Leland Hawking does."

It was like he'd slashed my tire of hope. "But..."

"But there *is* something odd going on."

"Oh?"

"I researched ownership of all the parcels on Hopper Street. Two houses and both of the vacant lots are owned by a company called Earl Clooney Management Systems."

"Wait—they're owned by them? Not just, you know, managed?"

"That's correct. And here's what makes me think something odd's going on: All four properties were acquired within the last three years, and they were bought dirt cheap."

"Wow," I said, and it came out all breathy.

"You understand why I find that odd?"

"Sure—why would someone buy up a string of slummy properties unless they thought they could turn around and sell them for a lot more."

"That's my girl."

I thought for a minute, then said, "So who's this Earl Clooney guy?"

"I'm not sure. The records show the address of Earl Clooney Management as a PO box in Santa Luisa. I don't find that in and of itself suspicious, but that, coupled with the fact that there's no number listed in the phone directory, leads me to believe that it's not a real management company. Or at least not one that handles properties other than those on Hopper Street."

"So how can we find out?"

"I called a friend who's doing some checking. It's too late for him to get anywhere today, but he'll look into it on Monday."

"Wow, Hudson. You're good!"

He chuckled, then said, "Now. What's this about cement?"

I couldn't believe it. "She told you about that?"

He chuckled again. "She *grumbled* something about it. Do you need help?"

"I don't know." I turned my back on Grams' door and whispered, "I only said that because I was feeling trapped."

"But why cement?"

"Well, Captain Patch keeps digging a hole in the same spot, and Mrs. Willawago can't fix it herself, and—oh, Hudson! Somebody threw a rock through her French door! It said 'sell or suffer!' Actually, it said sell or sufer, but the *point* is, it was a threat. Her neighbor got one, too. And get this—there was a reporter from the *Santa Martina Times* at her house when it happened. He saw the whole thing and said he might be able to get their story on the front page!"

"Say! That might really help them in the court of public opinion. . . ." Then he said, "Did you tell Annie your theory about Coralee Lyon owning part of Hopper Street?"

"I didn't have a chance. First the rock came crashing through the house, then the police were on their way, so I just got out of there."

"Hmmm," he said, then seemed to decide. "Why don't I come pick you up. We'll go to the hardware store and get some cement, then pay Mrs. Willawago a visit. If the police are still there, we'll work on plugging Captain Patch's hole, and when they leave, we'll tell Annie about your theory and what we've unearthed so far. I think we should wait to hear from my friend before we make any official accusations, though, okay?"

"Sure!"

"Okay, then. Go downstairs, I'll be right over."

So I got off the phone and headed for Grams' bedroom to tell her I was sorry about our spat, but before my knuckles hit the wood of her door, I stopped. Grams wouldn't let me just apologize. I'd have to *explain*. And just thinking about what it was going to take to patch things up with her exhausted me. And how could I do it in the few minutes I had before Hudson showed up?

Then the little voice was back, whispering in my ear, *Forget it. Just go. You can deal with her later,* and this time I listened—I called, "I'm taking off to pour cement. Bye." And before she could say anything back, I hurried out of the apartment and down the fire escape.

But the truth is, I felt sick inside. The lies. The spats. The deceit. As much as I tried to ignore it, the dark spot on my heart was growing.

Spreading.

Rotting.

And the awful thing is, I didn't know how to stop it.

NINE

It didn't take us long to stop at the hardware store, toss a couple of sacks of cement in Hudson's trunk, and haul them over to the Train House. And since the police and the reporter were gone, we wrestled them right up to the base of the cowcatcher.

"EZ-CRETE? Is that cement?" Mrs. Willawago asked when she saw the sacks. She reached out, held my cheeks, and said, "Oh, you angel!"

I hate to admit this, but it felt really good that she'd called me that. It also went a long way to making me forget that she hadn't believed me before.

She turned to Hudson and said, "And Hudson! How nice of you to help out. You have no idea what a lift this is. It has been such a rough day!"

"Sammy told me about the broken window and the problems you're having with your property being seized." Patch was at the door now, and Hudson gave him a ruffle behind the ears. "This fella digging holes is probably the least of your worries."

"But it is a problem. My neighbor came over and filled in the hole, but Captain Patch dug it out again." She rolled her eyes a little. "At this point he thinks it's a game, so I'm having to keep him inside." She opened the door wide. "Come in, come in! Can I offer you some refreshments before you get started?"

We both went inside, and Hudson said, "That's not necessary. But there is something Sammy and I would like to share with you."

"Oh?"

So Hudson started laying out our theory, and when he got to the part about Coralee possibly owning some of the property on Hopper Street, Mrs. Willawago's jaw dropped. "That would be just like Coralee!" Then she looked at me and said, "Oh, Samantha . . . I am mortified that I doubted you. Please, please forgive me!"

So much for being miffed at Mrs. Willawago.

"What do we do now?" she asked Hudson. "How can we find out?"

So Hudson explained that his friend was checking into the Earl Clooney Management connection and that he hoped to learn more soon.

"Is it possible to get the information by Monday night?" Mrs. Willawago asked. "That's when the city council's reconvening."

"That doesn't give us much time, but we'll do our best." Hudson pointed to the French door. The glass was all cleaned up, and there was a thick piece of white plastic taped onto the door frame. "That's where the rock came through?"

She nodded. "Someone from the glass shop will be out tomorrow—it was too late for them to do anything about it today."

Now, I could tell that even though Hudson was trying to keep his mind on rocks and conspirators and eminent domain, being in the middle of a house full of cool train stuff was distracting him. So I said, "Hey, Mrs. Willawago, I'm gonna go outside and do the cement—would it be all right if Hudson saw your parlor car? And the caboose? He would love that."

"*You're* going to do the cement?" she asked.

I laughed. "Piece of cake." Then I added, "Believe me, I have experience."

But Hudson said, "No, no, I'm going to help with that."

"Hudson . . . ," I warned, "I'm not a little kid. Take the tour."

One look at my face and he knew better than to argue.

Then I added, "You won't believe the parlor car—it's amazing."

Hudson turned to Mrs. Willawago. "Is it really an old Pullman?"

"Well, half of one," she said, leading him toward it. "But the interior is all authentically restored, and you'll see the luxury in which passengers on the Union Pacific line traveled."

So off they went to the parlor car, and off I went to haul around cement. And yeah, the sacks were heavy and dusty and hard to manage, but I waddled them into the backyard through the side gate and flopped them next to Captain Patch's lovely hole. And to tell you the truth, it felt good. Physical labor always seems to help me feel better when I'm mad or upset or just plain worried. And in this case it was doing wonders to edge out the dark-hearted feeling I had inside.

I didn't need much in the way of tools. A shovel, some water...that was it. And since there was a shovel standing in the Stones' compost heap, I reached right over the fence and snagged it.

First, I shoveled dirt back in the hole, which wasn't as easy as you might think because Patch didn't leave me a big heap of dirt—he sprayed it everywhere. But when I'd scraped together as much of it as I could, I ripped open the EZ-CRETE bags and dumped the powder in a trough I'd made along the fence line.

Ta-da!

All I needed was water.

Trouble is, I couldn't find a hose. Anywhere. I looked in the front yard, the backyard, the garage...no hose. But when I peeked over the fence into the Stones' backyard, I spotted a nice long one near their sliding glass door, easily long enough to reach over the fence.

And since I didn't want to interrupt Mrs. Willawago and Hudson and have them think I needed help when all I needed was a hose, I went out the side gate and around to the Stones' front door and knocked.

Nobody answered.

I rang the bell a bunch and knocked some more.

Still nobody answered.

Finally, I decided to go into the backyard through their side gate and just use the hose I'd seen. Like they would care, right? I mean, after all, I was doing them a favor, too.

But the gate was locked. So I looked around a minute, then decided what-the-heck and climbed the fence.

No big deal.

I walked along the house to the backyard, turned left, and headed for the spigot. But when I got near the back porch, I stopped short. Mr. Stone was sitting in a chair, getting ready to put on his boots.

Now, maybe I should have just snuck out of there and rung the bell some more, but I was standing right there. I'm talking close enough to see the trucker symbol on his hat and the filthy toes of his socks. His socks looked like vanilla ice pops where just the tops had been dipped in chocolate.

So leaving without being spotted seemed almost impossible, and besides, if he saw me jetting out of there, it would look like I was guilty of something, and really, all I wanted to "steal" was a little water.

So I said, "Uh, Mr. Stone?"

He looked up and froze.

"Sorry, but I rang the bell a bunch and knocked and everything. I just need to borrow your hose." I pointed to the fence. "I'm putting cement in the hole Captain Patch dug. Your wife was pretty upset about him maybe digging under and getting to your garden."

"Get out of my yard!" he says, his voice honking through his moustache like an angry goose.

"But . . . I'm just trying to help . . . !"

Does he care?

No!

He grabs a hoe that's leaning against the porch and comes chasing after me in his dirty-toed socks, honking, "Get out!"

So I take off like Peter Rabbit escaping Farmer McGregor,

only instead of squeezing under the gate, I scramble over it. And when I'm safely on the other side, I cut over to Mrs. Willawago's house quick. Mr. Stone, though, doesn't even bother to come out the gate.

So great. All that for a little water, which I *still* don't have. And I was just deciding to break down and ask Mrs. Willawago where she hid her hoses when what do I hear?

Whistling.

So I look up Hopper, and there's a mailman weaving through Appliance Andy's graveyard of washers as he flips through a stack of mail. He's wearing shorts and a safari hat, and his hair is long and blond, pulled back in a ponytail. "Here you go. Sorry it's late!" he says, cutting toward me and handing me a small bundle of mail. "It's my first day on this route!"

So now I've got no hose, two magazines, and four letters. This is really helping get the job done. But whatever. I head inside to unload the mail, only then I notice that one of the letters is addressed to Marty Stone. It's not junk mail, either. It's a check.

A *government* check.

Which I recognize because it looks a lot like the social security checks that Grams gets.

Only Marty wasn't old enough to be getting social security. So I'm thinking, What is this? Welfare?

And yeah, I got snoopy. I didn't *open* it or anything—I know that's some big federal offense. But I did sort of tap it around and peek in the address window and hold it up to the light.

Maybe just a *little* federal offense.

Anyway, what I discovered was that Marty Stone got paid a lot of money for his "long-term disability."

Yeah, right. Like his bad back had stopped him from chasing me with a *hoe*?

Whatever. There was no way I was going back to the Stones', even if it was to deliver money. I'd leave that to Mrs. Willawago. Instead, I went inside the Train House, put the mail on the kitchen table, and said, "Hello?" a couple of times. Nobody seemed to be around, and since I didn't want to go traipsing through the house looking for them, I went out to the backyard to make one last search for a hose.

But the second I'm out back, a voice calls, "Hey, there."

I turn, and there's Mrs. Stone, looking over the fence near Captain Patch's hole.

"Hey, there," she says again. "I hear Marty ran you off with a hoe!"

I move toward the fence.

"I'm so sorry! He didn't know who you were."

"But I told him what I was doing. And he's seen me before!"

She lowers her voice as I get closer. "Ya spooked him. But here," she says, then holds up the spray-nozzle end of a hose. "Is this what you were after?"

"Yes!" I laugh. "I've never had so much trouble finding a hose."

So I pull on the hose until I've got enough slack, but when Mrs. Stone sees that I've already emptied the cement bags into the hole, she says, "You can't just dump

104

cement and water together like that! You need a wheel-barrow and a hoe and some sand!"

I smile at her and turn the sprayer on the cement. "Not when you use EZ-CRETE."

"EZ-CRETE?"

Cement dusts into the air as the spray hits it. "Designed to just add water." I let the water puddle for a while, then I shut off the sprayer and say, "Hey, would you mind doing this while I mix it in? The directions say it works better if you stir a little."

She takes the hose and says, "How's a girl your age know so much about cement?"

I laugh and start jabbing at the wet layer of EZ-CRETE with the shovel, driving the water in deeper. "You don't want to know."

She laughs. "Oh, now I really do!"

"Go ahead and spray some more," I tell her. And while she moves the water across the cement, I say, "I learned about EZ-CRETE when I was trapped in a basement on the West Side—some gang guy tried to kill my friend and me, so we knocked him out and cemented his tush to a wheelbarrow before escaping."

She stares at me a second while the water gushes out. "I'd accuse you of jokin', but I don't think you are."

"Nope." I nod at the sprayer. "That's enough, thanks."

So she cuts the water and kids me with, "Remind me not to mess with you!"

I laugh. "I'm just hoping this'll stop Captain Patch from messing with *you*." I jab at the cement until all the water's seeped in, then take a step back and rest on the shovel handle. "I sure hope he doesn't move down and start another hole."

"Well, if he does, I guess I know how to fix it, huh?" She sticks out her hand and says, "Your name's Sammy, right?"

I shake her hand and say, "And you're Mrs. Stone."

She smiles. "Teri." But all of a sudden the smile vanishes from her face and she shouts, "Hey! Mind your own business!" across Mrs. Willawago's yard.

I whip around but don't see a thing.

"Hey!" she shouts again. "You think I don't know you're there? Quit slinkin' around!"

Andy the Appliance Guy's head pops over the far fence. "Who you talkin' to?"

"You! This is the third time I've seen you nosin' around!"

"Nosin' around? I'm in my own backyard, trying to find some parts!"

"You think I'm stupid?" She shoots a finger his direction. "I'll bet *you're* the one who threw the rocks!"

He squints at her. "Well, at least now I know why them cops asked me all them nosy questions. Thanks a lot, neighbor. I'll be sure to return the favor!" Then he heads back for his house.

"Good-for-nothin' bum," Mrs. Stone grumbles.

"Do you really think he threw the rocks?"

She gives a little shrug, a scowl, and a shake of the head. "Marty told me that bum's already gone and spent the money he *thinks* he's gonna get for that place. He inherited it and all the junk that went with it from his daddy. Claimed he was gonna fix it up and sell it, but all he's done for the past year is watch TV."

Now, just as I'm thinking that she seems to know a lot about Appliance Andy, Hudson and Mrs. Willawago come outside through the back door of the caboose. "How are you doing?" Hudson calls across the yard.

"Just about done!" I hurry to finish the job by scraping together some dirt and covering the cement with it.

"That was quick!" Mrs. Willawago says, and Mrs. Stone nods and tells her, "This girl could make a fortune sellin' people on this cement—I'd never even heard of it."

I spear the shovel over the fence, jabbing it hard into the compost heap. "EZ-CRETE, fast and neat!" Then I pick up the empty cement bags and say, "It should be set up in no time."

"Here," Mrs. Stone says, reaching out for the bags. "I'll throw those away for you."

I hand them over, telling her thanks, but just as Mrs. Stone's turning to leave, Mrs. Willawago stops her with, "Oh, Teri, this is Hudson Graham. He and Sammy have an interesting theory that would explain what Sammy overheard yesterday."

Mrs. Stone turns back. "What's that?"

So Mrs. Willawago explains about Coralee Lyon maybe owning some property on Hopper Street. And the more she explains the theory, the wider Mrs. Stone's eyes crank and the farther her jaw drops. Finally, she cries, "This is wonderful!"

"It's a theory at this point," Mrs. Willawago hurries to say, "but the good Lord willing, we'll have proof before the council meeting on Monday."

"But if it *is* true . . . why, that's crooked as all get-out, isn't it? That's called a . . ." She snaps her fingers a bunch of times, and Hudson comes to her rescue, saying, "A conflict of interest?"

"Yeah!" she says, doing a combination snap-point at Hudson. "That's exactly what it is! And when word gets out about that, there's no way they're plowing my house down!"

"But, Teri," Mrs. Willawago says, "we have to keep this under our hats until we have proof." Then she adds, "No sense charging Hell with only a bucket of water."

"Got it!" Mrs. Stone says, putting a finger to her mouth. "Got it, got it!" But all of a sudden her face clouds over. "*Now* what?" she grumbles, looking toward Mrs. Willawago's back fence.

Hudson, Mrs. Willawago, and I look, too, but we don't see a doggone thing.

But Mrs. Stone is already hurrying around her compost heap, shouting, "Hey! Put your hands up!"

Put your hands up? Like she's got what for a weapon?

Empty cement bags?

But, very slowly, hands come up over the back fence.

Then arms.

Then a face.

And when I see who it is, well, my jaw drops, my eyes pop, and I hate to admit it, but I about choke on a gasp of surprise.

TEN

"See if she has any rocks!" Mrs. Stone shouts across to us.

That snaps me out of it. "She's not the one who threw rocks!" I run over to the back fence. "Marissa, what are you doing here?"

Marissa crosses her arms and gives me a really hard look. "Trying to figure out what was sooo important that would make you hang up on me."

"Marissa, I'm sorry, I—"

"So I track you down and find out that what's sooo important is some little hole and a bunch of old people."

"But I—"

"No," she says, putting a hand up. "You know what? I don't care. I thought you were freaking out about the dance or...or something else, I don't know. You've been acting so spacey that I thought it was something real. I was even worried that you were mad at me! But no. You'd just rather play hotshot cement mixer than spend two minutes talking to me."

"Hotshot cement mixer? Wait a minute!"

"Forget it!" she says, then spins around and storms away.

I call over my shoulder to Hudson and the others,

"Sorry, I've got to go!" Then I climb the back fence and tear through the trees and down the embankment toward the ball fields, calling, "Wait up!"

She just keeps running toward the backstop, where she's locked up her bike.

"Marissa!" I call after her, and finally catch up in the middle of left field. And I start to pant out, "Look, I'm sorry...," but when I see her face, the words catch in my throat.

She's not just mad at me—she's *crying*.

"Why don't you just tell me you're sick of hanging out with me?" she says, flinging tears off her cheeks. "Why do you have to go make up excuses and act like you've got tons to do?"

"What are you *talking* about?" I ask, but I know darn well what she's talking about.

She spins on me. "I'm talking about the way you've been acting and the excuses you've been making!"

"Excuses? What excuses?"

She hmphs and rolls her eyes and snaps, "Homework! Let's start with homework—who gave you homework last night?"

I look away.

"Exactly." She puts her fists on her hips. "You think I'm stupid? You think I can't tell you're avoiding me? We've known each other since the third grade. You're like my *sister*. And now all of a sudden you treat me like you can't stand me!"

"I do not!"

"You do so!"

I look away again, and finally I choke out, "It's just...I've been..." But I can't finish. What am I going to tell her? More lies?

The truth?

No, not the truth.

It's too awful.

Too embarrassing.

Too...cowardly.

And all of a sudden I just can't take it. I don't know *what* to do. Inside it feels like I'm imploding. *Ex*ploding. Coming apart in every direction. And before I can find a way to hold it all together, I buckle up and fall to my knees, crying, *"Aarrghh."*

Marissa grabs my arm, saying, "Sammy! Sammy, what's wrong?"

I'm all folded up, holding my head, rocking back and forth. I can't seem to stop rocking back and forth. I feel angry. Helpless. *Possessed.*

And that's when it flashes through my mind that there's the me I'd always been, and the me I was turning into. They were both afraid, but of completely different things.

One was afraid of what I was becoming.

The other was afraid of what I'd done.

And I could feel that this was it—this was the point where I had to choose.

The truth—or the lie.

My head felt heavy. My whole body was shaky. My stomach felt like it was ready to hurl.

"Sammy?" Marissa whispered. She shook me a little. "Sammy!"

"I killed him," I choked out, but it was so quiet that I almost couldn't hear it myself.

"What?" She shook me harder. "Sammy, look at me!"

It was strange. Even though she hadn't heard me, saying the words out loud had caused a little jolt inside me. A rumble in the distance, a flash of light through a pitch-black sky. And the words...the rumble...had been quiet, way off in the distance, so the light felt distant, too. But inside me, in my heart, I could *feel* the light. And all of a sudden I wanted the rumble to be louder. Stronger. I wanted lightning to strike hard and bright inside me.

I looked up at Marissa and said, "I killed him!"

"What?"

"I killed him!" I wailed. "I...killed...Tango!"

And with that the skies inside me opened up, and tears flooded onto the outfield grass.

We sat there cross-legged, facing each other, for at least an hour. And after we'd finally hashed the whole thing out, Marissa shook her head and said, "You are so hard on yourself, Sammy." She held my forearms. "It was an accident."

"I know, but now Heather's on the hook for what I've done—"

"And this *bothers* you? You don't think Heather would be in total revenge heaven right now if the roles were reversed?"

"Yeah, but don't you get it? It seems like I'm *trying* to frame her. So it seems like it *wasn't* an accident."

"Look," she said all conspiratorially, "she deserves it.

What we've got to do, though, is tell Mrs. Ambler about the Class Personality ballots."

"No!"

"No? You're saying you want Heather to be Most Popular Seventh Grader?"

"Most *popular*? She wasn't even on the ballot for Most Popular!"

"Like that's going to stop her from writing her own name in? Come on!"

I frowned. "I hadn't even thought about that."

Marissa rolled her eyes. "It's been a whole year of her, Sammy. How come I've caught on and you, of all people, haven't?"

" 'Cause I don't think like that, that's why. Who's ever won from a write-in? That's like throwing away your vote."

Marissa just shrugged.

"And you know what? I don't care. If she wants to be Most Popular Seventh Grader that bad, let her."

"You have got to be kidding."

I shook my head. "I'm not."

"Man," she said with a snort, "this keeping-a-corpse-in-a-closet thing has really done a number on you." She looked me square in the eye. "We can't let her get away with it!"

I shrugged. "Is it as bad as getting away with murder?"

"You didn't murder the bird! You accidentally killed the bird." She shrugged. "And hid it. And framed Heather for it . . ." She laughed. "But you didn't murder the bird!"

I laughed, too, then took a deep breath and said, "I have to tell Mrs. Ambler."

"About the bird? Are you crazy?"

I shrugged. "As Hudson says, the truth has an interesting habit of finding its way to the surface. I'd rather she heard it from me than some other way."

"Wait a minute. Wait just a minute! Who's going to tell her? Not me, that's for sure! I swear, cross my heart hope to die, I won't tell a soul."

I shook my head. "Marissa, don't you get it? I can't do this anymore. Poor Tango's all decomposing under some clothes in a closet! How long's it gonna be before Mrs. Ambler cleans out the closet and finds him all shriveled up and rotten and full of fly larvae—"

"Stop! Oh, gross! You've been *thinking* about that? *Fly* larvae?"

I gave a helpless shrug.

"Okay, okay, whatever." She shivered from head to toe. "If you've got to tell her so you can get the thought of *fly* larvae out of your head, then fine. Tell her. But it's a tragic waste of *the* most perfect payback ever, if you ask me."

"But I don't want to *be* like Heather," I said softly. "I want to be me."

For some reason that made my eyes get all teary, and when she saw that, her eyes got all teary, too. "Oh, Sammy," she said, and gave me a hug. Then she sat back and said, "Well, at least you'll be able to tell Mrs. Ambler about the Personality ballots."

I shook my head. "I can't do that."

"What?"

"If I do that, she'll think I'm confessing about Tango so I can get Heather in hot water about the ballots."

"So? She *should* be in hot water about the ballots!"

"Yeah, but it's not why I want to confess, and I don't want her *thinking* it's why I'm confessing."

She threw her hands in the air. "Unbelievable. So you're just going to let her get away with it?"

"I honestly don't care if she does. And, Marissa, just because I'm planning to tell Mrs. Ambler about Tango doesn't mean you can tell anyone else. You have to *swear* you won't. If kids find out what I did, I'm going to be—"

"Most Gossiped-about Seventh Grader?"

"There you go."

She laughed. "Don't worry. I won't breathe a word to anyone." She stood up and dusted her backside, saying, "Now. Can we talk about something serious?"

I stood up, too. "Serious?"

"Yeah," she said. "Like what we're going to wear to the Farewell Dance."

I laughed. And even though I knew confessing to Mrs. Ambler was going to be one of the hardest things I'd ever done, inside I felt light and hopeful.

Almost free.

ELEVEN

The first thing I did when I got home was apologize to Grams. And since I felt so much better after confessing everything to Marissa, well, I confessed everything to Grams, too.

And you know what? The more I talked about it, the more stupid keeping it all inside seemed.

It had been an accident!

Followed by a whole bunch of really bad decisions, yeah, but still—it had been an accident.

So when I was all done confessing everything to Grams and she had forgiven me, I was on a total roll, man. I wanted to go to Mrs. Ambler's house! Knock on the door! Confess all my sins!

Well, the ones having to do with her munched lovebird, anyway.

Trouble is, there were no Amblers in the phone book. Or at 411.

"Do you know her first name?" Grams asked. "Maybe Hudson could do an Internet search for you."

I blinked at her. Sometimes my grams astounds me.

But I didn't know her first name. And the more I thought about that, the more strange that felt. Since school had started, I'd seen her every day, I'd said hi to her every day, I'd listened to her every day, but who was she? Until she'd started bringing birds to class, I'd actually known nothing about her.

And the fact that I still didn't even know her *name* was making me feel pretty stupid. But when I told all this to Grams, she sort of shrugged it off and said, "That's normal, Samantha. She's not supposed to be your friend, she's a teacher."

"But still. She's someone I see every day!"

"So are neighbors. So are people at the grocery store. So's the postman. You see lots of people every day and you *think* you know them, but you don't. Not really."

I thought about this a minute, then said, "I still feel stupid."

She laughed, then kissed me on the forehead. "I know you're dying to get this bird business off your chest, but it'll wait until Monday. The important thing is you've decided what you need to do and you're actually going to do it." Then she tried to give me a stern look, and said, "And the next time you're tempted to forge my forgery, call me first—we'll talk things out together, okay?"

I laughed and said, "Thanks, Grams," and I gotta tell you—at that point I was a total confession convert. I just knew everything was going to be okay.

Trouble is, Monday morning I started losing my religion.

Call it cold feet. Or a panic attack. Or just being chicken. But as I was getting ready for school, I started getting sick to my stomach again, and I played around with the idea of ditching.

"Samantha?" Grams said as I jabbed at my oatmeal.

"I can't do it," I whispered.

She reached over and held my hand. "Listen to your heart, not your fear." Then she pulled back and said, "Although I must admit—Heather getting the blame would make keeping it a secret verrry tempting." Then she added, "Would it be any easier on you if I went along?"

"No!"

"Okay. Just offering..."

So she forced me to eat a little, then coaxed me out the door. But the closer I got to school, the more my heart started telling me this was *not* a good idea. It was crashing around inside my chest like a cannonball stuck inside a pinball machine, and by the time I reached the walkway to Mrs. Ambler's room, I felt faint. Shaky. I couldn't *think*. It was like fear had vacuumed my brain right out of my skull.

And then all of a sudden Marissa comes flying out of Mrs. Ambler's room. She grabs me by the arm and yanks me aside, whispering, "You do not want to go in there!"

"Why?" I choke out, and believe me, this is not helping me one bit.

"She found him!"

"Tango?" I gasp.

"Yes! And she's got him clipped to the whiteboard!"

"What?"

"You know—on one of those poster clips? He's dangling up in front of the classroom! By his broken wing! And he smells!"

"Ohhhhh," I whimper.

"And the classroom's full of kids saying how gross it is!"

"Ohhhhhhhhh," I whimper again.

"So you can't tell her now. You can't tell her at all!" Then she straightens up, smooths her expression, and whispers, "Be cool. There's Heather."

Sure enough, Heather's coming up the walkway. And when she spots us, she sneers and says, "What are you two losers doing? Picking your nose?"

"Yeah," I say out of some primal survival reflex as I stick my finger at her. "We knew you'd be hungry for breakfast."

"Eeew!" she squeaks, and hurries into the classroom.

"Eeew is right," Marissa whispers, looking at me with disgust.

I shrugged, and for once I was grateful to Heather. Flinging booger insults had broken the cycle of panic.

Marissa was dragging me toward the classroom door, saying, "Now's the time to go in because all eyes will be on Heather. Just take your seat and be cool. We'll regroup after homeroom."

So that's exactly what I did. I tried not to look at the heaping mess outside the closet door. I tried not to look at Mrs. Ambler. Or Heather. Or anybody else for that matter.

I especially tried not to look at Tango.

Mrs. Ambler acted all perky as she took roll. Like, Gee—there's not a decomposing bird clipped to the wall right behind me, is there? Then she led the Pledge, enunciating clearly and calmly until the end, when her anger

119

slipped out and she said, "and justice for all!" fast and loud—and looked right at Heather.

Then she plastered a great big phony smile on her face and said, "And now for the announcements!" like, Aren't we having such a wonderful, wonderful time! But after a torturous minute of her reading them in a singsongy manner, Cassie Kuo breaks in with, "Mrs. Ambler! Mrs. Ambler, stop!"

"Stop what?" she asks in her oh-so-perky voice.

"Why are you doing this? Why do you have poor Tango up there like that? If we knew what happened to him, we would tell you!"

"Oh, is that so?" she says, still perkin' away.

"Yes!" Cassie cries, and a lot of people in the classroom nod like, We would! Honest, we would!

Then some clown from the back of the class calls, "Hey, she finally clipped his wing!"

Cassie spins around and snaps, "That's not funny!" in the general direction of Derrick Stern and Rudy Folksmeir.

Mrs. Ambler levels a look at Derrick and Rudy, too, but doesn't say a thing. Then she moves her gaze around the room, and when it lands on Heather, Heather snaps, "Don't look at me like that."

"Like what?" Mrs. Ambler asks.

"Like you're looking at me! I didn't kill your bird, and I think it's sick that you've got him hanging up there like that. I can smell him from here!"

Mrs. Ambler moves closer to Tango and sniffs the air. "Hmmm," she says with a little nod. "He is a bit ripe, isn't he?"

"Eeew," a lot of the girls say, but some of the boys are looking at each other like, Whoa, dude! Extreme!

When we were finally free of homeroom, Holly intersected my beeline toward Marissa and said, "Was that intense, or what? I've never seen a teacher act like that!"

Now, I couldn't exactly say, Please. Not now. I have to talk to Marissa! I mean, Holly and I have been through a lot together, and I felt bad that she was totally in the dark about what was going on.

Then Marissa says, "Holly, uh, we've gotta deal with something right now. We'll catch you up at lunch, okay?"

Holly tries to hide it, but she's a little hurt. And she says, "Sure," and starts to walk off, but I hate the way that's making me feel. So I grab her by the arm, yank her to the side, and whisper, "It's about Tango and Heather and ... and ... and I can't say any more right now."

"Do you have proof?" Holly asks me, all wide-eyed.

I scowl and say, "Yeah, but it's proof that Heather didn't have anything to do with it."

Holly gasps, then whispers, "Well ... so you know who did?"

I look her in the eye and *keep* looking her in the eye until finally she blinks, drops her jaw, and whispers, "No!"

Marissa's there, too, and she whispers, "It was an accident!"

I can see the wheels spinning in Holly's head. "Who else knows?" she asks.

"Nobody," Marissa and I say together. Then I add, "I'll explain the whole mess later, okay? I was planning to confess today, but—"

121

"*Confess?* Are you crazy? Everyone thinks it's Heather!"

I close my eyes and take a deep breath. "I can't live with it anymore. If it was anyone but Heather, I would have confessed a long time ago."

"There's more," Marissa whispers. "Sammy saw Heather steal Class Personality ballots."

"To cheat?"

"Of course," Marissa says.

"Well, *that* you've *got* to tell Mrs. Ambler!"

The next class was starting to file into Mrs. Ambler's room, so I said, "Look, just don't breathe a word of anything to anyone, okay? We'll regroup at lunch."

So off we raced to our classes, only I couldn't concentrate on anything. In English Miss Pilson gave us a busy-work assignment while she graded essays. "See how many words you can form out of WILLIAM SHAKESPEARE," she said, writing it out on the board, 'cause after a full year with the Bard most of us still can't spell his name. "One hundred words minimum, contractions don't count, plurals don't count, no talking or working in groups. More than one hundred words earns you an extra credit point *each*." She turned from the board. "Some of you desperately need points, so get to it!"

Normally, I would have loved this assignment. And I sure could've used the extra credit points. But after I whipped past the basics like *I* and *a* and *am,* I started finding words like *ill* and *kill* and *shame* and *liar.* And pretty soon I was obsessing about Tango again, seeing him crunched in the door, rotting under old clothes, dangling from the wall by a wing. I tried to shake it off, but the images kept coming back, and pretty soon I was sick to my stomach again.

At the end of class Miss Pilson told us, "How many of you would like more time to work on these at home?"

Instantly all hands went up as kids glanced at each other slyly like, You wanna share answers?

Then Miss Pilson said, "Fine. And any word that nobody else has is *three* extra credit points."

The glancing suddenly stopped.

So I packed up my twelve words and went to math, where Mr. Tiller gave us a sheet of brainteasers to solve while he called us up individually to discuss our grades and what we could do in the next week and a half to raise them. And of course, I couldn't care less what the Roman numeral LMXI is equal to if CXV is six and CMLMI is seven. Or what number in a series of numbers is least like the others, or what *ABCD* is when *ABCD* times nine equals *DCBA*. All I could hear was the clock.

Tick. Tick. Tick. Tick.

The more I listened to it, the louder it seemed to get. And maybe it was the combination of nausea, fear, anxiety, and dread, I don't know, but pretty soon the ticking started sounding like the clicking of a roller coaster. You know, when they're pulling you up the incline. You're pressed flat against your seat. You can't really see the top, just the seats in front of you. And you're click-click-clicking up, up, up. Then there's that moment of balance at the tippy-top where a scream starts to gather in your throat, and then *wham* you're off.

Only the tick-tick-ticking didn't stop. So it felt like I

was click-click-clicking up, up, up in torturous slow motion. There didn't seem to be a top. I just kept going higher and higher.

"Sammy!"

"Huh?"

Mr. Tiller smiled at me. "Your turn. Come on up."

I was all light-headed. Shaky. Ultrapukey. And that's when it hit me that the longer I let the ticking go on, the steeper, harder, and faster I was going to drop.

So I decided. Right then, I decided.

It was time to make the clicking stop.

"It's not that bad!" Mr. Tiller joked as I stumbled to his desk. But then he looked at me better and lowered his voice. "Are you all right?"

I shook my head. "May I use the restroom?" It came out all breathy. All chalky-mouthed.

He nodded. "Of course. Go!"

So I escaped the ticking, skipped the bathroom, and went straight to Mrs. Ambler's room.

I don't know what I was expecting. She's a teacher. She's supposed to have students. What was I planning to do? Barge in in the middle of class and ask her to step outside?

I guess I was hoping she'd be alone. You know, having her prep period or whatever they call it. But when I looked in the window, there was *nobody* there. And Tango was down from the wall.

I kind of tisked and whined and stomped a foot all at once.

And then around the corner from the service alley comes Cisco, the school's head custodian.

"Sammy!" he says to me, 'cause Cisco's cool that way. He knows everybody. "You forget something again?"

"Uh, no. I'm just looking for Mrs. Ambler. Do you happen to know where she is?"

"Sure. She's in the special-needs room." I guess I was looking pretty clueless because he says, "You know, next to the cafeteria?" I still must've been looking out of it because he scoops a hand through the air and says, "Come on. I'll show you."

So he leads me across campus, around the cafeteria, to the ramp of a propped-open door and says, "Right here."

Now, before I just barge in, I've got to check the situation out. So I head up the ramp and hang back a bit from the door as I look inside.

There's a woman I've never seen before working at a table with a girl in a wheelchair, plus three or four other kids and Mrs. Ambler, who's trying to calm down a gangly boy with jabby black hair.

"It's mine!" the boy is shouting. "It's mine and he took it from me!" His voice sounds like it's coming through foam. Like when you're in the middle of brushing your teeth and have to shout, I'll be there in a minute!

"It's okay, Josh," Mrs. Ambler tells him in a soothing voice. "Calm down and I'll get it back for you."

"But it's mine! It's mine and he took it from me!"

"I know, Josh, but first you must sit down and calm down."

"But it's mine! It's mine and he took it from me!"

"I know, Josh. Sit down and calm down."

"But it's mine! It's mine and he took it from me!"

125

"I know. And how do you get your spaceman back?"

"It's mine! It's mine and he took it from me!"

"You get your spaceman back when you sit down and calm down."

Less than a minute of this and I was ready to shout, Sit down! Shut up! She'll get you your stupid spaceman! But Mrs. Ambler just kept at it, calmly, patiently, saying it over and over again, "Sit down, calm down. That's how you get your spaceman back."

Finally, *finally,* he sat down.

And, thank God, he shut up.

Thirty seconds later Mrs. Ambler had gotten the spaceman from another kid and had it back in Josh's hands. "See?" she said. "You got your spaceman back. You got it back because you were calm and sat down."

"I got my spaceman back!" Josh shouted at the other kid. "You took it but I got it back."

The other kid just stood near a wall, sort of swaying, rocking side to side.

"I got my spaceman back! You took it but I got it back!"

"That's enough, Josh," Mrs. Ambler said, but it wasn't the way I would have said it—it was soothing. Calming.

Then the other woman noticed me and said, "May I help you?"

"Oh, uh, no. I'll talk to her later."

But Mrs. Ambler looked over, and I could see her eyes light up as she realized that I was there for a reason.

"Sammy!" she said, hurrying over to me.

I could feel my knees start to wobble, and I had that

light-headed, dizzy feeling again. The clicking had stopped. Sheer panic set in. But there was no turning back. No getting off this ride. I was strapped in by my own conscience, about to catapult over the edge, hard and fast.

I held my breath, closed my eyes, and prayed the drop wouldn't kill me.

TWELVE

"Is this about Tango?" Mrs. Ambler asked.

Like it had a life of its own, my head bobbed up and down.

"Come in," she says, grabbing me by the arm, looking both ways outside to make sure no one's watching. Then she says to the other woman, "I'm going to be in the office for a few minutes," and leads me through the special-needs room to a little cubicle, where she sits me down in a chair. "Talk to me," she says.

"It's a . . . it's a really long story," I tell her. "And I can't just jump to the end."

She looks at the clock on the wall, and just then the passing bell rings. I look at the clock, too, not believing what I'm seeing.

"It's okay," she tells me. "I've got special-needs kids for another period and I'll write you a pass." She pulls up a chair so that our knees are practically touching and says it again, "Talk to me."

So I take a deep, choppy breath and say, "You know what you told me before about Heather being vicious, right?"

"Is she threatening you? Because if she is . . ."

I shake my head real fast. "But she does have a certain *power* on campus. I don't really *get* it, but she does."

"So you're afraid of her."

I kind of look to the side and take another deep breath, trying to figure out how to word what I want to say. Finally, I decide on, "I'm afraid of what might happen if she finds out."

She leans back a little and says, "Oh, Sammy, you have nothing to worry about! No one has to know you've told me anything."

I hesitate again, then say, "It's not just that. I mean, I want to tell you, but *only* you. Will you promise that you won't tell anyone else?"

"But...why?" She leans forward. "And how will we ever get rid of Heather if I can't share what you know with the administration?"

"Please, Mrs. Ambler?"

She looks at me a minute, then finally shrugs and says, "If it's that important, okay. You have my word."

So I take another deep breath and say, "You know that Heather has tried to sabotage me all year, right?"

She nods.

"You know that she's a vicious gossip who can somehow work people into believing that she's turned over a new leaf when what she's really doing is angling for Friendliest Seventh Grader, right?"

She cringes.

"You also know that if she had the opportunity to pin something on me, she would, right?"

Mrs. Ambler gives a little shrug. "Impossible with Tango, seeing how you were absent that day."

Now it's my turn to cringe. "But I wasn't absent, Mrs. Ambler."

"You . . . weren't?"

"No. I was hiding from Heather." I look down. "In the closet."

Her face goes slack. Her color sort of drains away, then comes flooding back. But before she can say anything, I blurt out, "I came in to drop off my skateboard and I saw Tango flying free, making a beeline for the door. So I hurried to close the door, only the hydraulic closer wouldn't budge, and then when it finally did, it *slammed* shut and poor Tango got caught in the jamb. And I had just picked him up off the floor when I saw Heather through the window and panicked. So I hid in the closet from *her*, only then Brandy and Tawnee came in, and then *you* came in, and pretty soon the whole class was there, and you were accusing Heather, and I was . . . I was trapped! It would have been suicide to step out! Heather would have crucified me! And then when everyone was gone, I ditched school and came in late, and I thought I could live with what I'd done because nobody, *nobody* knew it was me, but I started lying to everyone that matters to me, and my heart felt like it was just rotting away inside my chest, and then the God of Dead Birds started sending around agents, and I, and I, and I just can't take it! I feel horrible about Tango and about being such a coward and upsetting you so much and letting you down. After all the nice things you said about me, I turn out to be a liar and a sneak, and I wouldn't blame you if you hate me forever! But it was an accident, and I'm so, so, sorry . . . !"

Mrs. Ambler's eyes are wide, and she's stunned into silence as she tries to absorb everything I've said. Finally, she holds her head in her hands and says, "I am in a world of hurt."

I whimper, "I'm *sorry*," and boy, do I sound pathetic.

"No," she says, "I'm in a world of hurt because of the way I've been railroading Heather." She shakes her head. "What am I going to do? I was so sure she was lying to me! How could I have been so *wrong*?"

I look down, and very quietly I tell her, "You weren't."

"What's that?"

"She *was* lying to you." I peek at her, then look down again. "Just not about Tango."

"Then what?"

"I . . . I can't tell you."

"*What*? Why not?"

"Because I don't want you to think I'm confessing what *I* did wrong so that I can tell you what *she* did wrong."

"Wait—are you saying you don't want to have mixed motives?"

Just then Marissa's head shoots through the doorway. She's all flushed and out of breath, and when she sees she's found us, her eyes get big and she just stands there sort of sputtering, "I was . . . Did you . . . ? Is everything . . . okay?"

"She knows?" Mrs. Ambler asks me.

I nod. "Holly does, too, but they're the only ones." Then I cringe and say, "And if you can find it in your heart to forgive me, please, *please* don't tell anyone else. Word'll get out and—"

She waved it off. "Sammy, I forgive you. I would have forgiven you the day it happened. It was an accident, and from what you've explained, I can see that things got out of hand."

"Oh, Mrs. Ambler, thank you!" I actually jumped up and hugged her but got embarrassed and sat back down. "And I'm so sorry you found Tango yourself. I tried to look you up this weekend, but you're not in the phone book or at 411 or even on the Internet."

"It's okay, it's *okay*. But, Sammy, you've got to help *me* now. What was Heather lying about? I need something! Something to distract her from suing me. Do you have any idea what I've been enduring with that mother of hers? She's a beast!"

Marissa backhanded me softly. "Tell her!"

I thought about it a minute, then said, "What does Heather want more than anything?" I gave a shrug and added, "Besides humiliating me, of course."

Mrs. Ambler knew the answer in a heartbeat. "Popularity."

"And if you were Heather, how would you go about convincing people you were popular, even if you really weren't?"

She just stared at me.

Finally, I said, "Okay, how about this: Were you missing anything the day Tango disappeared?"

She hesitated, then shook her head.

"It wasn't so much *missing* as it was *partially* missing. You probably didn't think anything of it 'cause you were worried about Tango."

"Good grief, Sammy, just tell her!" Marissa said.

But a little light sparked to life in Mrs. Ambler's eyes. "Wait a minute...wait a minute! The seventh-grade Personality ballots! I thought I hadn't made enough copies, but...but she stole some of them, didn't she!"

I gave her a little smile. "You didn't hear that from me."

She was putting it together quick now. "Not enough for me to notice, but enough to sway the election!" Her eyes were getting bigger and bigger. "Which explains why she got fifty-two write-ins for Most Popular!"

"No!" I gasped. "She wrote herself in for Most Popular? Like winning Best Style or Friendliest wouldn't have been enough?"

"Told you!" Marissa said, giving me a smug look. Then she added, "And it's Most *Unique* Style, Sammy."

"Who cares?"

Mrs. Ambler scowled. "And make that winning Most Unique Style *and* Friendliest."

"She won *both*?" I asked.

"That's right," Mrs. Ambler said, but then scratched her head and added, "But if I can't say you witnessed her stealing the ballots, on what grounds am I going to get them thrown out and start over?"

"That's easy," I said. "You ran off extra copies, right? So there are more ballots than there are kids. Just pull out the ones that have Heather written in for Most Popular and you'll probably wind up with the right number."

She nodded. "Can I say I got a tip from a student?"

"Sure!" Marissa said. "How about I write a note and put it in your box?"

"That'll work," she said. Then after a quick minute of thinking, she motioned us in like we were huddling up for a football play. "All right. Here's the plan: We don't tell anybody about your involvement with Tango or that Heather *didn't* kill Tango. I show Mr. Caan the suspicious ballots. He calls Heather in, and the pressure he puts on her will hopefully deflect the focus from my false accusation to her real crime." She leaned back a little. "I don't get sued, you don't get crucified, and Tango can rest in peace."

I was so relieved I couldn't believe it. But then I noticed that Marissa had a wicked look in her eye. "What," I asked her, "are you thinking?"

"I'm *thinking*," she said, drawing the word way out, "that it would have a bigger impact on Heather if you kept quiet about everything for now and then announced the *real* Class Personality winners at the Farewell Dance."

"Oooooh," Mrs. Ambler said. "That is diabolical!" She laughed. "All week she'll assume she won, then *bam*." She nodded, and I could see the wheels racing in her head as she added, "I'm sure I can get Mr. Caan on board . . . I just hope that I can keep that beastly mother of hers at bay until Friday."

I think my jaw must've hit my chest. "Mrs. Ambler," I said, "I can't believe you're being so cool about this. I was expecting you to be so mad at me! Look at the mess you're in, all because of me!"

"Sammy, I loved Tango. He was a sweet little bird. But what bothered me most was not knowing what happened to him . . . or the feeling that someone — Heather — had played a prank on me. But now that I know what happened"—she gave a little shrug and nodded out to the special-needs room—"well, in the scheme of what I deal with every day, it's minor." She grabbed a pad and a pencil and started writing us passes to class. "And I'm actually impressed. Most kids would have been happy to let their archenemy take the fall." She eyed me with a little smirk. "To tell you the truth, I don't know that *I* would have stepped forward had I been in your shoes."

When she was finished writing, I asked, "So, uh, how's Hula adjusting?"

She peeled the notes off the pad and passed them to us. "Hula's fine. We got her a new friend, Jitterbug." She laughed. "She harasses him just as much as she did Tango."

"Hula does?"

"Oh, Hula acts demure when people are around, but she's a fiend. I wouldn't be surprised if she's the reason Tango escaped."

My mouth was sort of dangling. "But I thought lovebirds seriously bonded to each other."

She stood up and gave a little shrug. "Lovebirds also fight."

I couldn't believe how much better I felt. I was all bubbly inside. Lighthearted. Free! And as we hurried over to math to retrieve my backpack, I couldn't help it—I started skipping.

Skipping.

"Wow, look at you," Marissa laughed. "You seem like a whole new person!"

135

"I can't believe how nice Mrs. Ambler was. She was *awesome*." *Skip-a-skip-a-skip-a-skip!* "And you know what?"

"What?" She laughed at the complete idiot I was making of myself.

"I cannot *wait*."

It must've been contagious because Marissa got in step, skipping right beside me. "For?"

"What do you think?" I eyed her and grinned. "The Farewell Dance!"

It was going to be a blast.

THIRTEEN

Marissa was right—I did feel like a whole new person. Everything seemed to make me laugh or smile or just, you know, skippity-do-dah inside. And maybe it was foolish or went against some verbal contract I had with Mrs. Ambler, but at lunch I caught Dot up on everything. Holly, Dot, Marissa, and I eat lunch together nearly every day, so trying to discuss it around her would be like saying, Sorry, Dot, but you're not really our friend. Besides, Dot's one of the nicest people I've ever met, and she's real good at keeping quiet about things.

Way better than Marissa.

So after telling her about Tango and Heather and Mrs. Ambler's reaction, I made Marissa, Holly, and Dot pile hands on top of mine and make a solemn vow that they wouldn't tell another soul how I'd tomahawked Tango with the door.

Now, it's happened before that I've told my friends secrets at lunch, only to discover that Heather—or, more likely, one of her witless spies—is eavesdropping. But this was such top-secret stuff that I'd made real sure that we were at a table safely away from where anybody could hear what we were saying.

137

But I guess that, in and of itself, was like waving a red cape at ol' Bull Brain Acosta 'cause right after we get done swearing to secrecy, Holly whispers, "Time to change topics," and nods a nose over my shoulder.

Sure enough, Heather's working her way through the benches. But instead of glowering like she normally does when it's killing her to know what we're up to, she's saying gushy hellos to everyone as she squeezes through, being really obvious about the fact that she's coming our way.

When she reaches us, she scoots onto the bench right next to Dot and says, "Hey, Dotty. Hi, Missy. Holly..." Then she looks at me and says, "Saw you *skipping* today."

"And your point is?"

She looks at her fingernails. "Looking forward to the dance?"

I hesitate a second, then instead of telling her to go eat bees or something, I grin a little and say, "Actually, I am."

"Do you even know *how* to dance?"

I grin a little broader. "Can't say that I do."

Now, I knew there was a *reason* she'd come to harass me. There's always a reason. And I guess the way I was answering her questions was irritating her, because she finally cut to the chase. "I hope you aren't deluding yourself into thinking you were Casey's first choice. He's only doing Danny a favor 'cause Missy can't go if you don't."

"Stop calling me Missy," Marissa said.

"Stop hanging around this loser," Heather replied with a shrug.

Marissa started to defend me, "Don't you call her a—"

But I cut her off. "Forget it. She's just jealous."

"Jealous?" Heather snorted. "Like I need to be jealous of a twerp in high-tops?" She shook her head and said, "You're gonna wear them to the dance, aren't you? I can just picture you stepping into a limo in worn-out holey shoes with knotted laces—"

"Hey, you should try some," I said. "You'd probably find it a lot easier to kick-start your broom."

One thing about Heather—she can dish it, but man, she can't take it. Her face bloomed like a red geranium, her lips twitched for something, *anything* to come back with, only before she could, Vice Principal Caan was towering over us. "Heather!" he barked. "What are you doing here? You're not supposed to be within twenty-five feet of Sammy."

Heather rolled her eyes, scowled, sighed, and finally got off the bench.

"Heather, where are you going?" Mr. Caan commanded. "I asked you a question!"

She threw her hands in the air. "I'm just getting twenty-five feet away," she said, trying to sound like the new "reformed" Heather, but sarcasm oozed through anyway.

"You wait right there!" Mr. Caan told her, then turned to me. "Are you really going out with Casey Acosta?"

"Going out? No!"

But Marissa sort of elbows forward, giving him a knowing look as she says, "They're get-together-ing."

"What?" He squints. "Are you going to the Farewell Dance with him or not?"

I shrug and try not to blush. "A group of us are going, yeah."

Mr. Caan's a big guy. A strong guy. But at that moment his whole body seemed to sag. He shook his head. He closed his eyes. He took a big breath. Then he looked at us and said, "Why do you kids make life so hard on yourselves? Why does there have to be all this drama?"

I hitched a thumb Heather's way. "She's the one you want to talk to about drama. We're just trying to eat lunch."

He sighed again and took off. And after he'd escorted Heather a safe distance from us, Holly snickered and said, "Kick-start your broom..."

Dot giggled. "That *was* pretty funny."

But Marissa was not looking too happy.

"What?" I asked her.

Her forehead wrinkled as she said, "I know what you're going to say. You're going to say that now you *have* to wear your high-tops. As a matter of principle or whatever."

"Marissa, it's the Farewell Dance, not the prom!"

"But we're going in a limo!"

I shrugged. "Casey said it was casual. High-tops are part of the deal I made with him."

"But, *Sammy*...!"

"That doesn't mean you can't wear what *you* want to wear."

"But we'll look stupid together!"

"So? Maybe you'll look good with the other girls and *I'll* be the awkward one. I don't care. I can't both go to a dance *and* dress up."

"So you can dress up and stay home? Or go dancing and not dress up? But you can't do both at the same time?"

"Hmmm. I could also stay home and not dress up. Actually, that sounds like the best choice yet."

"But you already said you'd go!"

I sighed. "I know. Foolish, huh?"

"Sammy!"

Dot looked at Marissa and said, "If I was going to the dance, I sure wouldn't wear a dress, Marissa."

"But—"

"Me either," Holly added. "Besides, it'd be pretty uncomfortable sitting on the gym floor signing yearbooks in a dress and heels."

"But we're going in a *limo*..."

I shrugged. "So do whatever you want. Get an updo! Wear ribbons! Rub glitter everywhere! I'll still talk to you."

"Thanks a lot," Marissa grumbled.

So Marissa was not too happy, and then when the warning bell rang and we were dumping our trash, Casey caught up to us and caused some more rain to fall on her parade. "Have you heard?" he asked.

"Heard what?" I asked back.

He broke into a wicked grin. "The limo has morphed into a stretch Humvee."

"A what?" Marissa asked.

But I said, "One of those jeep-meets-tank jobbies?"

"Exactly!" Casey said.

"You can rent those around here?"

He grinned. "There's exactly one in the whole Tri-Counties, and Danny got his mom to snag it. You should

141

see the picture! It's all stretched like a limo, sleek black with chrome detail…it's smokin'!" He turned to Marissa. "Danny hasn't shown you the brochure?"

Marissa shook her head, and I could tell—she was gagging on her tongue.

"So he also didn't ask you about ice-blocking?"

"Ice-blocking?" Marissa choked out.

"It's Billy's idea."

"What's ice-blocking?" I asked.

"You've never been?" He looked from me to Marissa and back again.

We both shrugged and shook our heads.

He grinned. "Basically, you get a big block of ice, sit on it, and slide down a hill."

Marissa winced. "And that's supposed to be fun?"

He laughed. "Actually, it can be. Depending on the hill." He grinned at me. "And who you're sliding with."

"But…," Marissa said, still cringing, "doesn't your…don't you get all wet?"

"You put a towel or a jacket or something on the ice." He scratched the side of his neck, saying, "Billy wants to do it in the cemetery—"

"The cemetery?" Marissa gasped.

Casey nodded. "You know, those hills at the back side of it? But I think the golf course would be way better."

"Danny and Nick want to do this, too?" Marissa asked, still pulling a face.

"They're up for it, yeah." Then he added, "Assuming you guys are…"

"What about the girls Billy and Nick are taking?"

Marissa asked, trying to buy herself an out. "Who are they, anyway?"

"Nick's taking Olivia Andrews. You know her, right?"

We both nodded—she was an eighth grader. Quiet, but nice.

"He says she's up for it." He laughed. "And Billy says he's taking his harem, but what I think that means is he hasn't asked anyone yet."

I scowled. "As long as his harem doesn't turn out to be your sister."

"He knows better than that. Besides, Heather'd never go for ice-blocking." He shrugged. "And she told me Hummers are 'revolting.'" Then he added real fast, "But if you guys don't want to go ice-blocking, I can totally understand—we could just go out and get dessert afterward or something."

His gaze landed on Marissa, who stammered, "Well, I . . . I . . . Whatever everybody else wants is fine."

So now they both looked at *me*. And yeah, maybe I should have bailed Marissa out and said, Uhhh . . . that's not exactly the picture we had in mind . . . do you really expect us to go ice-blocking in updos, dresses, and *heels*? But the truth is, it sounded like a blast to me. So I grinned and said, "Count me in!"

"Cool!" he said, and since the whole lunch area was vacant and the tardy bell was about to ring, we all said, "Later!" and raced off to class.

I was late to science, but it didn't matter 'cause Mr. Pence was busy picking up his prized model skeleton that Mason Oakley had knocked on the floor. Mason was going, "Dude, I'm so sorry! Dude!"

143

"Just sit down, Mr. Oakley! Just . . . sit . . . down!"

"Dude, if you say so. But here—I know where his arm goes. It's the femur and the ulvana, right?"

"The radius and the *ulna*," Mr. Pence snapped. "Now SIT DOWN!"

"Sure, dude, sure. Whatever you say."

So Mason was heading back to his seat, hamming it up for everyone but Mr. Pence to see, when only two steps past my bench he turns and says, "Hey, I heard you're going to the dance in a Humvee!"

I put my finger to my mouth, telling him to hush, but Roman Rivera on the bench behind me says, "In a Hummer, really? Who has one of those?"

"It's a *stretch* Hummer, dude," Mason says.

"You jivin' me?" Roman asks. "Around *here*?"

"Yeah! I saw the brochure. It's got surround sound, mirrored ceilings, three flat-screen TVs . . ."

Well, that was it. Within ten seconds the whole class was hummin' about the Hummer. Everyone, that is, except Heather. It was like someone had put her kettle on high and left her alone to boil dry. And, of course, she was glaring at me like it was all *my* fault. Like going to a dance in a vehicle she thought was revolting was somehow going to ruin *her* evening.

But whatever. That's just Heather.

Anyway, by the time school was over, Marissa was whistling a different tune about the Hummer, too. "Everybody's talking about it!" she whispered. "Even Tenille and Monet came up and asked me about it."

"Running reconnaissance?" I asked, 'cause Tenille and

Monet are Heather's little lackeys, although I don't know why they put up with her. Heather uses them like toilet paper.

"No," Marissa said, unlocking her bike. "I think they were just dying to know."

"So? Did you tell them anything?"

She shook her head, and as we headed off campus, her face fluttered a bit before finally breaking into a smile. "You were right, all right? I was being stupid. The Hummer'll be fun, and I'll just wear, you know, casual clothes."

"Hooray!"

But she was still all fluttery. All trying to contain something that she just wanted to blurt out but was sort of afraid to. So finally, I said, "What?"

"Well..." She fluttered some more.

"What?"

"I don't know...all the questions I got about the Hummer...all the people who came up and talked to me...I actually felt"—she cringed as she looked at me—"popular."

I eyed her.

"I knew you'd look at me like that! I knew it!"

"Like what?"

"Like *that*!"

"Well, come on, Marissa."

"I know, I know," she grumbled.

"You didn't even want to go in the Hummer."

"I know, I know!"

"And now you think it's cool?"

145

"I'm being totally shallow, huh?"

Her eyes were begging me to say no, so I said, "Nah." And I also refrained from saying anything about how Heather had been acting in science. Instead, I said, "Just remember—popularity around here lasts about as long as a Hummer rental, so don't start thinking it's *yours*." Then I frowned and kinda mumbled, "Who'd really want a Hummer anyway? Expensive, rotten gas mileage, lots to maintain . . . too much trouble if you ask me."

She grinned at me. "Only you would make some connection between being popular and owning a Hummer." She dug up a sorry-looking package of cheese crackers and said, "But I think popularity makes you hungry!" She wolfed some down, then held the package out to me.

I shook them off. "No thanks."

She ate some more, then tucked the rest away. "Well, how about I help you walk Captain Patch?"

"Oh!" I said. "I forgot!"

She swung onto her bike. "Come on! We'll walk the dog and talk some more about the dance, okay?"

"Thanks!" I said, tossing down my skateboard, because the truth is, I didn't really care *what* we talked about. I was just glad to have my best friend back.

Glad to feel like me again.

Glad to be believing that the mess I'd gotten into was finally over.

FOURTEEN

The whole way over to Mrs. Willawago's, Marissa rattled on about her vision of the Plan: After school we'd go over to her house 'cause obviously the Hummer couldn't show up at the Senior Highrise. We'd get ready there, and when the doorbell rang, we'd both answer the door so as not to get embarrassed by her parents—if they were actually home—or her annoying little brother, Mikey. She went on and on with details, and I just sort of agreed to everything because basically, I didn't care. I was just happy to be able to go to the dance as me, not some foo-foo version of me.

When we reached Hopper Street, Marissa got off her bike and I picked up my board. She was now on the subject of how generous Danny's mom was to spring for the rental and how it wasn't just that we were going to the dance in a Hummer, it was that we were *seventh* graders going with *eighth* graders to the dance in a Hummer.

"Hold on, hold on!" I said. "And what do you call Billy Pratt?" Because not only is Billy a seventh grader, he's probably the most immature seventh grader at William Rose Junior High.

"I call him crazy!" She laughed. "But he would have been an eighth grader if he hadn't been held back."

"Who told you that?"

"Danny did. They went to the same preschool."

"Danny and Billy did?"

"Uh-huh. You've got to ask them about the Nap Nazi sometime."

"The Nap Nazi?"

"Yeah," she laughed. "It's a crack-up."

Now, part of me was feeling really left out. I mean, when had she had these humorous encounters with Danny and Billy? Where was I when they were discussing Nap Nazis? But we were almost at Mrs. Willawago's, and the mailman was coming toward us, whistling away.

"Good afternoon!" he sings out as we converge in front of the Train House. He hands me Mrs. Willawago's mail and says, "Have a good one!" and continues on his way.

"Gee, Sammy," Marissa says, "if the mailman knows you, you're here way too much."

"I know," I said. "It's been almost a month of this, and I don't really see an end in sight."

"So? Are you just going to keep doing it forever?"

"I don't know. It's not like I *mind* . . ."

She whispered, "All that God-talk would drive me crazy."

"Aw, you learn to ignore it."

But then I noticed a strange letter in Mrs. Willawago's mail. The printing was in pencil and in all caps, which at first made me think it was from a grandkid or something. But then I started wondering because (a) it was addressed to Annie, not Grandma or even Mrs., (b) there was no return address, and (c) Willawago was spelled "Williwago."

And *then* I noticed something else, which made my heart start beating faster. "Mrs. Willawago!" I shouted, running up the cowcatcher. I opened the door. "Mrs. Willawago?"

"Merciful heavens, what is it?" she said, hobbling toward me.

"Look at this letter!"

She smiled at Marissa and said, "Hello, there. Nice to see you again," then took the letter from me. "What's this?"

"Look at the *L*s in Willawago!" I said, pointing.

"What about them?"

"See how they shoot up like that?"

"So . . . ?"

"That's what the *L*s in SELL OR SUFFER looked like!"

"I don't remember that . . ."

"Do you still have that rock?"

She blinked at me. "Why, no. The police have it."

"You've got to show this letter to them!"

"Samantha, honestly. I haven't even opened it yet." She frowned and grumbled, "And I don't know why you think you can tell so much from so little."

"So open it," I said with a shrug.

She did and pulled an odd-sized piece of paper from the envelope. It wasn't as big as binder paper or as small as a notepad. It was somewhere in between. It looked like old paper, too. A little discolored around the edges, and the lines on it were a real faint green.

The message, though, was loud and clear:

YOUR DAYS ARE NUMBERED.

Mrs. Willawago gasped when she read it. "Heavenly Father! It's another threat!"

I tried to wipe the I-told-you-so look off my face, but let me tell you, it wasn't easy.

"What's this about?" Marissa whispered. "Why is she being threatened? What rock?"

"I'll explain everything in a minute," I said, then I eased the paper out of Mrs. Willawago's hand and started inspecting it. Front side, back side, up to the light, sideways.

I didn't see a doggone thing.

"What are you looking for?" Mrs. Willawago asked, her voice kind of croaky.

I shook my head. "I have no idea." Then I checked out the envelope and said, "This is postmarked Saturday. That's the day after the rock was delivered."

Mrs. Willawago nodded, but she was staring at the paper. "This is a very ominous threat. It can mean two different things."

Then I saw the *Santa Martina Times* lying on the coffee table behind her. The headline read LOCAL MONU-MENTS UNDER SIEGE, LONGTIME CITIZENS RAILROADED FROM HOMES.

There was a picture of Mrs. Willawago in the parlor car and another one of the front of her house. "Hey! You made the front page," I said, picking it up.

Her face lit up. "And it's a fantastic article." She pointed to a section of it. "Read this right here."

So Marissa looked over my shoulder as I read the part she'd pointed out.

Willawago's Train House is a ferrophiliac's delight—full of antique equipment such as signal lanterns, inspection torches, coal picks, fire hooks, and surveying equipment as well as brass bells, headlights, and whistles. There is also a collection of clothing, ranging from a telegrapher's uniform to the hickory-stripe overalls, hat, and goggles of an engineer. The walls are decorated with nearly one hundred locomotive builder's plates dating back as far as 1875, and among these are mounted, framed ink-on-linen drawings of locomotive prototypes, employee record cards, telegrams, and photographs of the Last Spike ceremony.

To one side of Willawago's original house is a restored Pullman parlor car used now as a sitting room, and to the other Willawago has attached a Union Pacific caboose that is utilized as a guest bedroom.

A short walk away, the abandoned Santa Martina Railroad Office is likewise a hidden historic treasure. Behind the boarded-up doors and windows lie what Annie Willawago describes as "tools and toys of the trade," a museum waiting to open, an era yearning not to be forgotten.

"He really paints the picture, doesn't he?" she asked, beaming away. "And I love that last line right there."

"Lots of people in Santa Martina are into trains,"

Marissa said. "My dad has a friend who collects—he would love to own this stuff."

"You see?" Mrs. Willawago said. "There's a real value to these things. And I think it's important that kids today understand the historical significance of the railroad. Why, it's—"

"Uh, Mrs. Willawago," I said, because I could tell she was about to give us a little sermon on the toils and sacrifices of the men who gave their lives or limbs to tie our great country together. "Don't you think you should call the police?"

She blinked at me a minute. "Oh! Oh yes, of course."

"We'll be walking Captain Patch," I said as she headed for the phone.

"Thanks, angel. Thanks so much!"

The French door to the backyard had been repaired over the weekend, so I told Marissa, "This is the door someone threw a rock through on Friday. It was totally shattered."

Captain Patch yip-yap-woofed a happy hello as we stepped outside, and Marissa said, "So catch me up, would you? What rock? Who threw it? What's going on?"

I latched the leash to Captain Patch and led him down the street to Miller, instead of toward McEllen like we usually went. And I was explaining to Marissa about the city trying to seize the land and how Coralee Lyon was in cahoots with Leland Hawking, but I was talking really fast, and I'm afraid it came out kinda jumbled because Marissa's face crinkled up and she said, "Sammy, slow down. I'm not following any of this. Eminent doh-what?"

"Domain. Eminent domain."

"Wait a minute—didn't Mr. Holgartner talk about that in history?"

"Yeah. It was boring then, but it's interesting now."

"Coulda fooled me," she grumbled. "And why are you whispering?"

"Because this is Leland Hawking's office coming up right here. See?" I said, pointing over the hedge. "That's where Coralee Lyon's car was parked. And that's the window where I went up and heard them talking."

When we rounded the corner and Patch pulled over to sniff out any new "postings" on Leland Hawking's sign, I said to Marissa, "Hey, hold Patch for a minute, would you?"

She sighed and shook her head like she just knew I was about to do something she didn't want me to do. "Why?"

"I just want to go in for a minute."

"And do what?"

"And see if I can spot some paper like that threat was written on."

She scowled but put out her hand for the leash. "I'll meet you at the ball fields, okay?"

"Great!"

Trouble is, when I got up to the front door of Leland Hawking's office, there was one of those cardboard clocks in the window, and the time on it was 10:00.

Leland Hawking, Esquire was gone for the day.

I peeked through the blinds for a while anyway but didn't spot any odd paper anywhere. Just a big room with a little waiting area, an oversized desk, a few chairs, some plants, and a whole wall of books. Everything was in lawyer colors, too: greens, browns, and brass.

153

So I hurried toward the ball fields to find Marissa, only when I got to the edge of the hill that leads down to the backstop, I couldn't believe my eyes. Marissa was trotting Captain Patch around the bases, and he was staying right at her side. She took a U-turn at second base. He took a U-turn, too. No yanking. No dragging. No looking like a marlin on a line. She went fast, he went fast. She stopped, he stopped. And in between all these maneuvers, she knelt and ruffled his ears and told him, "Good boy!" Then she took off again, saying, "Heel!"

After I'd watched them go forward and backward around the diamond again, I came down the hill, shouting, "How'd you *do* that?"

"He's smart." She nuzzled him. "And he likes me, don't you, boy?" Then she grinned at me and said, "Plus, I bribed him with bits of cracker."

"That's amazing!"

She shrugged. "I'm not gonna walk a dog that yanks me around like that." She handed back the leash and said, "Find anything?"

I shook my head and started toward the sidewalk. "The office was closed."

"So hurry up and tell me the rest of the story so we can talk about the dance, okay?"

I laughed. "Nothing like being direct."

"Well, come on." She put her hands out like she was a scale, weighing two items. "Eminent domain, the Farewell Dance. Old people and their problems, our first date..."

Captain Patch was starting to pull my arm off again. "Stop calling it a date, would you? It's not like that."

"Yeah, yeah, yeah," she said. "Just finish the story. And tell him to heel! You're giving him bad habits."

"Heel!" I said, pulling on the leash. I might as well have been tugging on a tiger, though, 'cause he kept right on yanking.

"Oh, good grief," Marissa said, taking the leash from me. Then she commanded, "Patch, heel!" and two seconds later he was smacking on a microscopic piece of cheese cracker, walking by her side.

"How come you know how to train a dog? You've never even had one, have you?"

Marissa scowled. "No. But my mother made me go to obedience training with Brandon when *he* got a puppy. That was like four years ago, and she still doesn't think it's the 'right time' for us to get a dog."

I chuckled, 'cause just when I think my mom's the worst, I hear about something *her* mom's done, and I don't know—it sort of helps to balance things out.

"Now," she said, "would you tell me the story?"

So I picked up where I'd left off, telling her about Earl Clooney Management and Hudson's friend and all of that. And when we got to the corner of Miller and Cook, I pointed across the street and said, "See that building? It's haunted."

"Oh, shut *up*," she said, like I was dumber than dirt.

Now, usually *I'm* the one saying haunted stuff is bogus, and *she's* the one biting a nail, shivering in her shoes. And it's not like I was shivering in my shoes or anything, but I *had* actually said it like I believed it, and that's when I realized that I *wanted* to believe it.

So as we walked west on Cook, I told her about Goldie Danali and how the mall got built. The more I talked, the more her jaw dropped, and when I was all done, she just blinked at me and said, "I had no idea . . . !"

"Me neither," I told her. Then I grinned and said, "You still think it's boring?"

She just said, "Wow," so I added, "And now they're trying to do the same thing to Mrs. Willawago and the Stones."

Marissa shook her head. "It's too bad they don't want to sell. That neighborhood's a wreck. And batting cages and a rec center would be awesome."

"I agree." I shrugged. "But not if they're haunted."

So we walked down McEllen, and by the time we were past the pool complex, Marissa was pretty much caught up on everything. And she'd just said, "So. Can we talk about the dance now?" when I heard a sound coming out of the old railroad office. I stopped and whispered, "Did you hear that?"

"Hear what?" she said, looking around.

"*Shhh.*" I put up a finger and perked an ear. Then I heard it again. "That!" It was a strange sound. A muted sound. A slow, metallic *screeching* sound.

"So?" she said, looking toward the boarded-up windows of the railroad office. "And why are we whispering?"

"Because somebody's *in* there."

"It's probably just some homeless guy."

Sound *eeeeek*ed from the building again.

"Or maybe it's haunted . . . !" she said, making fun of me.

I eyed her. "Yeah? Well, come on. Let's go find out."

"Find out?" She grabbed me. "Wait a minute, Sammy. Wait just a minute."

"What's the matter?" I said, pulling her along to the rear of the property, where I'd spotted a gap in the chain-link fence. "You afraid of ghosts?"

"Stop it. No. I just don't want to go inside some boarded-up building and find some deranged homeless guy cooking a can of beans."

"Cooking a can of beans?"

"Yeah," she said. "Or whatever homeless guys do when they break into abandoned buildings." Captain Patch was back on the march now, yanking her along as he weaved in and out of the trees behind the property.

"Look," I told her, squeezing through the hole in the fence, "I'm not *going* inside, I'm just *looking* inside."

"Yeah, right! Do you remember the last time you said that? Do you remember how it almost *killed* us? Do you—"

"Take it easy, would you?"

"What if they've got a gun? What if they've got a knife? What if—"

"It's broad daylight, Marissa," I said through the chain-link.

"It was broad daylight *last* time!"

I hesitated. "It was, wasn't it."

"Yes!"

"Well..." I shrugged. "This is different." Then I smiled at her and said, "Wanna come?"

Captain Patch had wrapped the leash around her legs twice as he sniff-sniff-sniffed the ground. "No!" she said, trying to pull her legs free. "I'm going to stay right here so I can call the police when you get yourself in trouble again."

So off I went, zipping up to the railroad office. And I discovered that even though it still *looked* boarded up from a distance, the graffitied plywood that covered the back door had been pried back and was just leaning against the door frame.

I peeked behind the plywood and found that the door was slightly ajar. I'm talking *very* slightly—like an eighth of an inch. And maybe I should have just flung it open, looked, and run, but what I did was try to inch the door open a little farther.

Screeeeeech went the hinges.

I jumped to the side, ducked around the building, and waved at Marissa to take cover behind the trees.

We both held still and waited. But after a minute or two of nobody coming out, Marissa started asking me questions with her arms. You know, *flagging* at me. Shoulders up. Hands up. Hand in circles. Arm this way, arm that way, foot up, foot down . . . She was one big, bossy, semaphoring spaz.

And when I got sick of trying to explain with *my* arms that I didn't *know* what was going on, I just gave her a Forget-it! wave and tiptoed back to the door.

And great. Now I could see a whole wedge of nothing. Well, it *was* better than before—I could make out an old desk and a bunch of train stuff on the wall—but the door had only squeaked open about an inch, and I couldn't see any*body*. So maybe I'd imagined that someone was inside. Maybe it was just a draft causing something to swing on its hinges. Like the squeaky door. I mean, no one had come to see what the squeak was about, right?

But then I realized that because the whole place was boarded up, it should have been dark inside. But there was light.

And the light was *moving*.

Then I heard footsteps.

And a clang.

"Shhh!" someone whispered.

My heart started beating faster. *Shhh* meant that not only was there someone inside, there was *more* than one someone inside!

Then all of a sudden, less than four feet away, someone crosses my slice of view.

It's a woman.

A woman I *know*.

And when I see what she has in her hand, I inch away from the door, tiptoe away from the building, then scamper as fast as I can to the hole in the fence.

FIFTEEN

Marissa and I ran to Mrs. Willawago's as fast as we could. It would have been faster to hop the back fence, but since we had Captain Patch with us, we had to run back to McEllen and then down Hopper. There was a police car out front, which in this case was good. I ran up the cow-catcher, burst through the front door, and said, "Come quick! Appliance Andy and his Old Lady are ransacking the railroad office!"

Mrs. Willawago was in the front room with Mrs. Stone, who had apparently also gotten a threatening letter. Standing with them were two police people I'd never seen before—a blond-braided woman and a man who looked like an oversized boy playing policeman, his face was squeaky clean, and his cheeks were round and soft, even though the rest of him wasn't at all fat.

Now, even though I said, "Come quick!" none of them did. They all just stood there, staring at me.

So I said, "Hurry! Appliance Andy is stealing stuff out of the railroad office!"

The first person to move was the blond-braided cop, and you know what she did? She flipped to a new form in her report-taking notebook and hoisted a pen.

"Don't write a report! GO! It's happening right NOW! Right down the street!"

Squeaky Cheeks looks at the Police Chick, then asks me, "Who's doing what where?"

"The neighbor on that side," I tell him as I point to my right, "is stealing stuff out of the railroad office down that way," I say, pointing to my left.

And I can just see them thinking, What could someone possibly want to steal out of *that* place, when Mrs. Willawago says, "It's full of railroading treasures. They probably read about it in the paper."

So *now* Squeaky Cheeks and the Chick jet out to their car and take off, *ka-thump*ing over potholes as they try to zoom down the street.

I roll my eyes and say, "Broth-er," and head through the house for the French door, grumbling, "They don't know about the back fence, they don't know about the back door..."

"How do you know it's the Quinns?" Mrs. Stone asks, trailing behind Marissa and me.

"We heard them, then I found a break in the fence and looked in the back door."

"You went snooping around other people's property?" Mrs. Stone asks. *"Again?"*

She didn't sound too happy, that's for sure. But I realized that in the last couple of days, I'd eavesdropped on Leland Hawking, gone into Mrs. Stone's backyard for a hose, and ducked through the fence of the railroad office.

I hadn't exactly been minding my own business.

"Do you need me out there?" Mrs. Willawago calls from the French door.

"Uh, no!" I call back. "I just want to make sure they don't escape this way."

"Right!" she calls, and disappears inside.

So Marissa and I step onto the bottom frame of the back fence and look down toward the railroad office.

"Do you see them?" Mrs. Stone asks, but when I look over my shoulder to say no, it seems like she's more interested in Captain Patch than she is Appliance Andy. Patch is zigzagging around, sniff-sniff-sniffing the ground near where he'd dug before. "Sure hope it's not another dadgum gopher," she mutters.

Then all of a sudden Marissa cries, "There they are!" and when I whip around, I see Andy and his Old Lady trucking toward us along the corridor of trees, their stomachs leading the way, their hair flying, their fists clamped around pillowcases of loot.

"They're back here!" I shout at the top of my lungs, even though the railroad office is so far away that the cops for sure can't hear me. "Help, police!" I shout into the sky.

Mrs. Stone cups her mouth and calls over to her house, "Marty! Call the police!" But then Marissa bounces up and down on the fence brace, crying, "There they are!" and this time she's talking about Squeaky and the Chick.

The trouble, though, is that they're not moving very fast at all. Yeah, they're shouting, "Stop! Police!" but it looks like they're fumbling around with guns or holsters

162

or radios or who knows what, and they're sure not catching up.

"Oh, brother." I start to climb the fence, only Marissa yanks me back, saying, "What are you *doing*? Stay out of it!"

"But what if they get away?"

"How are they going to get away, Sammy? Get real!"

"But what if they make it home and stash the loot before the police catch them?"

"The police'll get a search warrant!"

"But what if Andy and the Old Lady *hide* it?"

"Sammy! The police are here—just let them do their job!"

Appliance Andy and the Old Lady are huffing and puffing along, looking over their shoulders, not quite believing they haven't been stopped yet. And the closer they get, the more I feel like I can't just stand there on the fence. I've got to *do* something!

Marissa was right, though—getting in their path wouldn't help. They'd just bowl me over. Plus, what if Squeaky Cheeks started shooting?

If only there was some way to trip them up.

So I look around, and when I spot Mrs. Stone's shovel sticking out of the far side of her compost heap, I climb over the dividing fence, scramble across her pile of plant manure, and yank out the shovel. And before Mrs. Stone can finish saying, "What are you *doing*?" I've half scaled her back fence and have speared the shovel blade over the fence so it's wedged in the V of a tree where a big branch grows out from the trunk. Then I hold on to the handle tight and check to my left for Appliance Andy.

Okay. I admit it was a pretty lame barricade. I mean, what was to stop them from going around it? Or under it? But Andy and the Old Lady were looking over their shoulders so much that they didn't see the shovel sticking out. And when they *did* see it, well, Andy's eyes got wide, he cried, "Aarrrghh!" and at the last minute he tried to limbo under it.

Well, good luck there. He lost his balance, and then the Old Lady plowed right into him and they both crashed to the ground like giant hairy bowling pins.

A few seconds later Squeaky and the Chick were upon them, shouting, "Freeze!" and "You have the right to remain silent" and all that jazz. So I yanked the shovel out of the tree and jabbed it back into the compost heap. And while the Chick sniffed the air and said, "Eeew. These perps need a bath!" I climbed back into Mrs. Willawago's yard.

Now, Marissa and Mrs. Stone were so busy looking over the back fence at the cops cuffing Andy and the Old Lady that they hadn't noticed Patch, digging away like mad in the corner of the yard next to where I'd poured the cement.

"Patch, no!" I said, yanking him back by the collar.

Mrs. Stone's head snapped to look, but all of a sudden Mrs. Willawago was there asking, "Did they catch them?"

"Yes, they did," Mrs. Stone said, but her eye was on Patch. Then she chuckled and pointed to the hole. "Looks like we'll be needing some more of that EZ-CRETE."

I peeked over the back fence, and since I could tell it

wouldn't be long before Squeaky and the Chick decided to detain me for questioning, I tapped Marissa and whispered, "Ready?"

She hesitated, then said, "You bet."

So I went over to Mrs. Willawago and said, "Uh, we're gonna get going."

"Now?"

I nodded. "And do me a favor. Don't tell the police who we are."

"But—"

"Please? I don't want to spend the night answering a bunch of questions when they have all the facts right there."

She didn't seem real comfortable with that but said, "I suppose . . ."

Then I remembered. "Hey! Have you heard anything from Hudson?"

"Not yet." She checked her watch. "I'll call him as soon as this is over because we're running out of time. The council meeting convenes at seven, and I would love to present proof that Coralee is trying to feather her own nest."

So Marissa and I grabbed our stuff and jetted out of there. And the funny thing is, Marissa didn't even bring up the dance. She was more into talking about Squeaky and the Chick and Appliance Andy and how every time you turn around in this town you find some new wacko that you can't believe actually lives here.

And you know what? Something about that made me kind of swell up inside about Marissa. Not like I was proud of her. More that I was just so glad she was my friend.

So when we got to the corner of Cook and Miller and it was time for us to go different directions, I gave her a hug—which is something I hardly ever do—and said, "Thanks."

"Thanks?"

I laughed. "Yeah. It's been some day."

Her eyes got wide, and I could see her remembering everything that had happened at school just a few hours before. "Oh, right—it has!" Her light changed, so she pushed off the curb, saying, "Well, you're free tonight, right? So recuperate 'cause tomorrow we discuss the dance!"

"I've got homework!" I called with a laugh.

She scowled over her shoulder.

"Really! I do! Math and English!"

"You'd better not be chickening out . . . !"

"Me? Chicken?"

"Brawk-brawk-brawk!" she crowed from across the street, which made me laugh again because I knew she was right. I mean, maybe I can strike down big ol' hairy bowling pins without really trying, but when it comes to boys, I'm one big wobbly gutter ball.

"There you are!" Grams said when I snuck through the door. "I've been worried all day about how it went at school. Did you tell her? Is everything okay? I tried calling Annie's but there was no answer. . . ."

I put down my backpack and skateboard and gave

Grams a big hug, too. Then I told her every detail of everything that had happened, from confessing to Mrs. Ambler, to her reaction, to her getting a new bird...everything. And when I got to the part about Mrs. Ambler not telling Heather until the Farewell Dance that she was on to her, Grams wiggled in her seat and said, "Oh! That is perfect!" Then she asked, "You're planning to go to the dance, aren't you? You've just got to!"

So I laughed and said, "As a matter of fact..." Then I told her how I'd been invited to join a group of kids who were going to the dance in a stretch Hummer.

"Really?" she said, but it was a pretty wary *really*.

So I figured what-the-heck and told her everything about *that*. And you know what? As soon as she knew the whole truth, her attitude totally changed. She went from Uh, really? to Way cool!

Or as close to that as a grandmother can get anyway.

And *then* I said, "But that's not all. Marissa and I went to Mrs. Willawago's today and—"

"Oh! That reminds me—Hudson called. He said to tell you no luck yet with..." She made her way over to the counter, peeled a page off the phone pad, and returned to the table, saying, "Earl Clooney." She handed me the paper and said, "He invited me to go to the council meeting tonight, but they are so terribly dull."

"But Hudson's not," I said with a little grin.

"Never mind. You were telling me about what happened today at Annie's, remember?"

"Oh, right!" So I caught her up on the railroad office

and the hairy bowling pins and all of *that*, so by then it was dinnertime and I hadn't even started on my homework.

"You go ahead and work on that, dear," Grams said when I moaned about it. "I'll fix dinner."

So I got busy on the math puzzles. And I was actually making pretty good progress—like I'd figured out that if CXV is six and CMLMI is seven, then LMXI is equal to "vein" and that if $ABCD$ times nine is equal to $DCBA$, then $ABCD$ is equal to 1089—when the phone rang.

Grams answered it, and the minute I heard her say, "Why, hello again, Hudson," I sat up straight and said, "I want to talk to him!"

She made me wait through an endless exchange of niceties, then finally said, "Yes, and she's eager to talk to you. Just a moment."

I didn't even say hello. I figured Grams had covered enough greeting ground for both of us. I just jumped in with, "Did you find something out?"

"No," he said. "There were problems with sealed documents and stonewalling. He's convinced that there's something fishy about this Earl Clooney character, but we're out of luck for tonight's meeting."

"Rats."

"But I was wondering if you were interested in coming along with me to the meeting tonight."

I looked at the clock. "Uh...maybe. But it starts in half an hour, and we haven't even eaten dinner yet. And I've got to do an extra credit assignment for English 'cause I'm borderline." What I didn't tell him was that even though I actually cared about what they were discussing, I'd seen glimpses of city council meetings on TV, and talk about boring—man!

He said, "Well, your grades come first, but if you find you do have time, why don't you just meet me at city hall?"

"Okay." I eyed Grams. "Meanwhile, I'll work on sending my envoy."

He chuckled. "That would be nice, but I won't hold my breath."

I laughed and said, "Well, if we don't see you there, call when you get home, okay?"

"Will do," he said, and got off the phone.

So I finished my math during dinner, then got busy on my English while Grams fussed around the apartment tidying things up. And I was on a roll, boy. I'd found dozens of words inside William Shakespeare's name. Some really stupid ones like *ape* and *are* and *am* and *pee*, but also some really great ones like *spasm* and *washer* and *miser* and *simile*. *Simile!* Miss Pilson would love that one. Maybe she'd give me bonus *bonus* points for it!

And I'd just realized that you can't get one single word of the phrase "to be or not to be" out of William Shakespeare's name—not *one*—when I noticed that Grams had changed her clothes and put on lipstick.

"You're going?" I asked her.

"Would you mind?" she asked back.

"Of course not—I want you to go!"

"Well, then..." She gave a worried look at the clock. "I've already missed the first part of it."

169

I snorted. "Lucky you." And I bit my tongue before actually saying, Besides, that's not why you're going!

"It's only a few short blocks . . . ," she was saying, "and it is still light out . . ."

She obviously needed a push out the door, so I said, "Go! And call me if you're going out afterward." I grinned at her. "I don't want to sit around here worrying."

She fluttered a little, then kissed me on the forehead and said, "Okay then!" Then she pointed to my list and said, "*Shale*. Did you get the word *shale*?"

"No!" I wrote it down. "Thank you!"

So off she went while I started jotting down a whole new slew of words inspired by *shale: shall* and *shake* and *shape* and *shark* and *shirk* and *shrill* and *shriek*. And then I saw *sphere*! What kind of great word was that to find?

Man, I was having a blast.

So I kept at it, sort of going through phases of finding a whole bunch of new words and then no words for a while. A group of new words, then no words. But then it got harder and harder to find words, and finally I just hit a wall.

So I counted my list: 126 words—not bad!

I got up, got a glass of juice, sat back down, and just sort of stared at the paper for a while. But my eyes must've drifted, 'cause I found myself looking at what Grams had written on the phone-pad paper that was still sitting on the table.

Earl Clooney.

Ear. Early. Loony. Coo. Cool. Coal. Core. Clone . . . My mind was making words out of Earl Clooney.

But then I pieced something together. Something I couldn't quite believe. "Holy smokes!" I whispered.

I checked it again.

"Holy *smokes*!"

I stood up and spun around twice, trying to decide what to do.

Then I grabbed my skateboard and tore out of there.

SIXTEEN

When I got to the steps of city hall, I jumped off my board and tore up to the door. I yanked it open and found the main corridor full of people milling around, looking very calm.

"Is the meeting over?" I asked a man by the drinking fountain. I was panting like crazy.

He sort of laughed at the state I was in, then said, "They're still in there." He checked his watch. "But it shouldn't be long."

"Where is it?" I asked. "Where's the meeting?"

He pointed down the corridor. "Council chambers are right down there. Past the lady in red."

It's a little embarrassing to burst into a room full of properly dressed adults when you're wearing what Grams calls rags and your hair's all wild from having ridden your skateboard a hundred miles an hour, but that's exactly what I did.

And I discovered something very surprising—the auditorium was *packed*. Not only was it standing room only in the back, but way down the center aisle there were reporters and camera crews. They were crouched around the edge of the speaking arena, where Leland Hawking was at a heavy oak podium, addressing the council through a microphone.

And even though I'd seen little snippets of council meetings on TV, being there felt nothing like seeing it from the apartment couch. It was much bigger. Much warmer. And in a very surreal way, much more real.

Anyway, there's Coralee and the other council members sitting like high-court judges behind a massive curved bench that's raised so that they're totally lording over everybody else in the room. And after I blast in, the sound inside the meeting room kind of grinds to a halt. It's like someone's slowing down the speed on an old vinyl record. And while the sound's winding down, waves of faces turn my way until it's completely quiet, and everyone—the council members, the people in the audience, Leland Hawking at the podium, the camera guys and reporters—*everyone* has turned to stare at me.

And I can tell what they're thinking: Who is this petrified girl with the wild hair and skateboard? Did she take a wrong turn, or what?

Coralee Lyon gives me a withering look over the top of her blue rectangular reading glasses, but she doesn't say a word to me. Instead, she turns back to Leland Hawking, and, like dropping the needle back on the record, she says, "Your point is well taken, Mr. Hawking, but if you have nothing *additional* to contribute, I think it's time we put this to a vote."

"Wait!" I cry, my feet moving me forward. It feels like I'm in a dream. A dream where you see yourself doing something and want to go in a different direction but can't.

173

Then a familiar voice floats through the crowd. "Sammy?"

I turn and see shiny hair.

Swimmer hair.

Brandon.

And there's a shiny blond girl next to him.

And a man wearing a polo shirt with COACH on it.

My feet keep moving, my voice saying, "You can't vote yet!"

From her perch at the center of the bench, Coralee Lyon sighs and sort of rolls her eyes. Then she takes off her reading glasses and says, "Young lady. You do not just burst into a meeting late, then disrupt the proceedings with presumptuous demands. The hearing portion of the meeting is over." Then, in an effort to dismiss me, she turns to the other council members. "I believe we are ready to vote. Can I have a motion?"

A man on the council says, "I move to adopt a resolution of necessity—"

"Wait!" I shout at the council. "I have something really important to say!"

Coralee Lyon turns slowly to face me. "*You*," she seethes, snatching up a gavel and pointing at me, "are out of order."

"And *you*," I say, pointing my finger at her, "are doing something illegal!"

"Oh, for heaven's sake," she says, putting down the gavel and waving me off. "It is not illegal. Have your history teacher explain it to you. Now—"

"I'm not talking about eminent domain! I'm talking about how you bought four properties on Hopper Street at rock-bottom prices and are in cahoots with Leland Hawking to sue for more money so you can make a big profit on them. *That's* what I'm calling illegal."

In her eyes I can finally see it dawn on her who I am.

I can also tell that she's worried.

But she snorts and says, "That's the most preposterous accusation I've ever heard! Would somebody remove this girl? She's friends with Annie Willawago, who is obviously stooping to new lows to hold on to her *Train* House."

I take a step closer. "If it's preposterous, then why don't you tell us who owns Earl Clooney Management Systems?"

She gives a sarcastic scowl. "How should I know?"

"You should know because *you* own it."

Other council members are starting to look at her like, Uh . . . Coralee? Is that true? And people in the audience are starting to buzz.

"Order!" Coralee calls, and she actually pounds the table with the gavel. "Of course that's not true!" Then she snarls down at me, saying, "Expect to be sued for slander."

This *was* a lot like dealing with Heather. And since I've got a lot of experience with *that,* it's like second nature for me to snarl right back at Coralee and say, "Yeah? Well, expect to be kicked off the council, lady, 'cause you're in some deep, deep doo-doo." I hurry over to a big easeled whiteboard, and while I'm erasing what's written on it and scrawling EARL CLOONEY across the top, I'm saying, "Earl Clooney Management Systems has bought four properties on Hopper Street over the past three years. Four slummy properties that they've done nothing with."

"Where's our security?" Coralee cries.

"Yes!" one of the other council members says. "We can't allow this girl to disrupt our meeting! We have a procedure. We have rules. We have decorum. She is completely and wholly out of order."

I sort of laugh to myself. I mean, please. What did they expect?

I'm in junior high!

But I've got no time to lose, so I get busy writing CORALEE LYON directly under EARL CLOONEY, which makes Coralee's bonny blue butt shoot right out of her chair. "This sort of disruption will set a precedent for future meetings," she shouts. "Somebody get her OUT of here! NOW!"

But it's too late, baby. By the time she's done with that little spiel, I've drawn lines that connect the letters of one name to the letters of the other.

They match exactly.

"Coincidence?" I call out to the audience. "I don't think so! And once someone cuts through the red tape that she's wrapped around the ownership documents, you'll see that Coralee Lyon wants this deal to go through *not* because it's good for Santa Martina but because it's good for *her*. She's planning to make a bundle of money on it!"

"But *we* want the deal to go through!" someone from the audience shouts. "We think it'd be great for the community."

"You know what?" I say, putting back the whiteboard marker. "So do I. But not like this. This is just *wrong*."

After that, it was all over. Everyone started talking at once. And when I heard one of the other council members bang the gavel and shout, "This meeting is adjourned!" I looked over and saw that Coralee was fleeing out a side door, being chased by reporters.

All of a sudden Hudson was there, hugging my shoulder with one arm. "I have never been so proud in my life!" And Grams was saying, "I held my breath through the whole thing. You were wonderful!" And Mrs. Willawago clasped my forearm and said, "You're a real angel, a gift from God!" while Mrs. Stone said, "Girl, you've got guts!"

Mrs. Willawago turned and said, "Teri! There you are! I looked all over for you earlier."

Mrs. Stone laughed. "We couldn't find you, either. What a turnout, huh?"

"Where's Marty?" Mrs. Willawago asked, looking around.

"He left about halfway through. He was so mad! Wait 'til I tell him how Sammy saved the day!"

Then reporters started sticking microphones in my face, asking me stuff like, "How'd you get involved in this?" "Are you friends with the train lady?" "What's your information source?" "When did you make the connection?" "What will you do if you're wrong?" "Are you planning to go into politics?"

The other questions I gave a not-gonna-answer-that shake of the head to, but that last one? Boy, did I pull a face.

A couple of them laughed, and then Hudson intervened, saying, "My young friend here cracked the nut, it's your job to pry out the meat."

They all looked at him like, Huh?

"Don't badger her," he said, "go investigate!"

The meeting room was still full of people, but it wasn't packed in solid like it had been. So Hudson and Grams led the way up the center aisle, with me behind them and Mrs. Stone and Mrs. Willawago behind me. And it was funny—nobody said, Nice going! or even, Interesting contribution! as I passed by. They just got quiet when I approached, moved aside, then started talking again after I'd passed.

It was like being in old-guy junior high.

But what did I expect? The Stones and Mrs. Willawago were probably the only people in the whole city who didn't want the project to go through.

So whatever. Let 'em glare.

I did look around for Brandon but didn't see him or his shiny-haired friends anywhere. Was he mad at me? Why would he leave without saying anything to me? Maybe *he* had given a little speech about how *great* the rec center would be. I mean, why else would he have been there?

And now what?

Was I uninvited to his pool party?

I tried not to think about that. I just moved through the crowd with my own little posse of seniors, feeling very relieved when we were finally outside. There were plenty of people outside, too, but at least there was air. Cool, damp air.

And then through the mist I heard someone calling, "Sammy!"

My heart recognized the voice before my brain did. "Brandon?"

"Over here!" he called from the sidewalk. "Isn't this that dog you walk?"

Even from the steps of city hall I could tell that it was indeed Captain Patch. But when I ran over, I saw that Brandon was holding him by the scruff of his neck. Patch's collar was gone. No collar, no tags, no nothing.

Patch wagged like crazy and yip-yap-yowled when he saw me. So I gave him a doggie ruffle and asked Brandon, "Where'd you find him?"

"He was crossing the street, over by the mall." He broke into a lopsided grin. "Quite a show tonight. And here I always thought you were kinda shy."

I could feel my cheeks turn red. "So you're not mad?"

"Mad? Why? Coach is bummed, but if that council lady's got her own agenda, they're going to have to think of a better way to make it happen." He started moving up the sidewalk, saying, "Coach is giving me a ride home, so I've got to boogie. See ya!"

"See ya!" I called back.

My over-the-hill entourage had been hovering a few feet away, and when Brandon was gone, Mrs. Willawago asked, "Who *was* that handsome young man?" like he was Superman or something. "And how did he know to give the Captain to you?"

"He's my best friend's cousin," I told her. "He saw me walking him the other day." I squatted next to Patch. "We're really lucky 'cause look—his collar's missing."

"Maybe he dug out." Mrs. Stone said. "His collar coulda got caught on the fence...."

"Oh dear," Mrs. Willawago said. "This is becoming a real problem. He could have been hit by a car!"

But I looked Patch over and said, "His muzzle's not

dirty...and his paws are clean...," because when he'd been digging before, boy, he'd been filthy.

"Oh, he must've dug out," Mrs. Willawago said. "The fence is very secure."

Then Hudson said, "Why don't I give you a lift home and we'll find out."

"Say," Mrs. Willawago said to the group of us, "why don't you all come over for a little celebration of tonight's victory. I've got some fresh baked scones...."

So everyone but me and the Captain went with Hudson to get a ride in his antique Cadillac. Hudson said it was fine for Patch to get a ride, but I handed him my skateboard and borrowed his belt for a leash instead. "I'll beat you there!" I called as I took off jogging with Patch.

I did, too. I even waited on the porch for a minute before deciding to go check out the backyard. Patch and I went through the side gate, but it was really dark. So I sort of felt my way along the corridor between the fence and the parlor car until I got into the open part of the backyard, where there was enough light from the ball fields for me to see where I was going.

And sure enough, there was a huge hole under the back fence, real near where we'd watched Squeaky and the Chick cuff Appliance Andy and the Old Lady. "Captain Patch," I scolded.

He yippy-yap-yowled and wagged his tail.

I looked in the hole. Under the fence. Over the fence. I couldn't find Patch's collar anywhere.

And I was in the middle of wondering if Mrs.

Willawago had some bricks or something that I could put in the hole before filling it when I noticed something odd—the dirt from the hole was in a mound. It wasn't sprayed everywhere like when a dog digs a hole.

It was like a *human* had dug the hole.

With a shovel.

Then I turned and saw something that gave me a creepy feeling inside. The Stones' shovel wasn't on the *far* side of the compost heap, where I'd stuck it after I'd used it to stop Appliance Andy.

It was on the *near* side of the heap.

Right by the fence.

SEVENTEEN

I stood there for a minute, thinking. Then the lights came on in the Train House, so I decided to fill in the hole so Captain Patch wouldn't run off before I could tell Mrs. Willawago about my suspicions. But when I went inside, Mrs. Stone was there and Mrs. Willawago was playing the perfect hostess, bustling around with scones and jams and pots of tea.

So I gave Hudson his belt back, then sat around listening to old people chitchat. Talk about dull. I don't know what it is—you get a bunch of old people together and the pacing of a conversation *kills*. Maybe it's their hearing, or maybe they're just more polite than junior high kids. I mean, when my friends and I are excited about something, we walk all over each other's sentences, jumping in with this or that, cutting each other off...it's fun. It's *alive*.

Old people don't converse like that. Even when they're not really listening to each other, they *act* like they are, waiting for their turn to put in their two cents. And then, since they've waited so politely, they feel justified in turning their two cents into about *fifty* cents, wandering down memory lane on some barely related story.

Anyway, I could tell Mrs. Stone was a little antsy, eating a scone and not saying much. And I sure didn't feel like chitchatting with *her*. Just being in the same room with her was making me very uncomfortable.

So when I finally got Mrs. Willawago alone in the kitchen and blurted out that I thought the Stones had tried to get rid of Patch, she listened very politely, then scoffed and said, "Oh, nonsense. The shovel was moved because Teri used it to fill in the hole Captain Patch dug earlier. You know, when the police were arresting Andy Quinn?"

All of a sudden I felt kinda stupid. "Are you sure?"

"Of course! I was right there."

"But . . . but the dirt wasn't sprayed out. It was in piles. And I can't find Patch's collar anywhere."

"That doesn't mean the Stones dug him a hole and re-moved his collar!" she whispered. "Besides, they were at the council meeting!"

"But Marty left early! And how do you *know* they were there? You didn't actually see Teri until it was all over, right?"

She held my cheeks gently and smiled at me. "Oh, lamb. Not everyone is as devious as Coralee Lyon—don't let her cast a shadow on the entire flock! Teri's our ally, remember? And no, she doesn't like Captain Patch dig-ging into her yard, but she's a long ways from purpose-fully releasing him."

"But what about Marty?"

She frowned. "Marty? Dig a *hole*?"

"Yeah! He knew you were at the meeting," I whispered.

"And don't tell me he has a bad back. He mows their yard, he works in their garden, and he chased me with a hoe! If you ask me, he's just using his back as a way to get paid for not working!"

"Shhh!" she warned. Then she frowned again and whispered, "He *was* injured on the job, and if his back has improved, well, it's not my place to meddle. Besides, he does have cancer now—"

"But don't they just take the cancer spots off and make you stay out of the sun? It doesn't stop you from digging a hole!"

"Skin cancer can spread to other parts of the body, Samantha. It can kill you!"

"Annie?" Mrs. Stone said, coming into the kitchen. "I gotta get going."

"Oh!" Mrs. Willawago said, fluttering a little. "Why don't I wrap up a scone or two for Marty?"

Mrs. Stone smiled. "That'd be nice."

Then Grams came into the kitchen and said, "We should be going, too. It's getting quite late." She turned to me and said, "Samantha? I think we should give you a lift home," pretending like I didn't live with her.

So I said, "Sure," and we got out of there in a wave of polite thank-yous. But once I was inside Hudson's car, I let my frump show in a big way. "I am so sick of people not believing me!"

"What *now*?" Grams asked. "People seemed to believe you just fine at the council meeting . . . !"

So I told them about the hole and the shovel and how I was pretty sure Marty Stone had dug the hole. And just like Mrs. Willawago, Grams tried to come up with reasons why he *hadn't* done it.

"See?" I said. "*I* think the hole was man-made, so you think I'm wrong. If it was someone with a Ph.D. in hole digging telling you the same thing, you'd think it was the gospel, but it's *me*, so you think it's my imagination."

"But someone with a Ph.D. in hole digging would know about holes," Grams said.

"Someone with a Ph.D. in hole digging should be put in the nuthouse! It's a *hole*. All you do is apply a little common sense to the surrounding dirt and the walls of the hole. I don't need to write a dissertation on holes to know when one's dug by a dog and one's dug by a shovel!"

"Well," Grams said, patting her hair. "Teri Stone *is* a little odd, I'll give you that."

Silly me, I thought I was getting somewhere. But when I asked, "What do you mean?" she said, "Well, for one thing, she should bathe more. And socks and Birkenstocks? Goodness."

See? That's what talking to Grams is like. You're discussing the science of hole digging and she turns it into a criticism of someone's personal hygiene and fashion choices.

But then Hudson looked at me in his rearview mirror and said, "Her socks were quite dirty. Perhaps *she* dug the hole."

Good ol' Hudson.

"Hmmm." But then I shook my head. "Her feet always look like that."

"She always wears those sandals?" Hudson asked.

I nodded.

"Well, that hippie look is very unattractive if you ask me," Grams said. "But to each his own."

I felt like saying, Who cares about fashion? I want to know who dug the *hole*. But I kept my mouth shut, and when we finally got home, I took a quick shower and went straight to bed. I was beat!

The next morning I actually watched the news 'cause I was on it. Actually read the paper 'cause Mrs. Ambler brought in a copy and I was *in* it. And I actually had an outside-the-classroom conversation with Mr. Holgartner on my trek between classes.

"Sammy!" he called from the admin building as I walked by.

Now you have to understand—Mr. Holgartner is not exactly Most Popular Teacher or anything. He's more like Most *Un*popular Teacher. He's boring, sarcastic, snide, and gives really confusing multiple-choice tests. And talk about needing to bathe more—pee-yew! He always smells like he's sweating garlic.

So having a teacher like this call your name with such enthusiasm across the campus makes you want to:

(a) Hide

(b) Pretend you didn't hear

(c) RUN

(d) Die of embarrassment

The correct answer?

(e) All of the above

I did go for option (b) for a second, but he called my name again, "Sammy! Samantha!"

"Uh, yes, Mr. Holgartner?"

He came up to me quick and stood a little too close. "Since when have you been interested in politics?"

"Uh . . . I'm not really."

"That was *my* impression," he laughed, oozing garlic.

"Ha-ha," I said back.

"No, seriously! I saw the news, read the paper . . . I was proud to see you taking a stand on the matter." Then he said, "We discussed eminent domain earlier in the year . . . ?"

Now, it's funny—it was like he was trying to take credit for my involvement. And maybe it would have been nice of me to say, Oh yeah. You totally inspired me to fight city hall, sir. But I wasn't in the mood to lie.

Too bad he hadn't talked to me the week before!

Instead, I looked right at him and said, "Actually, I got interested because of Mrs. Willawago's Train House and because I found out how the mall got built by the city kicking people out of their houses."

He nodded like he knew all about that.

Well, you know what? That really irritated me. So I kind of squinted at him and said, "Why didn't you tell us about that when you covered eminent domain?"

He shrugged. "We only have so much time to spend on each subject."

"But . . . but it would have made it *interesting*. You know, *relevant*."

He just stood there, blinking garlic fumes at me.

His face had totally fallen, and I felt kinda bad. Plus we were standing with this awkward silence between us. So I said, "Next year. Teach 'em about it next year." I gave him a little smile. "Kids might actually listen."

After my encounter with Mr. Holgartner, the rest of the day was very normal. Except for my little circle of friends, only teachers seemed to know anything about what had happened at the city council meeting, which made total sense. I mean, what junior high kid in their right mind gets up and watches the news or reads the paper? We're too busy rushing around from oversleeping to care about anything but not being tardy.

And for the rest of the week school was sort of a happy place. The teachers seemed to be in good moods, the kids were all buzzing about summer plans, there was hardly any homework . . . it was real *enjoyable*.

'Course, Heather was still lurking around, still making snide remarks, still plotting and conniving and pretending to be popular, but you could tell she was also counting the hours to Friday night, when she just *knew* she'd be ordained Friendliest *and* Most Stylish Seventh Grader. Maybe even Most Popular.

She couldn't wait.

And neither could we!

Hee-hee!

Things over on Hopper Street were also pretty mellow. Well, except for Captain Patch. He had a new collar and tags but was spending more time inside, which made our walks real athletic adventures. I tried to get him to heel like Marissa had, but he wouldn't listen.

And the whole thing with the Stones? I decided, Forget it! As long as Patch wasn't getting out and running the risk of being hit by a car, what did I care?

But Wednesday I asked Mrs. Willawago, "Hey, have you gotten any more threats since that letter?"

"No, thank God! And Teri hasn't gotten any, either."

Now, that should have been good, but something about it seemed strange to me. I mean, if the person who'd sent the letters and thrown the rocks was trying to make the rec center project go through, you'd think they'd be madder than ever after what had happened on Monday night, right?

But whatever. According to my number one news source, Hudson Graham, the rec center project was in limbo because there was now proof that Coralee Lyon owned Earl Clooney Management Systems, and instead of talking about batting cages and a sports café, people were talking about recalling ol' Blue Butt from the city council.

I played with the idea of sending her some suggestions for a new personalized plate. She could switch to CNCLCRK. Or LYNLYON. Or maybe just RECALME.

Anyway, Wednesday I also told Mrs. Willawago that I couldn't keep walking her dog forever and that Thursday would have to be my last day for a while. I mean, I like Mrs. Willawago and all, and I like Captain Patch, but c'mon, I'd been doing this every day for a month. My heaven insurance was more than paid up.

Besides, I'd promised Marissa that on Friday I'd go straight to her house after school.

Mrs. Willawago was very nice about it, actually. She said, "You've been an angel of mercy, lamb, and I will always be so grateful for your help." Then she told me that her physical therapist had been urging her to exercise her foot more and that she'd heard of a special harness you could put on dogs to make them easy to handle.

Now she tells me.

But anyway, Thursday after school Mr. Pence and his science club were selling supersour suckers to raise money for some Rocket Wars Camp they're attending this summer. And since I *love* supersour suckers, I broke down and let Marissa buy me one. Normally, I don't let her spend money on me, even though she always offers. I guess you'd say it goes against my philosophy of friendship.

But they had supersour apple, so I couldn't resist. And since these are big, square, chunky suckers, there was plenty of pucker power left to my sucker by the time I got to Mrs. Willawago's.

It was trash collection day, so I dragged her empty trash can into her garage, then waited for the mailman, 'cause he was whistling his way up the street.

When he reached me, he handed over Mrs. Willawago's mail and motioned over to Appliance Andy's. "Do you know if the folks next door are on vacation? Their mail's piling up."

I shrugged. "They're probably still in jail."

His eyes popped. "Jail?" Then he put up a hand and said, "Never mind—I don't want to know," and continued toward the Stones', whistling his merry little tune.

It did seem strange, though, that the Hairy Bowling Pins would still be in jail. Unless they hadn't been able to make bail or something. So I asked Mrs. Willawago about it when I went inside.

"Oh, lamb," she said. "I found out this morning that Andy is a swindler! He's wanted in thirteen states for insurance fraud! He's one of those deplorable people you hear about that preys on old people's fears. And imagine—him living right next door! I wonder if he ever phoned me. I get calls like that, you know. They were supposed to put an end to it, but I still get them!"

So. Appliance Andy was out of the picture. The threats had stopped. Maybe Mrs. Stone was right that it had been Andy making the threats. Maybe he wanted to sell his house and skip town.

Made sense.

I guess.

Mrs. Willawago squinted at me. "Why are your lips all green?"

I showed her my sucker, which I'd been holding politely by my side. "I'm supporting the science club," I said with a grin, then popped it back in my mouth.

She laughed. "I'm going to miss you, you know that?"

All of a sudden I felt bad. I'd probably miss her, too.

Just not tomorrow.

Or over the weekend.

Or—

"I know you have your own life to live... but maybe you can still come over once in a while?"

"Sure," I said. "I'll have lots of time this summer." Then I got the leash, and Captain Patch and I started our last adventure around the big block.

We went the way Patch always wants to go—west. Only this time he practically killed me, yanking me around the Stones' trash can. "Patch!" I shouted. "Patch, heel!"

"Yip-yap-arf! Yip-yap-arf!" he barked, wagging and

wiggling. Then he smelled something delicious on the sidewalk, and off he went again, following one scent until it led to another, to another, all the way around the block.

Like always, he lunged for Leland Hawking, Esquire's sign, but this time I let him add a posting while I grinned about the orange CLOSED sign in the front window. It had been there since Tuesday. And as we rounded the corner, it occurred to me just how many secrets had come out in the past week. Mine, Coralee's, Appliance Andy's, Leland Hawking's . . .

And then I giggled with the thought that there was one more secret that was coming out of the closet on Friday.

Heather's!

So I took a delicious chomp and shattered what was left of my sucker, thinking how nice it was not to be sweating anything out. And as I passed by Appliance Andy's house, it hit me that confessing to Mrs. Ambler might have been one of the hardest things I'd ever done, but it was probably the *best* thing I'd ever done. I'm not talking goody-two-shoes stuff. I'm talking the best thing I'd ever done for my*self*.

Anyway, by the time I made it back to Mrs. Willawago's, all that remained of my supersour sucker was a well-chomped, soggy stick.

It was pretty gross, let me tell you. And since the Stones' trash can was still at the curb, real near where I'd go in the side gate to put Patch away, I went over, opened the lid, and tossed the stick inside.

Only as I was closing the lid, my eye caught on something. Something stuck to the inside wall of the can.

I opened the can again. The inside was wet from trash ooze, which was working like glue on scraps of garbage. And near the rim, one of those scraps was a full sheet of paper.

It was smaller than binder paper but bigger than a notepad.

With discolored edges.

And faded green lines.

As I reached inside and peeled it off, a tingle ran through me like I'd touched naked wires.

There was nothing, not one word, written on it.

EIGHTEEN

"Sammy?" Mrs. Stone said, coming out of her house toward me. "What're you doin' in my trash?"

I put down the lid. "I was just throwing away my sucker stick, but then I noticed *this* stuck to the side of your trash can." I held out the paper and kept a close eye on her face.

Captain Patch sniffed the hem of her peasant dress. Her socks. Her sandals. And all the while Mrs. Stone stood stock-still, staring at the paper. No nervous fluttering. No snatching it from me. Some color had risen to her cheeks, but that was it.

"It's the same weird paper the threats were written on . . . ?"

Finally, she said, "*Where* did you find it?"

"Inside your trash can."

"Well, that's odd," she said, gently taking it from me. "That's very odd."

"Indeed," I said, sounding very English.

"I know what you're thinkin'," she said. "And I'd be thinkin' the same thing if I was you. But why would I send *myself* a threatening letter?"

"Maybe so nobody would suspect it was you sending the letters?"

"But why would I send Annie one? We're on the same side!"

"What about your husband?"

"He's on the same side, too!"

My mind was racing through the things that had happened in the last week. "Pretty convenient, don't you think, that the rock thrown at your house sailed through an *open* window?"

"It could've *killed* Marty!"

"According to Marty, right? I mean, did *you* see it happen?"

"Yes!" she said. "I mean no! I saw it just after it landed."

Now, I couldn't tell if she was covering for her husband or if she was in on it, too. So I said, "Well, I tell you what—why don't we go in and ask him? Why don't we find out why he's making death threats and chucking rocks and pretending like he doesn't want to move when maybe he really does? I mean, according to Mrs. Willawago, you guys hated living here until—"

"Stop it!" she says, glancing over her shoulder at the house.

"Are you *afraid* to? Then maybe I should just call the police."

"No!" She covers her face with her hands for a moment, then says, "Look. It beats me why that paper was in our trash. Maybe that jerk on the other side of the Willywagos' planted it there!"

"He's in jail."

"In jail? Still? Well, it really don't matter. Nobody got

hurt, right?" She glances over her shoulder again, then says, "I just wanna live in peace. Can you please just leave us alone?" Then before I can say, Uh, no, ma'am, she turns around and hurries back inside her house.

After standing there for a solid minute, I realized that for once I *was* in the mood to just let it go. I mean, it was my last day in this dumpy neighborhood, right? And whether her husband was a reformed abusive drunk or not, Teri Stone was obviously still afraid of him.

But there was one thing that made all the threats a lot more sinister than they might otherwise have seemed.

The hole someone had dug under the back fence.

I didn't care what anyone said, I knew Patch hadn't made that hole. And there was only one reason *for* the hole—someone was hoping Patch would follow a scent right up to heaven.

Or at least far enough away that he couldn't find his way home.

And maybe if the Train House had been stripped of all its precious train stuff while we were at the council meeting, well, it would have made sense for some burglar to spring the dog.

But why not just let him out the side gate?

No, someone had tried to make it look like Patch had escaped on his own. And since the Train House hadn't been burglarized, who else would have done it except Teri or Marty?

But talk about drastic! Did Patch really bug them that much? What was the big deal? Was their garden *that* precious to them?

So I didn't just forget about it. I put Patch in the back-yard, then went inside to tell Mrs. Willawago what I'd discovered.

Trouble is, Mrs. Willawago wasn't in the living room. Or the kitchen. Or the front room.

Then all of a sudden I hear a *thump* from down the hallway. Not a *sinister* thump. More just, you know, a *regular* thump.

So I mosey down the hallway, going, "Mrs. Willawago? Hello?"

Then I see that the door to the bedroom where I'd shoved Patch on Flying Rock Day is partly open, so I peek inside and what do I see?

The bottom half of Mrs. Willawago.

She *is* still attached to her top half, but she's standing on her tippytoes on a step stool, reaching into the closet, so all I can see of her is from the waist down. "Mrs. Willawago?" I ask, but she doesn't hear me because she's half buried in the closet, struggling to get something down off the shelf. Or put something away. I'm not sure which. So I say it again, louder. "Mrs. Willawago?"

Her arms stay up, but her head whips out of the closet, her eyes enormous. And I'm about to say, I didn't mean to startle you! when all of a sudden stuff comes tumbling off the closet shelf. A hat, a doll, a wreath . . . and as Mrs. Willawago tries to stop the avalanche, something else crashes to the floor.

A metal box.

Mrs. Willawago screams as it busts open, spilling gray-ish sand everywhere. I rush to help her, but she turns

197

on me and shouts, "Get out! Look what you've done! Get out!"

She's not hurt, but the sand's made a mess, and since I don't feel right just *leaving*, I ask, "Do you want me to get the vacuum cleaner?"

"No!" she screams, scooping the sand back into the box.

And that's when I realize that this sand is too dusty to be regular sand.

It's more like . . . ash.

But . . . Mrs. Willawago didn't have a fireplace . . . and besides, why would anyone keep ashes in a closet?

Then it hit me.

These *were* ashes.

Her husband's ashes!

She hadn't scattered them in her backyard—she'd just said that to get sympathy!

Man, talk about having a skeleton in the closet—this was the real deal!

Well, the powdered version of the real deal, anyway.

I left her alone, but I didn't leave the house. I sat in the front room thinking. Brooding. She had totally lied. To me, to the reporter, to the city council . . . And why? Did she think that was the only way to get people's sympathy about her property?

So what else had she lied about? What other secrets was she keeping?

The longer I sat there, the creepier I felt, and when she finally emerged from the bedroom and said, "Why are you still here?" I gave her a hard look and said, "You and the Stones were in on this together, weren't you?"

"In on what together?"

"The rocks, the letters... they were just for getting sympathy, like telling people you'd scattered your husband's ashes in the backyard."

Her face pinched into a pious frown. "I find your accusation to be brash and insulting. I had nothing to do with the threats."

I stood up. "Yeah, that's what Mrs. Stone said, too. But I found a piece of paper in her trash can that's just like the paper the threats were written on. And when we talked about it, she pronounced your name Will-*y*-wago, which goes with the way your name was spelled on the envelope of the letter you got. And wasn't it convenient that the rock crashed through your window when the reporter was here? Nice way to get yourself bumped up to the front page, wasn't it?"

"How *dare* you! I had nothing to do with the threats."

I scowled. "Yeah, and your husband's ashes are scattered in the backyard, too."

She pointed to the front door. "Leave."

I didn't hop to or anything, so she actually pulled me by the arm and started shoving me out the door, saying, "It is time for you to *leave*." She wasn't hobbling, either. And she was surprisingly strong.

After she'd thrown me outside and closed the door, I just stood on her porch for a minute, stewing. I'd walked her dog for a full month, I'd saved her bacon at the council meeting, I'd helped her get back at her archenemy, and after all that, I make one little logical accusation and she tosses me out on my ear?

Well, fine! If that's how she was going to be, what did I care? It's not like she'd been doing *me* any favors.

I stormed off, telling myself that it'd be a windless day in Santa Martina before I set foot back on Hopper Street.

The trouble with my brain is, it won't shut down. It can tune out fine. Like when Mr. Holgartner's talking about, well, about *anything*, or Vice Principal Caan's holding us hostage in the gym to lecture us about trash on campus, or Miss Pilson starts her little spiel about how we need to find a passion for something other than ourselves and that the work of Shakespeare is a very good place to begin...I can tune out quicker than you can click your remote. But turning my brain *off*? I haven't quite figured that out yet.

And the *other* trouble is, usually when I'm tuning *out*, I'm switching over to the puzzle channel. So even if I tell myself that I'm through thinking about something, my brain has this way of overriding that, and I find myself stewing or brooding or just running through different scenes in my mind. Like Coralee being in Mrs. Willawago's house. Or Appliance Andy and the Old Lady being cuffed behind the fence. Or Mr. Stone chasing after me with a hoe. Some things I play in slow motion, some I go through in double speed. And I find that the ones that I keep coming back to have something in them that doesn't quite *feel* right. Usually I don't even know what that is, but it's like my subconscious knows and it's trying to relay it to my conscious mind.

So that night I *tried* to get some sleep, telling myself,

Forget about it! You're through with Mrs. Willy-whatchamacallit and her wacko neighbors! It doesn't matter anymore. Who cares who sent the letters? Who cares who threw the rocks? Who cares who dug the hole? It's over!

But my mind had a mind of its own. It kept going back to Hopper Street. Kept telling me, Play it again, Sammy. Look at everything all over again.

So whether I wanted to or not, I did. And the funny thing is, I didn't spend much time thinking about Mrs. Willawago and her powdered skeleton—I sort of chalked that up to desperate times and desperate measures. It was the things Mrs. Willawago had said about the *Stones* that my mind kept drifting back to. The cancer. The quitting drinking. The changes in Mr. Stone.

If he'd become a better person, why was Mrs. Stone still so afraid of him?

Did he threaten *her* with a hoe?

Mrs. Willawago had said she'd heard screaming and crying, and had seen bruises, but all that had stopped when the drinking had stopped.

But maybe it hadn't really. Maybe Mr. Stone was just sneakier about it. I'd heard of men who were really controlling of their wives—didn't let them have friends or talk to the neighbors or even stay connected to their family—but I'd never actually *met* one before.

And I didn't understand *her* at all. She seemed scared of him, but she was protective of him, too. Why protect him? Was she embarrassed? Did she think *she* was to blame? Why was she hiding the way he treated her? Why

201

had she put up with it all these years? Why didn't she just *leave*?

So my mind was swimming with questions, wading through scenes from my encounters on Hopper Street. And the last vision I had before drifting off was of Mr. Stone.

Coming at me with a hoe.

NINETEEN

The next morning the phone rang early. It was Marissa, cock-a-doodle-dooing a list of instructions for me. "I was thinking we should bring hand towels. And mittens! You know, for when we go ice-blocking? And do you think we should get some special pens or something? For signing yearbooks? And what about a disposable camera? I don't want to bring a real camera, but a disposable one could be cool! And don't forget a jacket. You can borrow one of mine if you want, but if you *don't* want to, bring your own because if the fog comes in, it'll be cold! Especially if we're sitting on ice! Do you think we should bring extra pants? Or maybe a hair dryer for if our bottoms get wet?"

"Marissa?"

"Uh, yeah?"

"Have you been thinking about this all night?"

"Yes! Absolutely! I got like, *no* sleep. How about flashlights? Do you think we should bring those?"

"Why? You want your block of ice to have a headlight?"

"No! But what if we go ice-blocking somewhere really *dark*..."

I sighed. "Marissa, we don't need all that stuff. Don't

overpack, okay? If you come out with a giant suitcase, it'll be embarrassing."

"But . . . what if we need stuff?"

"Look. I'll talk to you at school, okay? I haven't even taken a shower yet."

I could practically see her jaw drop. "You're just getting up? Just *now*?"

"Yup."

"Are you packed?"

"I didn't know I *had* to pack."

"How can you be so nonchalant?" Then she added, "Whatever, whatever. You can borrow from me. Just hurry up, okay? You're going to be late! Oh! And don't forget your student ID!"

"Okie-dokie," I said.

"Okie-dokie? Okie-*do*kie? A day like today and you okie-*do*kie?"

I laughed and said, "Yup. Now toodaloo!" and hung up the phone.

All week Mrs. Ambler had been one cool customer. So much so that I was actually starting to wonder if something had gone wrong with our little plan. Maybe Mr. Caan had nixed the idea of exposing Heather at the dance. Maybe the ballot numbers hadn't worked out right. Maybe . . . who knows what? With adults it can be anything. They say we don't worry enough about consequences, but if you ask me, they worry too much.

But during homeroom, after she read the part in the announcements where they reminded us *again* that all

William Rose Junior High dances are *closed* dances where

you have to be there by a certain time and then can't leave until a certain time, and that you can't get in unless you have your student ID or a special visitor pass, well, after *that*, she paused and a little smile crept across her face. Then she looked out at our sea of tuned-out faces and said, "I am *so* looking forward to chaperoning the dance tonight."

All of a sudden kids snap to. And Tawnee blurts out, "You know who the Class Personality winners are, don't you?"

"Ah," Mrs. Ambler says with a smile. "*Those* are in a sealed envelope in the vault in the office." She opens her eyes wide and drops her voice like she's telling us a scary story instead of a lie. "Only Mr. Caan knows! But *he* tells me that there'll be some interesting surprises tonight!"

Everyone's leaning forward, looking at her like, Really!

"Mmm-hmmm." She drops her voice even further. "*Apparently* there were some write-ins!"

After a few seconds of wide-eyed waiting for her to say more, Heather breaks down and asks, "Write-ins who *won*?"

"That's what he tells me," she whispers. Then she straightens up and says, "I guess we'll find out tonight!"

After that Heather could barely contain herself. And it was pretty obvious that she had spent a lot of money and time prepping for her evening of glory, too. Her hair was still flame-throwing red, but now it had dramatic blond streaks in it. And her nails were done with those fake white tips that are supposed to look real but look like fake white tips. Her eyebrows were all waxed, and she was sporting new glittery eye makeup. Even her teeth looked whiter.

After homeroom she was so full of herself that she couldn't help it—she caught up to Marissa and me and said through an inch of lip gloss, "I'm showing up in a *real* limo tonight—nothing like that butch thing you classless losers are riding in."

I probably should've just kept my mouth shut, but what else is new? I said, "I'm sure it'll be a real memorable evening for you, Heather."

Now, the words were fine. But the trouble is, I couldn't help attaching a smirk *to* the words. "What do you mean by that?" she said, grabbing me by the arm and spinning me around. "And why are you looking like that?"

"Why, Heather...!" I gave her a Who-me? look as I removed her hand from my arm. "If I didn't know better, I'd say you were worried about something." I put a finger to my chin. "But no. That can't be. That's the old Heather. The *new* Heather's learned so much from her mistakes. The *new* Heather's grown so much as a human being that she wouldn't do anything that might cause her to be worried." I smiled at her and wiggled my eyebrows. "See you at the dance tonight." Then I linked arms with Marissa and walked away.

"I didn't kill her bird!" she called after us.

"I belieeeeve you!" I called back.

"I didn't!" she shouted.

"I belieeeeve you! Honest! I do!" Then I smiled and waved. "See you tonight!"

For a second, nothing. Then she screamed, "I hate you!"

I blew her a kiss.

Ah, what wings the clean conscience brings.

So I was in a great mood, but even after Marissa got over scolding me for egging Heather on, she was in an absolute state all day. It's been a long time since I've seen her bite her thumbnail with, as Miss Pilson would say, such *voracity*.

"Stop with the cannibalism already!" I finally told her.

"I can't believe you're not nervous, Sammy. Our first date and you're—"

"It's not a date. It's a fun time with friends. Get over the idea that it's a date and you might actually have a thumb left in case something happens and you have to hitchhike home."

"Hitchhike home? Why would I have to hitchhike home?"

I rolled my eyes. "It's a joke, Marissa."

"But it's not funny! I don't want to have to hitchhike home!"

"That's still no reason to chew off your thumb."

She didn't think *that* was funny, either. "Sammy! *Promise* me you're not going to do something that's going to ruin tonight."

"Ruin it? Me? I'm not the one in danger of being hospitalized for self-mutilation."

So that's how it went all through school and the whole way over to her house. And once we were *at* her house, it got even worse. Her bratty little brother, Mikey, figured out that something important was going on and wouldn't quit harassing us. Marissa complained to Simone, their "nanny," but Mikey still kept following us around, making stupid comments and spying on us.

Then he let an alligator lizard loose in Marissa's room. Marissa hit the roof, then stayed on top of her bed, squealing, "There he goes!" "Stop him!" "Catch him!" while I chased after the beast on my hands and knees. That sucker was big. And any time I cornered him, he hissed at me like a cat.

When I finally caught him, I held him tight behind the neck, cornered Mikey in his room, and shoved the lizard in his face. "Do you have any idea what this is?" I asked him through my teeth. My eyes were squinty-mean. My nose was flaring.

"It's just an . . . an alligator lizard!"

"Nuh-uh," I said, shoving it closer so it hissed at him. "It's a *barracuda* lizard."

"Aarrrghh!" he cried, cowering farther into the corner. Then he tried to puff up a little as he said, "N-n-no it's n-n-not! It's an alligator lizard! I found him outside!"

"Oh, but you're wrong." I turned the lizard to the side. "See this pattern on its neck? That's how you can tell— it's a *barracuda* lizard." I gave him a wicked grin. "Do you know what barracuda lizards *love* to eat, Mikey?"

"F-f-flies?"

"Nuh-uh." My grin became downright evil. "F-f-*fish*."

Mikey's eyes got all wide 'cause if there's one thing on earth Mikey loves, it's his fish.

"That's right, Mikey. Barracuda lizards are great swimmers. Great predators. They can pick the flesh off a fish in two-point-eight seconds. You hear what I'm saying? Two-point-eight seconds." I eyed his fish tank and said, "Now, I'm gonna do you a favor, Mikey. I'm gonna keep this barracuda lizard in Marissa's room, faaaaar away from your fishies. If you stay out of her room, this guy stays out of your fish tank. But if you bug us again, get ready, 'cause you'll be starting a fishbone collection. No more warnings, no second chances. You got it?"

He gulped. He nodded. Then the lizard hissed again, which made him choke on a scream and cry, "I promise!"

Marissa had been watching from the doorway, and once we were safely in her room again, she whispered, "That was amazing!" Then she giggled, "Barracuda lizard." *Then* she said, "But we're not keeping that thing in here, are we?"

"Nah," I said, then opened the window and put him on the wall outside.

So we were finally able to get ready to go, which for Marissa meant tearing her entire closet apart, only to wind up in the outfit she'd laid out in the first place—jeans and a bell-sleeved shirt.

I was actually very cool about everything until six o'clock, when we were supposed to be picked up. Then all of a sudden, all at once, I got nervous. My stomach started fluttering. My hands started getting all clammy. I looked at myself in the mirror and thought I looked stupid. I pulled my hair back in a ponytail. Took it out. Put it back again. Took it out.

"It looks better down," Marissa finally told me.

I wasn't convinced. I pulled it back again.

"I tell you, it's better down." She was kneeling on her window seat, looking down the street.

I left it up anyway. "Do you have any gum?" My mouth felt all chalky.

She found some, then went back to looking out the window. It was already six-fifteen. "Maybe they're lost?"

"Everyone knows where East Jasmine is."

"Maybe they can't make it up the hill?" But then she gasped and said, "There they are! Ohmygod, look at that thing!"

So I went to the window, and man, my heart was beating like it had twelve chambers instead of four.

"Oh my *God*," she said again, then she squealed, grabbed me around the shoulders, and jumped up and down. "*Look* at that thing!"

It was sleek but tough-looking. Like a shark in a tuxedo. And as music from it pulsed through the neighborhood, I found myself getting more and more nervous. This wasn't just a get-together.

This was a *date*.

The chauffeur stepped out of the Hummer and went to open the back door. He was wearing a tailored black suit, only he didn't have a shirt on under his coat—just lots of gold chains where a shirt was supposed to be. He was also wearing narrow wraparound shades and had a shaved head, which made him look more like a rap star than a driver.

"Come on!" Marissa squealed, grabbing her duffel bag.

"What's in that?" I asked.

"All that stuff I told you about!"

"But—"

"Come on!"

"Wait!"

She turned to face me. "For *what*?"

"Aren't we supposed to let them ring the bell?"

"Who cares! I want to get out of here before my parents get home!"

"But—"

She blinked at me. "Ohmygod, you're nervous!"

My hands were *pouring* sweat. "I have to go to the bathroom."

"Sammy!"

The doorbell rang as I charged for the bathroom. "Oh great," she groaned. "Now I'm gonna have to deal with Mikey and Simone and . . . Sammy, would you hurry?"

I hurried. And I dried my hands real, real well. Then I pulled my hair out of the ponytail and followed Marissa downstairs, where she intercepted Simone from answering the door. "I got it, thanks!" she said.

And all of a sudden there we were, face to face with Danny. And Casey. And Billy and Nick and Olivia. And they were all sort of craning their necks inside, looking at the high-polish way the McKenzes live. "Wow," Olivia gasped. "You *live* here?"

"Nah," Marissa said, squeezing outside. "I rent a tent out back."

Danny laughed, then pointed to her gym bag. "What's in that?"

"Ice-blocking supplies," she said, and the funny thing

211

is, she said it with such confidence that you'd swear the girl was an ice-blocking pro.

"Cool!" Billy said with a goofy grin.

"Hey, where's your harem?" Marissa asked him.

"Waitin' for me at the dance," he said.

Meanwhile, Casey was trying to make eye contact with me, but I was having trouble looking at anything but my feet. "Hey," he said softly. "You okay?"

I nodded. A little too hard. A little too fast.

Then I filed in behind Marissa and entered the mighty Humvee.

TWENTY

"This is *awesome,*" Marissa squealed once we were inside. "This is amazing! I can't believe this is a car!"

The seats ran along the perimeter instead of across in benches. They were slick black leather and had compartments and speakers and cup holders behind them and actual coffee tables in between them. Everything was black or chrome and definitely high-tech.

We all scooted in, me next to Casey; Marissa and Danny across from us; Nick and Olivia next to us; and Billy lounging across the whole backseat.

"Where to next, m'man?" the driver said through a speaker.

Danny keyed a button on the wall. "Just cruise, dude."

"Broadway? Main?"

"Both!" Danny said back with a laugh.

Billy clicked the televisions on with a remote but kept the volume muted. Nick turned the stereo on. Olivia leaned toward me and said, "Guys and gear—it just cracks me up."

I nodded and smiled but didn't know what to say.

"Nervous?" she whispered.

I nodded a little.

She laughed. "Don't worry—it'll go away."

"Bubbly anyone?" Danny asked, and that's when I noticed the bottles of champagne in an ice bucket.

All of a sudden I was doubly nervous. They were going to *drink*?

But when he pulled a bottle out of the ice, I saw that it wasn't champagne—it was carbonated apple cider. Pretty soon everyone had pretzel sticks and cider, and I was feeling a lot better. It was just nice to have something to hold on to. Something to *do*.

Then Billy started clowning around, acting like his pretzel was a cigar, hoisting his glass, and talking in an English accent. "I say there, lads and lassies, this is a bonny good batch of cider! Another round! On the house!" It didn't go at *all* with the CD that was thumping in the background or what was playing on TV, but that didn't matter. Billy's Billy, and there's no way TV or CDs can compete.

Then when we were downtown cruising along Broadway, Billy hung out a window and started yelling, "Cheerio, my good man!" to old men and "God speed, fair lass!" to old ladies as we passed by. Then *Casey* got the bright idea that they should act like pirates, so pretty soon *all* the guys were hanging out the window, going, "Ahoy, matey!" and "Arg!" and "Shiver me timbers!"

Then they *really* started getting carried away. Especially at red lights.

"Yield to the Black Pearl!"

"Move, ye lazy landlubber!"

"All hail the sea doggies!"

"Spare me pieces of eight, can ye?" Billy shouted at a man in an SUV next to us. The man kept looking straight ahead, so Billy said, "Nay? Well, perhaps pieces of seven then!" No reaction. "Pieces of six? Five? Four...?" The light changed and the man pulled away fast, and Billy shouted out at the next car, "Are ye a buccaneer? Arg! That makes ye two bucks in all!"

Marissa looked at me like, Huh?

"A buck an ear?" I told her.

She laughed out loud, and Olivia just groaned.

Then our driver rolled down the glass partition and called, "Belay the chatter, ye landlubbers, or I'll keelhaul the lot of ye! Look to yer starboard side! We be chased by the Queen's own men. Handsomely now, or we'll all be tossed in the clink!"

Danny said, "Huh?" but Casey pointed out the window and said, "Cops."

"Following us?" Danny asked.

Casey nodded, and we all scooted over so we could see.

"Oh no!" Marissa and I said at the same time.

"What?" Danny asked.

It was Squeaky and the Chick.

"Those cops are *idiots*," Marissa and I said at the same time. Then we both busted up.

"How do you know them?" Casey asked.

Before I could answer, Marissa shook her head and rolled her eyes. "Don't even ask. Just believe us—they are." Then she yanked on Billy's shirt 'cause his head was still sticking out the window. "Billy! Get in here!"

Squeaky and the Chick tailed us up Broadway, down

215

Main, down Miller, and along Cook. And when we neared a turn-in to the mall, Billy scrambled forward to talk to the driver. "Go in here!"

"Aye, aye!" the driver said, then cruised along to a passenger-unloading curb and said, "Shall I drop anchor, matey?"

"Aye!" Billy cried, and when we'd stopped, he added, "You are one cool dude," and jumped out of the Hummer.

"Hey!" Danny called after him. "Where are you going?"

Billy ran toward the big glass doors of the mall, shouting, "Don't set sail without me, mateys!"

So while Billy disappeared inside the mall, Squeaky and the Chick left their squad car idling behind us and came around both sides of the Hummer.

"Evening, Officer," our driver said, rolling down his window.

"Nice rig," Squeaky said back. He looked in back at us, and we all sort of waved and smiled.

"Underaged minors?" Squeaky asked the driver, one eyebrow up.

"Hmmm," the driver said. "They're minors, yes, sir. And that's just cider they have back there."

Danny held up an empty bottle. "See?"

"Between you and I?" Squeaky said to our driver. "It would behoove you to keep them contained within the inside of the vehicle."

"Uh, yes, sir."

"Very good, m'man," Squeaky said, trying to act hip as he gave the window frame a chummy pat. Then he and the Chick headed back to their squad car.

"Landlubbers," the driver grumbled as he watched them in his sideview mirror. "Like I could contain you within the *outside* of the vehicle?"

All of us snickered. Then Danny said to the driver, "Leave the partition down, man. You're too funny."

"Aye, aye, Cap'n," he said back.

As we watched Squeaky and the Chick zoom off, Danny asked Marissa, "So how do you guys know them?"

Marissa took a deep breath, looked at me, took another deep breath, looked at me again.

"It's not a big deal," I finally said. "There were these people stealing stuff out of the old Santa Martina Railroad Office and Marissa and I—"

"You, not me," Marissa said.

"You were there, too."

"I know, but I didn't knock them down with a shovel."

"Wait," Olivia said. "You knocked those two cops down with a shovel?"

"No! The people raiding the railroad office."

"What railroad office?" Casey asked.

"You know—on the corner of McEllen and Hopper? It's all boarded up." They just kind of stared at me, so I said, "Never mind. It doesn't matter. The point is, *we* wound up stopping the thieves, because those cops almost let them get away."

"So where's the shovel come in?" Nick asked.

I shrugged. "We used it to block their escape route."

"A *shovel?*"

"They could've gone under it, but they were looking over their shoulders so much they crashed right into it."

217

"Wow," Olivia said.

I shrugged again. "It was no big deal."

Billy came out of the mall wearing an eye patch, a hook hand, and a fake parrot on his shoulder. He waved a skull-and-crossbones flag as he ran toward us. "Ahoy, sea doggies! Hoist the Jolly Roger!" He clipped the flag to the Hummer's antenna and scrambled back inside. "Here ye go, mateys!" he said, passing out eye patches and skull-and-crossbones bandannas.

Olivia looked at him like he was a few trinkets short of a *real* treasure, but Marissa and I shared a grin, then tied bandannas around our heads like do-rags. "Arg!" we said to each other. "Arg!" we said to the guys.

"Gar!" they said back at us with eye patches on.

"G'on, wench!" Billy said to Olivia. "Or we'll make ye walk the plank!"

So Olivia laughed and tied on a bandanna. "Arg!"

"All right then, mateys!" the driver said. "The Black Pearl is set to sail. Where to, Captain?"

Danny looked around at the rest of us. "Where do you want to eat? We'd talked about going to the Grill, but—"

"Arg!" Billy snarled. "And leave the Black Pearl? I say we get a bucket o' bones and sail the seven seas!"

"Aye!" we all cried, so Danny laughed and told the driver, "Set sail for Crispy Chicken, matey!"

So that's what he did, and on the ride over Billy lifted his cup and said, "Another round of grog!" and when we all had more cider, he started singing, "Yo ho, yo ho, a pirate's life for me!"

Casey actually knew some of the words to the song, so he

threw in: "We're rascals and scoundrels and villains and knaves. Drink up, me hearties, yo ho. We're devils and black sheep—really bad eggs. Drink up, me hearties, yo ho!"

Then we all joined in, singing, "Yo ho, yo ho, a pirate's life for me!"

"We're beggars and blighters and ne'er-do-well cads. Drink up, me hearties, yo ho! Aye, but we're loved by our mommies and dads. Drink up, me hearties, yo ho!"

"Yo ho, yo ho, a pirate's life for me!"

The Hummer couldn't make it through the drive-through at Crispy Chicken, so the guys all jumped out and brought back two big buckets of chicken legs. No other parts, just legs. Which, of course, we had to eat like a bunch of ravenous pirates, ripping the meat off the bone, going, "Arg!" and "Gar!" and tossing bones back in a bucket.

Meanwhile, the driver cruised around town whistling the yo-ho song. And even though we all would have been perfectly happy *not* to go to the dance, that *is* where we were supposed to be going. So we headed for school, and by the time we arrived there was no doubt about it—crazy or not, we were going in as a jolly band of pirates.

Arg!

TWENTY-ONE

So at our school dances they don't let you into the gym until a certain time or *after* a certain time, and then once you're in, you're not allowed to leave until the dance is over. It's Mr. Caan's way of controlling the situation, and believe me, he's big on control.

Even though there were only about five minutes left before they closed the gym doors, there were still a whole bunch of kids outside when the Black Pearl sailed into the drop-off zone. I guess that's the thing about being controlled—you avoid it any chance you get, even if that means shivering outside when you could be inside out of the wind.

There were also two other limos ahead of us—both white. Heather, Monet, and Tenille were just getting out of one of them, and they were all wearing dresses. I'm talking spaghetti straps, wraps, jewelry, updos, the whole nine yards. I nudged Marissa and whispered, "Do you wish you had gone with them?"

"Are you kidding?" she whispered back. "This is the most fun I've had in my entire life!"

I grinned. "Me too."

Anyway, as we eased into the drop-off zone, all the kids

shifted their attention from the white limos to the Hummer. It was a total teen magnet.

Danny made us wait for the driver to open a door for us, and when he did, we all piled out, going, "Arg!" and "Gar!" and "Ahoy there, matey!"

Real classy, huh?

Everyone laughed, especially at Billy, who was carrying the bucket of chicken bones, going, "Don't cross us, landlubbers, or this be yer fate! Arg!" as he shook a bone. Then he snatched off the Jolly Roger flag and led us all to the gym, saying, "Come along, buccaneers! Come along, wenches! Time to walk the plank!" So a whole bunch of kids followed the seven of us as we marched toward the gym, singing, "Yo ho, yo ho, a pirate's life for me . . ."

Now, as we were waiting in line to have our student ID cards checked, Marissa nudged me and cocked her head toward the parking lot. "Look at her," she whispered in my ear. "She's in a rage already."

Sure enough, Heather was talking to Tenille and Monet, hands clenched, face pinched into a frown. Then some girls behind us started gossiping about them.

"Why are they dressed like they're going to the prom?"

"Why'd they get a limo? Aren't they all seventh graders?"

Pretty soon a lot of people in line were talking about them, making the typical cutting junior high remarks.

Now, part of me was surprised by this. From the way I'd been processed through the gossip machine for most of the year—thanks to Heather—I figured kids just bought what she sold.

But now here I was listening to the machine turn on *her*, and I couldn't help feeling a little . . . sorry for her. And Casey. I mean, he was standing right beside me and could hear all the acidic remarks, too. And even though he always acts like Heather is a pain, she *is* his sister, and how could you *not* be embarrassed by what everyone was saying?

But when I looked at him like, Ouch! he just rolled his eyes and said, "I tried to warn her, but you know Heather."

Then he looped an arm around my waist and smiled. "You're the last one who's supposed to be feeling sorry for her, y'know?"

I tried not to jerk. Tried not to look totally freaked. But his hand was warm. And heavy. And all of a sudden it felt like everyone was watching and whispering about *us* instead of Heather.

But then we were in the foyer and it was our turn to show our IDs, so his hand dropped away.

The people checking IDs and handing out yearbooks turned out to be Mrs. Ambler and Vice Principal Caan.

"There you are!" Mrs. Ambler says to me, but when she sees who I'm with, her eyes sort of bug. She recovers quickly, though, and says, "Well!" as she checks a list. "Sammy ordered a yearbook," she says to Mr. Caan, "and Mr. Acosta . . . gets one, too."

So Mr. Caan hands over two yearbooks and two pens and says, "What's with the pirate theme tonight? I had to confiscate Mr. Pratt's hook hand and his 'bucket o' bones.'"

"We sailed in on the Black Pearl, sir," Casey tells him.

Then he hitches a thumb toward the parking lot and says, "Courtesy of Danny's mother. Check it out when you get a chance."

"Well, have a good time," he says, then eyes me with a sigh. "And promise me you'll stay out of trouble tonight, all right?"

"Arg!" I say with a little squint, then laugh and add, "Of course."

So into the gym we went. The lights were off except for a disco ball in the middle of the room, some light-up palm trees, and spillover lighting from the foyer and the locker-room hallways. There were chaperones posted at every exit, and balloons, streamers, and painted butcher-paper signs that said FAREWELL 8TH GRADERS and HAVE A GREAT SUMMER decorated the walls. Music was thumping through speakers on either side of some tables where a DJ had set up, but no one was dancing—they were all gathered in little groups off to the sides, poring over their yearbooks.

Billy had already attracted a covey of girls and was entertaining them by pretending to converse with his parrot, while Marissa and the others were standing near a light-up palm tree, checking out their yearbooks.

"Come on!" Casey said with a smile, then grabbed my hand and led me over to the others.

Now, Casey *has* held my hand before. Actually, he's *kissed* my hand before, but that was at a Renaissance faire when he was playing the part of some Renaissance guy. It didn't mean anything, but my hand was freaked out about it for a week anyway.

So what I'm confessing here is that my hand is real

good at making a huge deal out of nothing. Like one time Brandon McKenze let me borrow his catcher's mitt, and my hand thought it had died and gone to heaven.

Stupid, sweaty appendage.

And now with the way Casey had grabbed it and was pulling me along, well, you'd think that I'd stuck it in an electrical outlet or something. There it was, spazzing away, while the rest of me was too paralyzed to yank it free.

Luckily, you need two hands to look in a book, so once we were with the others, our hands just sort of went their separate ways. We all wound up sitting on the floor in a circle, checking out our yearbooks, laughing at the wacky collage pictures and how dorky we all looked in our beginning-of-the-year photos. Then we passed our books around, signing each other's, which was easy for me to do in Nick's and Olivia's because I barely knew them:

> It was fun getting to know you aboard the
> Black Pearl. Arg!
> > Good luck in high school,
> > Sammy

But Danny's was harder 'cause what I really wanted to say was, Don't trifle with the affections of my best friend, dude, or there'll be hell to pay, but I knew that Marissa would kill me if I did. So I made some dopey comment about how lucky he was to be getting out of junior high jail before us and just passed it on.

Marissa's I couldn't do right then and there. We'd had such a wild year that I didn't even know where to begin.

So I made a border design around an entire autographs page in back and wrote SAVED FOR SAMMY on top of it. Then I started writing stupid stuff in Casey's. I thanked him for being different from everybody else I knew, and for standing up for me when it could have gotten him in a lot of trouble, and for being funny and calm and patient and protective—even though I didn't need him protecting me—and for making junior high a whole lot more enjoyable than it would have been.

I didn't want to say a bunch of mushy stuff—like how he's got the most chocolaty eyes I've ever seen, or how he's noble and dashing and strong, or how I wear the little lucky horseshoe he gave me everywhere 'cause it makes me happy to know I have a friend like him.

Nope. Sure didn't want to say any of that.

So I was trying to figure out how to wrap it up when I noticed that everyone else was already done.

So . . . what had Casey put in mine?

Have a nice summer. Be cool?

God, was I being embarrassing, or what? I was taking this whole yearbook-signing thing way too seriously.

So real fast I wrote a bunch of *Arg!*s and *Gar!*s and *Ahoy!*s and signed off, "Drink up, me hearty, yo ho!" and scrawled my name.

Then the DJ cut into the end of the song he'd been playing and announced, "All riiiight! Enough with those books, it's time to get this party started!" He cranked up the volume and "Get the Party Started" came thumping over the P.A.

"Let's put the books in our gym lockers!" Marissa shouted over the music.

"Good idea!" we all said.

So the boys went to the boys' side, and we girls went to the girls' side, and since Olivia was an eighth grader, she went to her section of the locker room while Marissa and I went to ours.

And of course, the first thing we did when we were alone was paw through our yearbooks to see what Casey and Danny had written.

"That's it?" Marissa said when she found hers. She seemed crushed, so I looked to see what he'd written.

Hope you had a good time at the dance.
Danny

She turned to my book and said, "What did Casey say in yours?"

Now, I could tell that if Casey had written something equally boring in mine, Marissa would somehow feel better about what Danny had written. So I said, "I haven't found it yet, but I don't think he wrote much, either."

"Guys," she grumbled. "I tell you." But then she spotted it. "Wait! Go back!"

I didn't want to because I'd glimpsed enough of it to know that it was *not* going to make her feel better. But she flipped the page back herself, and we both read what he'd written:

Sammy—
You're amazing!
Love, Casey

"Ohmygod!" she whispered. "That is so . . . romantic!"

"Stop it, Marissa," I warned.

"Sammy, he *worships* you!"

"Stop it!" I said through my teeth.

"And he signed it *Love*."

I shoved the yearbook in my locker and slammed the door shut. "STOP IT!"

Just then a voice snakes into our alcove. "You losers having a little problem?"

We both whip around, and there's Heather and her sidekicks, sneering at us through *way* too much lipstick.

"Let's go," I say to Marissa.

But the three of them spread out, blocking our way out of the alcove.

"What's with the do-rags, losers? Tryin' to look like gangsta girls?"

"Lighten up, Heather," Marissa says. "We're just having fun."

"What you're doing is looking dumb."

"Fine," I tell her. "We're looking dumb. Now will you please just step aside?"

But she doesn't step aside. She sneers and says, "I heard you went to Crispy Chicken for dinner." She snorts. "Hot date."

Now, I'm trying hard not to get caught in a war of words with her, but Marissa's already a little backcombed because of what Danny had written in her yearbook, so *she* snaps, "It's not where you go, it's who you're with," as she tosses looks at Tenille and Monet.

So, good friend that I am, I can't let Marissa wage war

227

alone—I pull the pin on a little word grenade and toss in, "Yeah. Where'd *you* guys go to dinner? Sour Krauties? Oh wait—that was for your *facials.*"

Sure enough, Heather explodes. "You guys think you're so hot, coming to the dance with eighth graders in that butch-mobile! Well, I've got news for you—you're nothing but classless losers!" She sneers at Marissa. "Danny's mom thinks you're a real good connection for her son 'cause you're rich"—she turns to me—"and my brother's just trying to get me mad by going out with you! You may *think* you're smart and hip and cool, but nobody on this campus likes you. Neither of you got nominated for *anything*. You're just a couple of dorky losers!"

Marissa's number one weak spot is her parents' money. She's had a real problem with friends because she can't tell whether they like her for her or for her money. So what Heather said struck where it hurt. And combined with the detached thing Danny had written in her yearbook, I wouldn't have been shocked to see Marissa just break down in tears.

But I learned right then that Marissa's not the same timid person that she was at the beginning of the school year. Instead of backing down, she takes a step forward and says, "Nominated? Oh, you're talking about the Class *Personality* categories."

All of a sudden the situation feels like it's slipping out of control. I look at her like, Don't say anything, Marissa. Don't! but it doesn't do any good. She says, "I heard there was a problem with the ballots."

I'm looking at her like, SHUT UP! but she's not seeing me. She's too ticked off at Heather and Danny and junior high life.

She takes a step closer to Heather. "Uh-huh. I heard there was a problem with someone *cheating*."

Heather backs down a little, her face doing tiny twitches. Like a marshmallow on a stick held above a fire. Roasting. Sizzling. Melting on the inside. Getting ready to burst into flames.

"What's she talking about?" Tenille whispers, and Monet adds, "Do they know something we don't?"

Marissa snorts, then gives Heather a deadly look as she says, "Count 'em and weep, loser."

Then she pushes past Heather and out of the alcove.

TWENTY-TWO

I chased after Marissa and whispered, "Do you have any idea what you just did?" sounding just like *her* talking to *me*.

"I don't care, okay? I don't even care."

"But now she's going to think *we* ratted her off."

"I tell you—I don't care."

"Marissa!"

Her head snapped to face me. "*We* didn't lie and steal and cheat and deceive! *She* did. And if she wants to get in a brawl over it, well fine. Bring it on." She looked over her shoulder and snarled, "Coming in here like she's some prom princess, putting *us* down ... give me a break!"

"Marissa," I whispered. "*You* may feel that way, but I don't!"

Her face scrunched up. "Why not?"

"Does the name Tango ring any bells?"

Her eyes got wide. Her mouth became a little, Oooh! Then she grabbed me by the arm and said, "I'm sorry! That was really, really stupid of me! I forgot about that part of it!" Then she tried to be optimistic, saying, "She'll never figure it out."

"Heather's not stupid, Marissa. I mean, who was absent the day Tango went missing?"

She cringed. "You. But don't think about it. Don't worry about it. Look, if anyone takes the fall for it, I will."

I let out a long, puffy-cheeked breath. "She really got to you, didn't she?"

Her eyes welled a little with tears. "Because I think it's true."

"Why?"

"Because he *has* said stuff about how I live in a mansion and how my parents can afford stuff. . . ." She looked down. "But mostly it's what he wrote in my yearbook—it's so *lame*."

Now, if Marissa hadn't had a heart-stopping crush on Danny since elementary school, I would have told her to take a step back and that time would tell. But she was so *emotional* about him that I really did feel sorry for her.

So instead, I said, "Do you think what Heather said about Casey is true?"

"No!"

"But see? I've spent a lot of time wondering if that *is* his motivation for hanging around me! And if I let myself, I could get all worked up about it right now. But that's how Heather operates—she uses poison, and if you just go ahead and swallow what she says, it's bound to make you sick."

She stood there nodding and blinking and thinking. "You're right. You're absolutely right." Then she about floored me by saying, "And you know what? I'm not going to let her ruin tonight. Time will tell what Danny's real feelings are. For now, I'm just going to take a step back. There's no way I'm going to be some dopey, star-struck fool."

I laughed. "Sounds like a really good plan."

"Plan schplan," she said. "Let's go have some fun. Arg!"

I laughed. "Arg!"

Casey and Danny had ditched their books *and* their eye patches. "What took so long?" Danny wanted to know when we found them. "Nick and Olivia have been dancing for half an hour!"

"Blame Heather," Marissa grumbled. "And it hasn't been half an hour."

Casey gave me a worried look, so I said, "Everything's cool."

"Whatever. Come on!" Danny said, grabbing Marissa by the hand.

We followed them over to the crowd of dancers and started moving around. Danny obviously knew what he was doing, and I don't know if she'd been practicing at home or what, but Marissa looked real natural jammin' around with him.

Casey and I, on the other hand, were terrible. It's like he beeped while I bopped, if you know what I mean. And just when we seemed to get the feel of a song, the song would be over. It happened again and again. And it would have been real embarrassing, only Casey and I both knew we were terrible, so we just started hamming around. I mean, if you're a geeky dancer, you might as well go with it, right? So we did square-dance moves during a rap song, kind of chugging them up, you know? But we were still square-dancing to a rap song. Then we did squatty Russian kick-out steps to a metal song—that was tiring, but Billy joined in with his parrot bouncing around on his shoulder, and pretty soon we had a whole circle of people laughing and doing this crazy Russian dance to a metal song.

When that was over, Billy shouted, "Line!" and automatically all the Russian dancers put their hands on the waist of someone in front of them, and we followed Billy around the gym, going step, step, kick, "Arg!" step, step, kick, "Gar!" step, step, kick, "Arg!" And at the end of that song, Billy shouted, "A pirate's life for me!" and the whole student body shouted, "ARG!"

So we were all laughing and panting and feeling wonderfully ridiculous when the DJ announced, "And now we're gonna bring it down a notch with this oldie-but-goldie special request..."

The opening chords of the song gave me goose bumps. Not 'cause it was a slow song and I was freaking out. No, because it was my new favorite song and I knew who'd requested it.

Casey.

He grinned at me and stepped in closer. "May I have this dance, m'lady?"

"Aye," I said, "but watch yer feet, matey. Ye may need a peg leg by the time I'm done with yer!"

He laughed and then put his arm around my waist and pulled me in closer. And I don't know if it was because we'd been having so much fun hamming it up or what,

233

but him holding me like that wasn't awkward or uncomfortable, it was...nice. And we actually *didn't* step all over each other. We just kind of swayed back and forth in slow circles like we knew what we were doing.

But the more we swayed around, the closer we seemed to be getting. I could feel his breath in my hair and his cheek against my temple. And even though his arms were loose enough for me to pull away from him, they were definitely there, keeping me close.

My heart started to panic. My hands went sweaty. Then he pulled back a little and looked me in the eyes.

All that chocolaty sweetness.

That beautiful smile.

There was only one thing to do.

Bolt from the gym!

But in that instant before I broke free, he started singing along with the song, "Maybe it's all been hard on you, Pushed against the wall, But there's no need to close your eyes, Waitin' for rain to fall..." Then he spun me out like some ballroom dancer, spun me back, and *dipped* me as he mimicked the bluesy guitar riff, *"Waah-waah-waaaaaaaaaah, waah-waah, whoa-whoa-waaaaaaaaah-waah-waah."*

I got upright as quick as I could, and then the song was over and the DJ was saying, "That was Darren Cole and the Troublemakers from *way* back when. And now, let's get this place kickin' again! Here's one by Queen that'll never grow old."

The opening rhythm of "We Will Rock You" started shaking the gym, and once again Billy got everybody going.

Stomp-stomp-clap! Stomp-stomp-clap! Pretty soon everyone was moving slowly forward, stomping their left foot twice, then clapping, then stomping their right foot twice, then clapping. And the further into the song we got, the more together we got and the *louder* we got. We could barely hear the song over the noise we were making.

Which, I've gotta tell you, was cool. It is the only time this entire year where I've seen everybody *together* on something. Usually it's seventh graders against eighth graders, this clique against that...but here we were all just following Billy in this crazy stomping pattern, shaking the roof right off the gym.

When the song was over, Marissa grabbed me and said, "That was awesome!" Then she hitched a thumb toward the water fountain, where Heather and her cronies were standing by themselves, looking very sullen. "They probably think we're idiots."

"Aw, forget about her." Then, since Danny was talking to Casey, I leaned in and asked, "Is everything cool?"

She nodded, but then she grabbed me and said, "I thought Casey was going to *kiss* you!"

I turned red as a radish. "You were watching?"

"Of course!"

"So you weren't in any danger of being kissed yourself?"

She laughed. "I've decided—that's gonna wait. But you! That was electric!"

"Shhh! No, it wasn't—it was..." I gave in and told the truth. "I thought I was going to die. I almost just tore out of the gym."

"So what happened?"

235

"He *sang* to me."

"Oh! 'Cause that's your song!"

"It's not *my* song."

"Not *yours*. Yours and Casey's! The one that will always remind you of him! The one they'll play at your wedding! The one—"

I shut her up with a punch to the arm.

"Arg!" she said, holding her arm, but she was laughing.

Everyone was thirsty, so we took a break and got some punch. There were also snacks like brownies and cookies and party mix, which the guys devoured, but all I was, was thirsty.

After I'd downed about four cups of punch, some sort of flamenco-y, cha-cha-cha-y music came on, and we all looked at each other like, Huh?

But then I saw that Mrs. Ambler had taken the floor with a sorta paunchy, sorta balding man in sorta tan slacks and a Hawaiian shirt. He took Mrs. Ambler's hand and started dancing, and an amazing thing happened—his stodginess completely disappeared. He was *smooth*. Really light on his feet. And dramatic, too. They danced cheek to cheek for a little while, then *whoosh*, he spun her out and pulled her back, and then with a silent turn and snap, he had her cheek to cheek again.

"Wow!" Marissa and I gasped when the song was over. And everyone, even the ultracool around us, whistled, cheered, and clapped.

Then a familiar voice came over the sound system. "Good evening, Bullfrogs! Looks like you're having a ribbiting good time tonight."

You have to endure greetings like this when your school's mascot is a warty, fly-snagging amphibian. Why we don't all just leapfrog off campus in protest is beyond me.

But anyway, it was Vice Principal Caan, sounding more jovial than he had all year. "Let's hear it again for the awesome Amblers!" So we all clapped and whistled again, and then he said, "Well, Bullfrogs, the time has come!"

"This is it!" Marissa whispered.

Our group moved more toward the middle of the gym as Mr. Caan continued. "It's time for us to announce Class Personalities. And elected or not, I want you to know that I think you're *all* personalities." He sort of rolled his eyes as he said it, which got a little chuckle out of some of us.

"Before I turn the microphone over to Mrs. Ambler, who will pass out the medals, I have an announcement to make."

"Shark alert," Marissa said through her teeth. "At eight o'clock."

I glanced over my shoulder and spotted Heather, back about twenty feet.

Mr. Caan took a deep breath, then let it out and said, "Every year the teachers and I put together a list of students that we think best fit each category. But this year we had a little, shall we say, *mutiny*. You let us know loud and clear by your write-ins that we should turn this process over to you, the students."

A cheer went up through the crowd, and then Mr. Caan continued. "So next year, seventh graders, we'll have a pre-election where *all* students are on the ballot, followed by the final election where the top five kids in each category are voted upon. Sound more fair?"

"Yes!" a lot of us cheered.

Marissa nudged me, and I chanced a look over at Heather, who was practically splitting at the seams with excitement.

"All right," Mr. Caan said. "So without further ado, take it away, Mrs. Ambler!"

So Mr. Caan hands the mic over to Mrs. Ambler, who takes a large, green-sashed medal out of a cardboard box. She smiles at the crowd and says, "Starting with the seventh-grade recipients, in no particular order..." She reads the back of the medal, then announces, "Oh. This one's for Class Clown but—"

A girl in front of us starts chanting, "Bil-ly! Bil-ly! Bil-ly!" and pretty soon the whole gym's echoing, "Bil-ly! Bil-ly! Bil-ly!"

"No surprise there," Mrs. Ambler says with a laugh. "*But,* this is the first year eighth graders have written in a seventh grader as *their* Class Clown."

"Bil-ly! Bil-ly!" the cheer starts again.

"That's right. And considering Mr. Pratt's history, we have decided to make an exception and award him both. So, Billy Pratt? I hereby bestow upon you the dubious honor of William Rose Junior High's *School* Clown."

Everyone cheers and Billy does a handstand, then walks through the crowd with his feet waving in the air. When he gets up front, he flips onto his feet, takes a grand bow, and accepts his medal like a pirate Bullfrog should.

"Arg!" he says, then gives Mrs. Ambler a giant smoocheroo on the cheek. "Bonny wench!"

The whole gym—even Mrs. Ambler—cracks up.

"Next up," Mrs. Ambler says, still laughing as she produces another medal from the box, "is Most Popular Seventh Grader, which goes to . . . Tyra Estavan!"

Tyra was the obvious choice. She participated in *everything*. Sports, leadership, community-service clubs—she was always trying to get people *involved*.

Anyway, while we're clapping, Marissa and I are sneaking peeks at Heather, watching her face twitch its way into reality.

She had not won Most Popular.

After Tyra got her medal, Mrs. Ambler announced, "Seventh Grade Brainiac goes to . . . Caldwell Lisske!"

Caldwell hadn't come to the dance, so Mrs. Ambler continued. "Friendliest Seventh Grader is . . . Elizabeth Reins!"

"Oh, I'm so glad she won," Marissa said, bouncing on her toes. "I was afraid it would go to Demitria."

Again, I checked Heather. She was trying to hide it but she was upset, and I could see her calculating her odds: Had her extra fifty-plus votes really not topped Elizabeth's votes? Were they onto what she'd done? But how could they be? No one had seen her! She hadn't told a soul!

And stupid me, she caught me looking. I turned around farther, like I was looking for someone else, but she knew I'd been checking her out.

Next Mrs. Ambler announced Most Athletic, which went to Lance Rodriguez, who's a star in every sport. And then when she announced, "Next up, Most Unique

Style," Marissa tugged my sleeve and said, "Shhh, shhh, listen!" even though I wasn't saying anything.

"This category," Mrs. Ambler said, "was very close. The votes were almost evenly split. But winning, with sixty-eight write-in votes, is . . . Sammy Keyes!"

The whole world seemed to spin. *What?*

Marissa jumped up and down, squealing, "It worked! It worked! I can't believe it worked!"

"What did you *do?*" I gasped, and believe me, I was *not* jumping up and down.

"Holly, Dot, and I talked about it, and we all agreed that you were *way* more unique than the other nominees. So we decided to tell everyone we knew to write you in!"

This was absurd. Ridiculous. *Embarrassing.* My face pinched up as I looked at Marissa. "But . . . I don't have *style* . . . I'm just me!"

"You are so stupid, you know that? What do you think style is?"

"Sammy?" Mrs. Ambler was saying into the mic. "Sammy, where'd you go?"

"She's right here!" Marissa shouted, pointing at me.

"Well, walk your high-tops up here!"

So like in a dream I went up, and when Mrs. Ambler looped the medal around my head, she whispered, "I want you to know this was completely legitimate."

I thanked her, then staggered back to my group, where Marissa was bouncing around, giggling, laughing, acting not at all the way a pirate should. And out of nowhere I've got lots of friends, patting me on the back and congratulating me and telling me they voted for me.

"Wow," Casey said with a grin. "And here I thought this school was full of morons."

I looked at my medal—it had a big goofy bullfrog with a crooked crown on top, and on the back was stamped:

MOST UNIQUE STYLE

SAMMY KEYES

I shook my head and said to Marissa, "I don't know whether to hit you or hug you."

She decided for me with a bone-crushing hug. Trouble is, as she's crushing my bones, I see Heather charging at me like a bull in a tutu. "Uh-oh," I say, breaking free of Marissa.

"What's wrong?" she asks, but Heather's already there, grabbing for me, saying, "You rigged this, I know you did!"

I pivot to the side, so all she catches is air.

"She rigged this!" she screeches out at the crowd. "Who in their right mind believes this loser has *style*?"

"Back off, Heather!" Casey says.

Heather doesn't back off, but everyone else does, and that creates a dense circle around us. "It's okay," I tell Casey, because I can see Mr. Caan plowing through kids, trying to get to us.

But Heather's seen him, too, and at this point she doesn't care—summer's right around the corner, and she's not going quietly into the seventh-grade sunset. She lunges for me again, and I'm so busy telling Casey not to get tangled up in things that she gets hold of my left arm and digs her nails in *hard*. Then she tries to punch me in the head, but I manage to duck out of the way in time.

Some moron yells, "Chick fight! Yeah!" and I'm telling

241

Casey, "Stand back!" 'cause how lame is that? Having your attacker's big brother come to your rescue.

But fake or not, Heather's nails are *gouging* me, and then *swish,* she swings at my head again.

So I'm actually *dying* to end the year the way I started it—with a nose-splatting punch to Heather's face. Right there. In front of the whole school. *Smack.* She'd go down, blood would squirt everywhere.

It would be a beautiful sight.

And who could blame me?

Trouble is, I don't *want* the year to end the way it started. I don't want to feel like I'm back at the first day of seventh grade. I want to feel like the year has brought me forward, not just back to where I began.

Besides, if Heather's a hundred percent wrong now, I want to keep it that way. Punching her out would confuse things.

So the next time her fist comes at me, I grab it with my free hand, twist her wrist 'til her arm goes with it, then pin it behind her back, hard and tight.

Not nearly as much bone-cracking fun as punching her lights out, but oh well.

Mr. Caan breaks through the crowd, so I shove Heather at him, saying, "You got a medal for Biggest Psycho?"

"She rigged it!" Heather wails. "I heard someone cheated—it was her! Her!" She points to my brassy bull-frog. "I bet she stole some ballots! I bet she filled in her own name! There's no way she really won that! Count the ballots! I'll bet there's more than there's supposed to be! Count the ballots!"

"Heather," Mr. Caan says, "you and I need to have a little talk."

So Mr. Caan gets her out of there, and Mrs. Ambler goes on to announcing the eighth-grade Personalities. And through it all I could tell that Casey was bummed about his sister. "I can't wait to be in a different school than her," he said. "I can't wait."

I felt sorry for him. I mean, how would you deal with a sister like that? I sure don't know. It's hard enough dealing with her as an archenemy.

So it was good to get out of the gym and back to the Hummer. Especially since Billy was still hamming it up. "Shiver me bum, mateys!" he said, having retrieved his hook hand and bucket o' bones. "Are we up for an icy slide?"

We all laughed and said, "Aye!" then he held the Jolly Roger high, and we all followed him into the Black Pearl.

And as we pulled away from school, calling "Arg!" and "Gar!" and "Ahoy!" to all the people gawking at the Hummer, I was sure we were leaving choppy waters behind us.

Turns out, we were sailing straight for trouble.

And this time, it was *real* trouble.

TWENTY-THREE

I don't think Olivia or Nick really wanted to go ice-blocking. They'd done a lot of slow dancing, even during fast songs, and were now more into locking lips than anything else.

It was making the rest of us kind of uncomfortable, but Billy shook his hook at them and said, "Ye got the rest of yer lives to drop anchor, swabbies! We got seas t'sail! Villages t'pillages! Lootin' t'doin'! Off yer miserable arses, sea doggies!"

Olivia looked at Nick like, Oh, honey, do we really *have* to? And Nick sort of scratched his head and looked from her to Billy to Danny to Casey.

"Arg!" Billy growled, his unpatched eye squinting.

So Nick said, "Come on, Liv, it'll be fun," but Olivia kept giving him that look and whimpered, "It's going to be *cold,* and I don't *want* to go to the graveyard!"

"We're going to the graveyard?" Marissa asked.

"Arg!" Billy growled. "I got me a bucket o' bones t'bury!"

"Billy," Nick said, "they're *chicken* bones. You don't need to bury 'em."

"Aye, I do!" Billy said. "Or their souls will haunt these parts 'til the moon fergets t'rise!"

"You know what?" Nick said. "Just drop us at my house."

"Aw, come on," Danny said. "We can go somewhere else . . ."

But Nick said, "Nah—that's all right, we're just not really into it."

So when we dropped Nick and Olivia off, Billy grumbled, "Off with ya, ye poxy landlubbers," as they left the Hummer. "Walk the plank, then." But we were actually all kinda relieved to see them go. There's only so much togetherness you can witness before you want to jump overboard yourself.

Anyway, after they were gone, we picked up some ice blocks at Reeba's Liquors 'cause Billy swore they had the biggest, slipperiest blocks in town. And after we'd loaded them into the Hummer, Danny said, "I think we should go to the golf course instead of the cemetery."

Casey agreed. "The golf course is way better, Billy."

"What about me bones?" Billy asked, rattling his bucket.

"Bury 'em at the golf course."

"Aye!" Billy said. "Eighteen holes to choose from!"

Everyone groaned, "Bil-ly!" but we set sail for the golf course. The driver had napped in the Hummer while we'd been at the dance, so it had taken him a little while to liven up. But he got back into whistling the yo-ho song, so thanks to him and Billy Bonkers Pratt, it didn't take long before we were all in a good mood again, singing and *arg*ing and acting like swashbucklin' pirates.

When we got near the golf course, Danny guided the driver through Country Club Estates, down some back roads to the end of a dead-end street, where the Black Pearl could park and not be noticed.

The guys lugged the blocks of ice through a break in the fence while Marissa carried her gym bag and I squeezed through with Billy's flag, his hook, and his bucket o' bones.

It was dark on the golf course, but the houses from the neighborhood to our right cast enough light on the grass to make it seem like we had just entered some secret fantasy world with rolling hills of moss.

"This is cool!" I whispered.

"It is, huh," Casey said as we walked along.

"Do you do this a lot?"

"We used to," he whispered. "It's been a while." He grinned at me. "And never with a girl."

I hadn't even thought about that. And now, knowing that it had crossed *his* mind could have made me feel uncomfortable, but it didn't—it made me feel good. This wasn't something they did with girls.

This was something they did with *friends*.

But we'd barely gotten onto the greens when all of a sudden megawatt lights snap on, totally blinding us. We all just stand there, squinting and using an arm to block the light like we're watching some alien ship descend. It's not an alien ship, of course, it's floodlights mounted to the back fences of some of the country club homes.

Dogs start barking. Then some guy we can't see because he's behind the lights shouts through a bullhorn, "This is a private facility. Get yourself and your stuff off the golf course!"

"We're not hurting anything!" Danny calls back. He hefts his bag. "It's just ice!"

"I said it's private! Get off the golf course or I'll call the police!"

"Great," Danny grumbles, lowering the ice.

So we get out of there as fast as we can, and when we're back inside the Black Pearl, Billy says, "To the cemetery then?"

Casey and Danny are looking at each other like, I *guess* so . . . , but Marissa pipes up with, "How about the ball fields? You know, the ones on Miller? By the courthouse? There's a great hill—"

"Oh, by those trees!" Casey says. "That would be perfect."

"Is there some place we can park?" Danny asks. "This thing isn't exactly inconspicuous, and that part of Miller's always crawlin' with cops."

So I say, "We can park by the old railroad office."

"That's right," Marissa says. "There's a path that cuts behind it, clear through to Miller."

"Is it dark?" Billy asks.

We nod.

"Deserted?"

We nod again, but this time Marissa and I look at each other like, Uh, maybe this isn't such a good idea after all . . .

"Perfect!" Billy pronounces, then adds, "Sounds like a bonny good place to bury me bones!"

247

"Stop with the bones already, would you?" Danny says.

"Arg!" Billy replies.

So I give the driver directions, and off we go. And on the ride over Danny asks, "Is this that same railroad office you were talking about before?"

"Right," Marissa says.

"So this is the place you knocked those guys down with a shovel?"

She rolls her eyes a little. "Right again."

"What were you *doing* over there, anyway?"

Marissa looks at me, so I tell them a little about Mrs. Willawago and my job walking Captain Patch. And I wasn't planning to say much more, but Marissa pipes up with, "Tell them the story about Goldie Danali."

"Who?" Danny asks.

"Goldie Danali . . . it's a ghost story!"

All of a sudden Billy's way interested. "Do tell!" he says, leaning forward.

So I start to tell them about Goldie, but I get on this huge sidetrack about Mrs. Willawago and the houses on Hopper Street because, well, to me that's part of the story. So by the time I finish telling them about Goldie, and how her property got seized, and how now they can't rent the offices because people think they're haunted, Billy's shaking his head, going, "You done?"

I shrug like, Yeah.

"That is *not* how you tell a ghost story." He drops his voice and gives it a spooky quiver as he says, "Goldie Danali. A simple soul. A quiet soul. Went to work each day in a golf cart . . ."

248

Everyone stifles a laugh, but just then the Black Pearl lurches to a stop, and when we turn to see why, we hear clanging and see lights flashing as the crossbars come down, blocking the railroad tracks.

We watch and wait, and finally Danny says, "What the heck?" 'cause with all that flashing and clanging and blocking the road, there's no train in sight.

Then the driver says, "I didn't think trains ran through Santa Martina."

"They don't," I tell him. "We just get the occasional locomotive." He eyes me in his rearview mirror, so I shrug and say, "We don't understand it, either."

The clanging and flashing continues for two minutes.

Three.

Then all at once it's quiet, the lights stop, and the bars lift.

The driver double-checks to make sure no locomotive's heading our way, then proceeds over the railroad tracks, muttering, "Must've been a ghost train."

Now, I'm not one of these people who's all *wooooooo*, scared of ghosts. But something about being in that part of town in the dark and hearing him say *ghost train* sent shivers down my spine.

It did the same for Marissa, I could tell. And as the driver pulled to a stop alongside the abandoned railroad office, I started thinking that maybe we should find someplace *else* to go ice-blocking, but the guys are all, "Oh, dude, this is *perfect*. No one's gonna bug us here."

So we haul the blocks of ice, the stupid bucket o' bones, and Marissa's duffel bag out of the Hummer and hurry to the corridor of trees behind the Hopper Street properties.

Billy zips ahead, then ambushes us from behind a tree. "*Woooagh-ha-ha-ha-ha!*" he roars, practically scaring the punch out of Marissa and me.

He, of course, thinks he's funnier than a whoopee cushion in church, but Danny's getting kinda irritated. "Shhh!" he says. "I don't want to get kicked out of here, too!"

"Who's gonna care about here?" Billy says. "It's public property, right? And we're the public, right? And what are we hurtin', huh?"

"Well, if you're too *loud*, they'll call the cops on us for disturbing the peace. Besides," Danny grumbles, "I'd like to get a few rides in before the ice melts."

"It's not gonna melt. They're big!"

"Mine's dripping all over the place! And so's yours, look!"

Billy says, "Who cares? They work better when they're a little melted."

So we walk along with the two of them arguing until all of a sudden I see something strange up ahead. I grab Billy's sleeve and hold him back. "Shhh!"

"What?" he whispers. Then he opens his eyes wide and peers around. "Is it a ghost ye see?"

The others have come to a stop, too, and are looking where I'm looking.

"What *is* that?" Casey whispers.

My heart's racing like it *is* seeing a ghost, but it's something much more real than that. "That's a shovel," I whisper back. We could see the handle going up and down, up and down in the corner of Mrs. Willawago's backyard.

"Who'd be digging at this time of night?" Casey whispers.

"Good question," I say back.

Then Billy pipes up with, "Hey, is that the infamous, criminal-clonkin' shovel?"

"Yes! Now shush!" I whisper.

Up and down, up and down the shovel handle's going. We can't see hands or a head, and it's a weird sight because even though it's not reflective or anything, the handle seems very *white*.

Very *eerie*.

I've taken the lead now, moving closer, hugging Billy's stupid bucket o' bones with one arm as I sneak forward along the Stones' back fence.

Billy's doing an exaggerated tiptoe, chicken-walking his neck and high-stepping his legs like some cartoon character, and I can hear Danny whisper to Marissa, "What's the big deal?"

"Shhh!" Marissa whispers back.

Smack, smack, smack, the shovel goes, hitting the ground. Then when we're about ten feet from the fence that divides the Stones and the Willawagos, the shovel stops.

I flatten against the fence with a finger to my lips. Every hair on my body feels like it's standing at attention. The air through my nose feels cold and hard, and even though I could just rush forward and pop my head over the fence to see who's working the shovel and why, inside I can feel that there's something bigger here than I understand.

Something deeper and darker than I've imagined.

And, my goose bumps are telling me, a whole lot more dangerous.

TWENTY-FOUR

The four of them are mouthing things to each other in the dark, but I've got my eye on a hole that's been dug under Mrs. Willawago's back fence. This one's right *at* the corner, not a few feet over like the other one had been.

I inch closer, wondering if Patch is already gone or if someone's digging him a way out. The others follow, hugging the fence. And then I feel something hard and cold being put in my hand.

A flashlight.

I smile at Marissa and nod a thanks, then put down Billy's bucket o' bones.

"What's that gross smell?" Danny asks.

"Mother Nature passing gas," I whisper, and Marissa adds, "A compost heap."

"That's brutal," he says, his face all scrunched.

"Shhh!" I whisper.

Whoever's on the other side of the fence is using the shovel again. I can't see it, but I can hear it going *scraaaaape thump. Scraaaaape thump.*

"What's the big deal?" Danny whispers, and Casey touches my arm and says, "Why are we doing this?"

253

We're close enough now, so in one swoop I spring forward and up, latching on to the fence as I look over.

"Aaah!" Mrs. Stone gasps, falling back on her fanny.

I flick on Marissa's flashlight and aim it straight down—straight at the place she's been digging.

And what do I see?

Cement.

"Sammy?" she asks, her eyes huge while she holds on to her heart.

I scan the flashlight over the whole area, and boy, I've got to tell you, I'm pretty embarrassed.

Casey and the others come up from their crouched positions, and when Mrs. Stone sees them, her eyes get even bigger. "What're you *doin'* here?" she asks, her voice gaspy and shaky.

"What are *you* doing?" I ask her, trying to sound like I've got a right to scare her half to death.

"I'm plugging these doggone holes," she says.

"In the middle of the night?"

"Yes!" She stands up and dusts off her backside. "I heard a noise and came out here and found an enormous hole. So I set about fixin' it, just like you showed me."

"In the middle of the night?" I ask again.

"I couldn't sleep," she grumbles, picking up the shovel. "And what're *you* doin' here in the middle of the night? *Spyin'* on me?"

"No! We're going ice-blocking."

"Ice-blocking? What's that?"

"It's sledding for the snowless," Billy tells her.

She frowns and heaps some dirt on top of the cement

she's put in the hole. "Well, you scared the livin' daylights out of me."

"Arg, the livin' nightlights!" Billy says.

She drives the shovel into the dirt with her foot and throws him a scowl, and that's when I notice that she's not wearing her usual Birkenstocks. She's got on her husband's work boots. But I tell myself that that makes sense—I mean, who'd pour cement in sandals, right? And it flashes through my mind that maybe she's out here plugging up a hole in the middle of the night because she doesn't want to get in a fight with her husband about who should fix the hole, and it's just, you know, *safer* to do it while he's asleep.

"Hey, can we get going?" Danny asks. "We're running out of Hummer time."

"Sure," I tell him, even though this whole thing with Mrs. Stone is feeling really disconnected. Really *odd*. And it's not just that she's out there in the middle of the night plugging a hole—which is plenty odd enough—it's more than that.

But I don't really have the time to put my finger on it 'cause everyone else wants to get ice-blocking. So I say, "See ya later," to Mrs. Stone and tag along through the trees to where the ground dips down to the ball fields.

Danny picks out a spot and says, "This is perfect!" and starts ripping the thick plastic off his block of ice. "And you know what? I think these pine needles are going to make us go *fast*."

Marissa pulls towels out of her duffel bag and hands them around while the guys get their blocks into position. And I'm starting to get the picture that this isn't just

255

riding a block of ice for the ridiculous fun of it—this is a competition.

"So what do you do?" Marissa asks.

"You put your block like this," Danny says, moving his ice about four feet from Billy's so it's facing down the hill lengthwise, "then you get on, hold your legs up, and *go*."

Then Casey adds, "First one down to the bottom without falling off wins."

"We'll demonstrate for you," Danny says. He puts a towel across his ice and gets on like he's mounting a mini ice bronco. Then he looks right and left at Casey and Billy, who've done the same, and says, "Blockers, on your marks . . ."

"Wait!" Marissa cries, grabbing the Jolly Roger flag. She hurries to the side of them and holds it in the air.

"Arg!" Billy cries, pulling his eye patch back over his eye. "*Pirates,* take your marks!"

The other two pull their eye patches out of their pockets and put them on, too.

"Get set . . . ," Marissa says, then whisks the flag down as she cries, "GO!"

So the guys push off, stick their legs out, and slide down the hill. And it sure doesn't *look* like they're going very fast, but they're all shouting "Arg!" and stupid pirate stuff, and Billy's heading for Danny, trying to kick him off his block. So they're laughing and yelping, and then Casey's block catches on something, and he winds up going down sideways. And then Danny falls *off* his block, leaving Billy to slide in first.

"Shiver me timbers!" Billy says. "I've won the first round!"

So they push the blocks back up the hill, and now it's Marissa's and my turn to slide. But since there are three blocks, Billy decides to go again, and he positions himself right between the two of us.

A little too *close* to the two of us.

I eye Marissa and she eyes me. We've seen how Billy operates, and knowing him, he'll show no mercy on us because it's our first ride. So I give her a little signal and she gives me a little nod, and when Danny drops the flag and calls, "GO!" we push off and immediately start kicking Billy off his block as we slide.

"Wenches!" he cries as he spins sideways and falls. "Black-hearted wenches!"

Marissa and I laugh, and boy! Even though I know we're not going that fast, it sure feels like it. I mean, there you are, on a fat block of frozen water, twisting and turning out of control, slipping downhill with nothing to hold on to.

It was *way* more fun than it looked.

And I think Marissa would've beat me, only she tried to pump the ground with her legs to get some speed and wound up catapulting instead.

"Shiver me tush!" I cried at the bottom of the hill. "I won me first round!"

The guys all laughed, then came down the hill to help us push the blocks back up to the top.

"Who goes now?" Billy asked.

"Sammy, Casey, and me!" Danny said.

The three of us saddled up our ice ponies, and I could tell from the way they'd positioned themselves on either side of me that I was on the menu. So when Marissa dropped the flag, I acted like I was pushing forward but didn't. Instead, I waited for them to get some speed and look back at me like, What happened? *Then* I pushed forward hard and tried to knock them both off at once—one with each foot.

Too bad for me, *I* fell off and my block slid down without me. Danny claimed victory, and when we had the blocks back up, Casey, Billy, and Marissa went, then Danny, Marissa, and me, and then the three guys again.

After that Danny said, "Do you want to double up?"

"We won't fit!" Marissa laughed.

"Sure we will." So Danny and Marissa wedged onto one block, Billy and his parrot got one all to themselves, and Casey and I scrunched onto the third. By the time Billy tossed the flag into the air and started the race, we were laughing so hard from just trying to fit on the blocks that it was a miracle we went anywhere at all.

Doubles is definitely not the way to ice-block. Billy beat us by a mile. But since Casey and I beat Marissa and Danny, we declared a doubles victory, which of course made Danny and Marissa demand a reslide. So we tried it once more, but it was just as slow, so we went back to riding solo.

Now, it finally got to a point where the ice blocks had melted so much that the towels were soaked and dragging, *we* were soaked and dragging, and basically, we just couldn't ride anymore.

And that's when Billy says, "Hey! Where's me bucket o' bones?"

I look around, then remember. "Oh, yeah! I left it by the fence." I point toward the Stones' house. "Up there."

So he Billy-goats up the hill to get his bucket o' bones, but when he returns, not only does he have his bones, he has the Stones' shovel. "Mateys, it's time for a proper burial!"

"Uh . . . ," we all say, sort of eyeing each other.

"The Hummer turns into a pumpkin in about ten minutes," Danny says, checking his watch. "Can you do it quick?"

"Aye, aye, Cap'n!" he says. "Follow me!"

But when he starts down the hill, Marissa asks, "Where are you going?" because it looks like he's heading straight for the baseball diamond.

"Home base!" Billy laughs, pointing.

"No way!" Marissa and I cry, because we both play softball, and digging up home base to bury a bunch of *chicken* bones seems really sacrilegious.

Casey shakes his head. "Besides, we'll be too visible." He points to the trees on the back side of the sports complex. "How about over there?"

So we wring out Marissa's soggy towels, stuff them in a plastic bag she's brought along, take one last look at the shrinking ice blocks, and cut over to the spot Casey had pointed out.

Danny makes Billy hurry up and pick a spot, and as he starts digging, Marissa whispers, "You want to change pants?" because our soggy jeans and the lack of activity are making us cold.

"You brought extras?"

"I told you I would."

"Yes!"

"Let's go over here," she says, heading behind a group of trees. Then she calls to the guys, "Don't come back here!"

So there we are, hiding in the trees, peeling down our jeans, when all of a sudden a fierce growl comes out of the darkness behind us.

Marissa screams and yanks her pants up, and believe me, I choke on a scream of my own.

"Are you okay?" we hear Casey call.

I grab Marissa's flashlight and shine it toward the sound, then about collapse from relief. "We're okay!" I call back, then tell Marissa, "It's just Captain Patch!"

Marissa's hyperventilating, and her eyes are enormous. "That's Patch? He looks like a *wolf*."

He did look pretty spooky with the light glassing up his eyes like it was. But I knew it was him, so I wasn't scared at all anymore. I took a few steps toward him. "Hey, boy! You got out again?"

Trouble is, Patch doesn't seem to recognize me. He growls again, this time louder.

"Get the light out of his eyes!" Marissa says. "You're blinding him."

So I lower the beam, but now it's shining on something between his paws. Something he's been gnawing on. Something long and white. Like a thick, bleached stick.

And then I hear Danny say, "Forget it, Billy, we don't have time for you to dig down six feet."

"Ye can't be rushin' a proper burial, matey! Else sea dogs'll sniff 'em out and dig 'em up! We'll be haunted forevermore by the souls of crispy chickens!"

260

My heart landed with a thunk in the pit of my stomach, then tried to lurch out my throat. My knees were suddenly shaky, and I started shivering so hard I could barely stand.

"Oh my God," I panted. Suddenly my lips felt like they were going to crack off of my face. I licked them. Licked them again. Tried to catch my breath. Tried not to shake into a puddle of fear. *"Oh my God!"* It came out strangled. Quivery. Like I was about to cry.

"What?" Marissa asked. "What's wrong?"

The flashlight shook like crazy as I shone it between Patch's paws. And like a time-lapse scene in a movie where clouds morph across the sky, turning black and heavy before erupting with rain and thunder and bolts of ripping lightning, the odd little events of the past few weeks tore through my brain, then zapped my soul with the truth.

Everything suddenly made sense.

Horrible, bone-chilling sense.

TWENTY-FIVE

I wanted to explain everything all at once, but it's like I couldn't quite believe it myself. So what came chattering out of my mouth was, "Did you bring gloves?"

Marissa cocks her head a little. "Shouldn't we first—"

"I need gloves. Or one of those towels..." Patch was ignoring the light now, gnawing on his prize.

Marissa digs through her duffel bag and hands over a pair of mittens, whispering, "Sammy, why are you being so intense? Are you afraid he's going to get away?" And while I'm pulling on the mittens, she adds, "He's not going anywhere—he likes that stick!"

"It's not a stick, Marissa," I say, moving in closer to Patch.

"So...so what *is* it?"

Patch lets out a low growl as I get within grabbing distance. "It's a bone."

She takes a few tentative steps closer. "A... *bone?*"

There's no way Patch is letting me get any nearer. Even when I tell him, "Hey, boy, it's me! How are you? Come here...thata boy, come here!" the only thing that budges is the tip of his tail, slapping the ground like a little part of him wants to, but not enough to give up his prize.

Then I get an idea. "Hey, Billy! I need a couple of those chicken bones!"

"Arg!" he calls back at me. "Ye can't have 'em!"

"It's an emergency!"

"That *is* a bone, huh?" Marissa says.

Crunch-crunch-crunch. Patch keeps a watchful eye on us as he works his jaws over the end of it.

"Billy!" I call down the hill. "We need those bones! NOW!"

Casey and Danny come running toward us with the bucket o' bones, Billy in hot pursuit, shaking the shovel at them.

"What's the deal?" Casey asks, all out of breath. Then he sees Patch, chomping away. "Whose dog is that? What's he got?"

"It's Captain Patch. Mrs. Willawago's dog." I grab a chicken bone out of the bucket and offer it to Patch, going, "Here, boy—check this out. Mmm, mmm, chicken!"

"Chicken bones aren't good for dogs," Marissa says. "They splinter and can get stuck in their throats and—"

"Shhh," I tell her as I wiggle the chicken bone a few inches from Patch's nose. "Come on, fella. Yum-yum. Much tastier than human."

"Than *human*?" Casey asks.

"Did she say human?" Danny whispers.

"Arg!" Billy cries. "Now that'd be booty worth sacrificing me bucket o' bones fer!"

Danny says, "Aw, c'mon. How can you tell? It's probably just a deer bone or a soup bone or a—"

"It's a human bone," I tell him. "I'm sure of it."

Just then Patch takes the bait. He stretches forward and

263

stands, letting go of his hard-earned prize. And while he reaches for leftover morsels of Crispy Chicken, I reach forward and grab the bone.

And as I pick it up, Marissa screams and jumps into Danny's arms, because on the end of the bone is something dangling and dirty.

Something creepy and gross.

Something Patch hadn't gotten around to picking clean.

A *hand*.

"Ohmygod," Marissa squeals. "Oh my *God*."

"Put it down, Sammy," Casey says.

Patch is in hound heaven now—there are bones, bones everywhere! He's yip-yap-yowling, spinning around and tossing chicken parts around like he's hit the crunchy-munchy lottery.

And between me shouting for diversionary bones, Marissa squealing to God, and Patch's yippy-yappy happiness, we gave away our location, because as I turn to tell them that I can't just leave this arm here—that I know whose it is and where it came from—through the misty darkness I see a figure moving toward us.

A figure in blue coveralls.

Work boots.

A safari-cloth ball cap.

Glasses and a moustache.

Carrying a hoe.

Coming *at* us with the hoe.

"Stop!" I shout, holding the arm up. "We know what you've done!"

But the hoe comes whacking through the air, hitting the ground. *Swish, whack! Swish, whack!*

Marissa screams. Danny pulls her away to safety while Billy abandons piratese and yells, "Everyone meet back at the Hummer!" and takes off running.

But I can't leave. Not yet.

Swish, whack! Swish, whack!

I keep my distance from the hoe and shout, "Stop! It's over! Don't make it any worse than it already is!"

Swish, whack! Swish, whack!

"Sammy!" Casey's pleading, staying with me as I get chased across the grass. "He wants the arm. Put it down!"

Just then we run by the shovel. So I toss aside the arm and snatch the shovel off the ground, and instead of retreating, I hold the shovel like a samurai pole weapon and charge forward, deflecting the hoe as it comes slicing through the air.

Then I lunge forward, tear off the cap, and shout, "It's over, Mrs. Stone! I know your husband's buried in the compost heap!"

And just like that, she drops the hoe and wilts into a blubbering heap of denim, sobbing, "I'm sorry! I'm so, so sorry."

"That's a *woman*?" Casey gasps.

I nod, and after she cries for a minute, Mrs. Stone peels off her glasses and moustache and looks at me, whimpering, "I wouldn't have hurt you, Sammy. Honest, I wouldn't have. I was just tryin' to scare you away."

I crouch beside her. "I guess I don't need to ask why you killed him."

265

"He was a beast!" she wails. "A cruel, heartless beast!" She wipes tears from her face, saying, "How many times did he almost kill *me* in one of his drunken rages? How many times should *I* have been put in the hospital?"

I watch her cry for a minute, then ask, "But why didn't you just *leave* him?"

"I was afraid to! Over and over he told me I was worthless, and I don't know... after a while I *believed* it. 'Who'd want to hire you, Teri—you're stupid. You're homely. You've got hands like a man.' He got between me and my friends, between me and my family. A few years with him and I had no one. No one! Just him and his terrifyin' mood swings."

"But... why'd you cover for him? Mrs. Willawago told me you always denied he'd hurt you."

She gave me a pathetic shrug and shook her head. "He was always sorry after. Always beggin' me not to leave him. And I thought if I could just be a better person somehow, he'd quit gettin' so mad. But then one night I was fixin' supper and he came at me with a chair." She snorted. "Why? Because I'd made him toast instead of biscuits. Before I knew what I'd done, I'd run him through with a knife."

"So you panicked and buried him in the backyard."

"I was afraid no one would believe me! I'd never once called the police on him! So I buried him quick, only I didn't put him down deep enough."

We were both quiet a minute, then I said, "But there was also the disability money, right? I mean, if he was *dead,* his disability checks would stop, but by pretending he was alive, you still had money coming in."

She looked so miserable. So broken. "He never let me have any cash. I always had to beg for every nickel. And since we were cut off from everyone, I thought I could pretend and just go on the way I had been for a while. But then that whole mess with the city council came up and I was trapped. I couldn't *un*bury him. Not in the state he's in now." She shivered. "I had to wait 'til he was nothin' but bones. And if they took the property, they'd for sure find him when they did the gradin', and I'd wind up in jail!"

"So you don't really want to live there, you just didn't want them to find the body."

"I hate that shack! Bein' there gives me nightmares! It's haunted with hateful words and deeds." She shivered, then said, "Why I thought jail would be so much worse is beyond me." She looked at me with pleading eyes. "No one wants to lose their freedom—especially not after finally gettin' some."

I thought about that, then said, "You know, maybe you won't have to go to jail."

"Oh, I'm going. After what I've done?"

"Well, maybe it won't be for all that long. Mrs. Willawago's a witness—she knows how mean he was to you. And if you just tell the jury the truth, maybe it won't be so bad."

Her eyes welled up, but then she sniffed back the tears and said, "So what gave me away? How'd you know it was Marty in there?"

I sort of cocked my head at her. "A lot of things—but specifically? Your socks."

"My *socks*?"

"Remember when I ran into you in your backyard? You were dressed up as Marty, getting ready to put your boots on? Your socks were dirty in a weird way. On the toes, mostly. Then tonight when I saw you were wearing your husband's shoes, something sorta clicked. But we got busy ice-blocking, and I didn't put it all together until I saw Patch with the arm. That's when it hit me that the socks were dirty like they'd be after doing some gardening in your sandals. And *then* it clicked that I'd never seen the two of you at the same time, and how troubled you'd been about my, you know, *trespassings,* and that the big changes in Marty—no more beer cans, no more shouting, him shielding himself from the sun—those weren't changes in *him,* those were changes because he was *gone.* And then, of course, those threats made total sense—you were trying to get the public on your side." I shrugged. "And being upset enough about Patch to get rid of him made sense, too."

"I was desperate! I knew he'd reach Marty if I didn't do something. So the night everyone was at the council meeting, I dug him a way out." She rubbed her forehead. "That was a terrible thing to do, I know, but that dog wouldn't quit! And tonight he finally reached his mark."

"Did you know he'd gotten away with . . . part of Marty?"

She shook her head. "I *feared* so. He'd dug that whole corner of my yard up, clear under my back fence. So I figured he was on the loose, and I did look all over for him, but I had to get back and hide Marty again."

I checked around for Patch—he was having a golden time demolishing chicken bones, but Marissa was trying to get them away.

"So tell me this—was Mrs. Willawago in on the threats?"

Her eyes bugged a little. "The Church Lady? You've got to be kiddin'." Then her eyes sharpened down on me a little and she asked, "Why would you think so?"

I gave a little shrug and said, "Let's just say she hasn't always lived by 'Thou shalt not lie.' "

"Oh?" she asked, and let me tell you, it was a very interested *oh*.

So I laughed and said, "It's kind of funny, actually. You tried real hard to convince people that your husband *wasn't* buried in the backyard, and she tried real hard to convince people that hers *was*."

She hesitated. "You mean to say Frank's *not* scattered in her backyard?"

"That's right." I sort of grinned because I couldn't really help it. "Last I saw he was scattered all over her closet."

She started to say, "What—?" but just then we heard Billy's voice going, "Right over here!" and saw flashlights bobbing along the tree corridor.

It was Billy with the Hummer driver, and bumbling right behind them were Squeaky and the Chick.

"Where's the perp?" Squeaky says, hand at the ready on his holstered gun.

"There he is!" Billy says, pointing to Mrs. Stone.

Billy is totally amped—ruddy faced, out of breath,

269

wide-eyed—he looks a lot more like a little boy than a swashbucklin' pirate, that's for sure. So I tell him, "It's okay, Billy—the he's a she, and she's all done fighting." Then I take Marty's grotesque arm and put it down in front of Squeaky, saying, "I don't think you want the remaining remains to remain staying where they're presently harbored at this time."

"Eeew!" the Chick squeals when she sees what it is. And when Squeaky realizes it's part of a corpse, he backpedals like crazy, shouting frantically into his radio for backup.

"No need for that," Mrs. Stone says wearily. "The rest of him's in my backyard." She heaves a sigh, then stands and says, "I'll show you."

"What about...the *arm?*" the Chick chokes out. She looks at Squeaky. "We can't just leave it here...."

Mrs. Stone sighs and waves it off, saying, "Aw, let Patch have it."

"Eeew!" we all say.

She lets out a bitter laugh. "It's the kind of end that hand deserves."

Squeaky's pretty green around the cheeks as he looks at the arm, but he says, "No, we need to, uh, properly execute the collection of this, uh, physical and material evidence."

Marissa pulls another plastic bag out of her duffel and holds it out for him. "Does this help?"

He nods and swallows hard as he accepts the bag, but it's obvious he doesn't know how to get the arm inside the bag. And really, who wants to touch a corpse arm?

Well, besides Patch, of course.

So since I still have Marissa's mittens on, I decide to help him out. I pick up the arm, shove it in the bag quick, and say, "There you go." Then I peel off the mittens and eye Marissa like, Wash or dump?

"Get *rid* of them!" she says, wrinkling her nose.

So I shove them in the bag, too, and Squeaky doesn't seem to mind. He nods and says, "I appreciate the help."

So Marty's gross arm is now out of sight and, apparently for Billy, out of mind. "Ahoy then, mateys!" he says to the cops. "Carry on!"

So the cops follow Mrs. Stone back to her house, and after Marissa gathers the rest of our stuff, we get Patch to follow, and we traipse along behind.

And somewhere along the corridor of trees, the driver shakes his head and says, "I've had some wild nights in that Hummer, but yo ho, man, nothin' compares to this."

Then Casey waves the Jolly Roger flag a little and grabs my hand. "Yo ho, yo ho, a pirate's life for me," he sings softly, looking at me with a smile.

But Billy overhears and starts the song in earnest. And there's something about that song that makes it impossible *not* to join in. So there we are, in the middle of the night, waving the Jolly Roger, marching along behind cops and a killer, laughing and singing at the top of our lungs.

It was a first date none of us will ever forget.

Arg!

TWENTY-SIX

Mrs. Stone did wind up going to jail. Hudson, Grams, and I visited her there, which was really weird, let me tell you. For one thing, being at the jail is freaky. It's all steel doors and block walls and echoing halls.

Mrs. Stone, though, didn't seem like a caged animal, sitting in her cell. She was acting like she had when she'd shown Squeaky and the Chick where her husband was buried—calm.

"I'm glad it's over," she told us, and that's when it really hit me that there *is* real freedom in the truth.

Even if it puts you in jail.

To a small degree I knew how she felt. I mean, getting my "little" secret out of the closet had been a huge relief. I guess there's something about not carrying the burden of the "sin," as Mrs. Willawago would call it. Something about getting it out that lets you breathe again.

And speaking of Mrs. Willawago, she was coming to visit Mrs. Stone just as we were leaving. No one had woken her up the night we'd discovered the truth—I'd just put Captain Patch in her backyard while Mrs. Stone confessed her crime.

So bumping into Mrs. Willawago was pretty uncomfortable after the way she'd thrown me out of her house. But she just ignored me as she spoke to Grams and Hudson. "Poor lost lamb," she said about Mrs. Stone. "But the Lord is watching over her. He will help her through this time." Then she told them how she'd offered to post Mrs. Stone's bail, but Mrs. Stone had refused. "She's repentant, I know, because she told me jail was a fine place for her to stay." She pulled some brochures out of her purse. "I've been to the battered women's shelter for ideas on educational opportunities and work-training programs. I'm hoping this will help her prepare for a decent life after her sins have been accounted for."

So it's nice that she's trying to help Mrs. Stone and all that, and if Willy-wag-a-Bible wants to stay mad at me, well, let her. If she can't balance the nice things I did against one understandable accusation, well, *amen*. I'm not gonna lose any sleep over it.

Anyway, enough about them—on to my pirate pals! This last week of school has been amazingly fun. No weirdness at all. Well, except for the number of people who have asked me where I get my high-tops—that's been *really* weird. But where the *pirates* are concerned, it's been cool. Danny and Casey and Billy chum around with us at lunch. Nick and Olivia don't, but that's just fine by me. We've started calling them Nickolivia and liplubbers because they're *way* too into each other.

The first couple of days we just talked about our night out as pirates—after all, we had *lots* to catch Holly and Dot up on. But after a couple of days we started talking

273

about other stuff, too. Like sports and summer plans and Heather.

Actually, I was the one who finally asked, "Where *is* your sister? She's been absent all week."

Casey scowled. "In London."

"London!" we all cried.

"With my mother," he grumbled. "She thought Heather needed a positive experience after what she'd been through."

"Oh, please," I said.

"Exactly." He shook his head. "I get to go camping, she visits London."

I grinned. "Any chance she'll stay there?"

He grinned back. "One can always hope..."

Then on Thursday I dropped by Hudson's after school. I had myself some cookies and iced tea and some more cookies and iced tea, and what I found out was that Coralee Lyon refused to step down from her position as city council chair, so *talk* of a recall had turned into *action* toward a recall.

"I gathered eighty-two petition signatures this morning alone," Hudson told me.

"*You* did?"

"Why, sure. It doesn't happen on its own, you know."

"But...you mean you were like one of those guys out in front of the supermarket with a clipboard, asking, 'Are you a registered voter'?"

"I wasn't *like* one of those guys, I *was* one of those guys. I'm part of a whole committee of 'those guys.' We're called the Recall Coralee Lyon Committee, and we

274

still have a lot of signatures to gather." He grinned at me. "Want to join?"

"Me?" I said, pointing to myself like a dodo. "I'm not even old enough to vote!"

He shrugged. "That doesn't mean you're not old enough to help. If you really want things to change, you have to get involved." He smiled at me. "Little strokes fell big oaks, you know."

When I left Hudson's, my head was swimming with that idea. I always figured I was too young to be heard. I mean, considering my experience with adults? Please. They listen about as good as wood.

But then it hit me that things *had* changed this past year. Maybe not radically, but they had changed. I mean, my first day of seventh grade I got suspended for punching Heather's lights out. After that all the teachers and Mr. Caan thought I was trouble. And since Heather was so clever and I was so hotheaded, it had taken nearly the entire year for them to start seeing that I was more than a quick-fisted delinquent.

I was a kid fighting to be heard.

And in the beginning of the year Heather had convinced everyone that I was weird. Some kind of thrift-store-scroungin' loser. But now I have in my possession a green-sashed brassy bullfrog that says I've got unique style.

Talk about miracles!

But that miracle only happened because my friends decided to try a new way to make a change. And the amazing thing is, people *listened*.

So last night I started thinking about different ways of making the rec center happen. I mean, now that Teri Stone no longer has her terrible secret to hide, the only property owner on Hopper Street that *doesn't* want to sell their land is Mrs. Willawago. And even though she isn't my best friend or anything, I still don't think it's right to force her out. So why not just build *around* her?

They could start by moving the old railroad office next to the historical society—there's room for it there, and it sure would be historical.

But then it would probably turn into one of those boring field-trip places where you went only once in your life and forgot.

So, what if they kept the railroad office where it is and turned it into the Railroad Café—you know, part of the rec center, where kids could go have refreshments *and* soak up some Santa Martina history. Maybe Mrs. Willawago could even work there and tell stories about the old days—like a barkeep for teens, pulling sodas or sports drinks or holy water or whatever.

I was so excited, I spent the whole night thinking about it. And the more I thought about the café and the rec center, the more ideas I got. They could figure out a way to do it—it could be really, really great!

So you know what? Today may be the last day of seventh grade, but inside it feels like it's the first day of something bigger. Something broader than myself or my friends or my problems at school. And I've decided—I *am* going to help Hudson collect signatures.

Coralee Lyon needs to go.

And I *am* going to take my ideas about the rec center and work them into a real plan. There's got to be a way to build the rec center without bulldozing history or seizing property that isn't for sale. Why wait around and hope that things will change on their own or that someone else will figure it out?

Because you know what? I've decided Hudson's right.

Little strokes *can* fell big oaks.

It may take time, but I'm willing to give it a try.

Have you read
SAMMY KEYES and the WILD THINGS
yet?

Turn the page for a sneak peek.

PROLOGUE

Summer's supposed to be a time of freedom. Freedom from school, from homework, from junior high head games . . . freedom to hang out with your friends without adults constantly hovering around, telling you what to do.

But it seemed like school had barely let out when all my friends suddenly flew the coop. Marissa's family went to Las Vegas. *Again.* Holly took off on some road trip in a motor home, and Dot went to Holland to visit her grandparents. *Holland.*

Me, I was left trapped in this freak-fest of a town, in an old-folks' apartment where I live with my grandmother, next door to a whale of a woman who has supersonic hearing and the charming habit of falling off her toilet.

I was desperate to get away.

The trouble is, when you're desperate, you do dumb things.

When you're desperate, you might as well face it— you're doomed.

ONE

If Marissa *or* Holly *or* Dot had been around, I wouldn't have been thinking about Casey Acosta at all. But since they weren't around, and since Casey *does* qualify as a friend (even though he's my archenemy Heather's brother) okay, I admit it—he had crossed my mind.

More than once.

Partly that was because I'd seen him at the mall a couple of times during the first few days of summer break. Marissa was with me the first time, and she practically choked my arm off with her grip when she spotted him coming out of Sports Central. "Sammy, look! It's *Casey*."

I wanted to say, So? but it just didn't come out.

Then *he* spotted *us,* and the three of us wound up cruising through the mall, laughing the whole afternoon away.

It was fun.

Like being with friends should be.

The *second* time I was by myself. I'd escaped the Senior Highrise, cruised the whole town on my skateboard looking for something, *anything* to do, and finally I'd wound up at the mall.

Did I go to the arcade?

No.

Did I go to the music store?

No.

To any of the clothing stores?

No.

Like a moronic moth to the flame, I fluttered over to the only place I'd ever bumped into Casey at the mall— Sports Central.

Now, I've got every right to go into a sporting goods store. I *like* sports. But I didn't go inside. I stood *outside*, pretending to window-shop, with my heart racing and my hands sweating, a shouting match going on inside my head.

"What are you *doing*?"

"I don't know!"

"Why don't you just go inside!"

"Because I don't need anything!"

"So what! Just go inside!"

"*Why?*"

"Because standing out here is the lamest thing you've ever done in your whole entire life!"

It was, too. I felt like one of those dingbat girls who walks back and forth past some guy's house, hoping he'll notice her. How stupid did I want to be? And what were the chances of Casey being here again? Why didn't I just call him up if I wanted to hang out with him?

So there I was, in the middle of a total mental spaz-out, when all of a sudden someone sneaks up behind me and pokes me in the ribs.

Before I can even think about what I'm doing, my elbow jabs back, punching deep into someone's stomach, and then *wham*, my fist flies up and back, smacking them in the face. And when I spin around, who do I see doubled up on the floor with blood coming out of his nose?

Nope, not Casey.

It's his goofball friend, Billy Pratt.

Casey *is* there, though. And even though his eyes are popped wide open, his words are really calm. "Dude, I told you not to startle her."

I drop to my knees and say to Billy, "Oh, man! I'm so sorry!"

He chokes out, "I'm good," but he's still totally winded, and blood's getting everywhere.

So I run to the pretzel stand, snag a bunch of napkins, and run back. "Here. Put some pressure on your nose. It'll stop the bleeding." Then I add, "I'm *really* sorry! It was . . . you know . . . a reflex."

He pinches the napkin against his nose and sits up, moaning, "No problem." He gives me a goofy grin. "I've had a stomach massage and a realignment. . . ." He shoves a corner of the napkin up his nose, and with the rest of the napkin dangling, he staggers to his feet and says, "I am totally ready to rock."

The thing about Billy Pratt is, you can't *not* laugh when you're with him. He is always, *always* "on," even when he's just been smacked to the floor by a girl. So being around him made the spastic thoughts I'd been having magically disappear. I followed him and Casey into the sporting goods store, where Casey picked out camping supplies while Billy harassed a clerk, acting like he was some hoity-toity British polo player instead of a kid with a bloody napkin dangling from his nose. "I say there, chap! These shorts say 'one hundred percent cotton,' but I must have combed *Egyptian* cotton or I break out in rashes. Absolutely wretched rashes! You wouldn't want to see, not at all! So I must know. I absolutely *must* know . . . are these combed Egyptian cotton?"

I whispered to Casey, "Do they even grow cotton in Egypt?"

"You got me," Casey whispered back. "Probably just Billy being Billy."

He'd turned and looked me in the eyes when he'd said that, only he didn't look away when he was done talking. He just kept right on looking me in the eyes.

Which of course made my heart skip around funny while glands everywhere burst forth with sweat. "Uh . . . so you're . . . uh . . . going camping, huh?" I said, showing off my brilliant intuitive talents.

He laughed, "Yup," and went back to picking out freeze-dried food. "Backpacking, remember?"

He had mentioned it at the end of the school year. Like twenty times.

"You've really never been?" he asked.

I shook my head.

He shrugged. "My dad and I got into it a few years ago. It's like camping, only cooler."

I hesitated, then said, "I've never been camping, either."

He stopped flipping through foil packages. "*You?* Never been camping?"

I shook my head again.

He stared.

I shrugged.

He went back to his freeze-dried selections. "Sorry. You just seem like . . ." His voice trailed off, and then he chuckled and said, "Now, *Marissa*. That I would believe. But you? You'd love camping."

"I don't know." I picked out a foil pouch of vegetable lasagna. It weighed hardly anything. "You actually eat this stuff?"

"That right there's pretty vile. But some of these are almost good." He grinned. "And after about day four, even the vile ones start tasting all right."

"You going with your dad?"

"Nah. He was planning to come, but then he got some big audition in L.A." He hitched a thumb in Billy's direction. "So now it's just me and Mr. Entertainment."

"You and *Billy*? And you expect to survive?"

He laughed out loud. "Yeah, my dad wasn't too hot on the idea, either. But I know what I'm doing, and he trusts me. And Billy's a good camper, believe it or not." He hesitated, then eyed me and said, "I don't suppose your mom would let you come along?"

It was my turn to laugh out loud. "I don't suppose . . . !"

And see? That's the stupid thing about trying to be friends with the opposite sex. How can you be friends when you can't *do* anything together? Even going to the movies becomes a big deal. Voices drop. Eyes bug. Gossip flies. "She went to the movies with him?

Alone?" All that gasping and gossiping over what? A movie? Sharing some popcorn? Sitting next to each other and laughing? Maybe accidentally touching elbows?

Hmm.

Anyway, it made me mad that I couldn't go camping. Not because I wanted to go and couldn't, but because I couldn't go even if I wanted to. I was a girl and he was a boy and the idea of going camping together was just insane. No, it'd have to be just him and Napkin Nose in the woods eating from shriveled foil pouches, warding off bears with nothing but sticks and their wits.

Okay, so it was probably a good thing that I couldn't go, but still, it didn't stop me from being royally ticked off about it.

So a couple of days later I went *back* to the mall because I was bored to death, and I went *back* to Sports Central. It was on beyond insane, because yes, I was hoping to run into Casey again, and no, I had no idea when he was actually leaving on his backpacking trip or how long he'd be gone.

Little details I'd neglected to gather.

I can be so bright.

Anyway, this time I didn't stare at the lime green biker shorts display and have an argument with myself. This time I just moseyed inside. And who did I find over in the camping department holding on to an empty shopping basket?

Not Casey.

It was a girl from school named Cassie Kuo. Or Cricket, as she likes to be called.

And maybe she wasn't Casey, but at least she was some-one I knew.

Sort of.

I mean, I'd had her in homeroom all year, and she had been my Secret Santa at Christmastime. She'd made me a little macaroni angel to hang on my tree, so I probably *should* have known her better than I did, but she's quiet and shy and I never saw her at the lunch tables or after school; she didn't hang out around town or at the ballpark. . . .

Not that this was anything I'd ever given any thought to, but now all of a sudden there she was, sifting through the same foil pouches that Casey had gone through, and it hit me that it was truly weird to see her anywhere out-side of homeroom, especially here.

"Cricket?" I asked, because I still couldn't quite believe it was her.

She jumped a little, then her head snapped to face me. "Sammy?" she gasped, like I was a long-lost friend. "It's so great to see you! What are you doing here?"

I shrugged. "Trying to get over perpetual boredom."

"You're bored? How can you be bored? It's summer!" Then her eyes got really big and she said, "Oh! It's be-cause Heather's in England, isn't it? She's gone and you just don't know what to do with the peace and quiet, is that it? But where are Marissa and Dot and Holly and . . . all your friends?" She looked around, like, where was I hiding my posse of friends.

I couldn't help laughing, because (a) she was being really hyper and (b) the stuff she'd said about Heather was so . . .

bizarre. Like I would be bored because the world's most evil, conniving, mentally deranged teenager was half a world away?

I don't think so!

Cricket leaned in and said, "I bet Heather comes back with a phony English accent! I bet she tells everyone that she had breakfast with the queen and a private tour of Buckingham Palace. I bet she starts complaining that there's no high tea offered in the school cafeteria! I bet she starts using words like *brilliant* and *loo*! I bet—"

I busted up so hard that everyone in the store turned to look at me. I mean, Heather's *my* archenemy, not hers, but everything she was saying was so spot-on that it was like *she'd* been the one harassed by Heather all year.

When my laughing wound down, I asked, "What did she do to *you*?"

"What did she do to *me*?" She seemed to take a step back, even though she stayed right where she was. "She tortured *you*."

"But . . ."

"She was evil! Awful! How can anyone be so terrible?" She shook her head. "All year I just wanted to smack her." She grabbed my arm. "But you stood up to her and won! And now her brother likes you and she's insane over *that*." She rubbed her hands together. "It's all so . . . satisfying!"

All of a sudden I was not laughing. I was staring at Cricket and feeling very, very weird. She was treating me like the star of some teen-drama reality show that she hadn't missed one episode of. She knew a *lot* about my life—about my archenemy and her brother and my friends and all the action that had gone down at school—but I knew nothing about her.

She was just Cricket Kuo, Quiet Girl.

Macaroni Angel Girl.

"So what are you buying?" I asked, suddenly wanting to change the subject.

"Backpacking food!" she said, like she'd been saving up all year for this very moment. "We're hiking out to Vista Ridge to see condors!"

"Condors? I thought they were extinct or . . ."

Her eyes got wide. "They were *almost* extinct, but they're making a comeback! We hike out to a tracking station where we can monitor them." She tossed a couple of freeze-dried pouches into her basket. "Everyone who's seen a condor soaring over the canyon says it's the most amazing sight, and this time I'm not leaving until I spot one!"

"So how far do you have to hike?"

"Aaaactually . . ." She pulled a little face. "We drive most of the way. There's a road clear up to the tracking station, but it's steep and full of potholes, and there's a gully you need a four-wheel drive to ford. So we just get as close as we can and hike the rest." She shrugged. "It's only about five miles."

"Your whole family's into this?"

She stopped cold, then seemed to thaw from her fingertips, up her arms, to her shoulders. "I'm going with my Scout troop," she said quietly, then gave me a shy smile. "Remember? I told you about it once?"

11

I racked my brains, and yeah, I kind of remembered her inviting me to go on an outing with them. It was when she'd given me the macaroni angel. Or thereabouts.

"We don't wear uniforms or anything. We're just a group that likes to camp." She was looking down, and her voice had dropped to a whisper. "We don't look like the girls you see on cookie boxes."

I didn't know what to say. She was acting apologetic and so *embarrassed*.

"You would like it, Sammy," she whispered. "You really would."

I shrugged. "Probably so."

Mis-take! All of sudden her face is twitching and popping and lit up like fireworks, and she says, "Why don't you come! You'd have a blast! Vista Ridge has the most amazing views! You could share my tent! You could share my food!" She turns over a pouch of freeze-dried Santa Fe Chicken with Rice. "See? Serving size: two! I don't mind! I'll buy more!"

"Whoa, Cricket, hang on! I've never been backpacking. I don't know how. I don't have any gear!"

And what does she do with this camp-killing news flash?

She looks at my feet.

"What's your shoe size?"

"A seven . . . ?"

She hops up and down. "You can borrow boots from me! And a pack from my brother! And Robin has extra sleeping bags! You'll love Robin—she's our leader and she's good friends with Coach Rothhammer!"

Now, the fact that her leader was good friends with my softball coach was a plus. I respect Ms. Rothhammer. As Grams says, she's got backbone. But still, it wasn't reason enough to go backpacking.

So while Cricket's whipping around the store, tossing one thing after another into her basket, I'm trailing behind her going, "But I, um . . . I don't know if I can. . . . Cricket . . . ? Hey, Cricket! Hold on a minute. . . . Cricket?"

But there's no stopping this girl. When she's done filling up her basket, she grabs me by the arm and yanks me toward the checkout line. "Come on! There's a ton to do before tomorrow!"

"You're leaving *tomorrow*?"

"*We're* leaving tomorrow."

I didn't really want to, but I *was* desperate to do something, *anything*, besides hang around the mall.

So yeah, I was doomed.

I was *so* doomed.

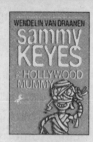
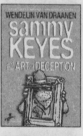

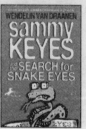